RETURN TO TOPIC BAY

A Novel

H. Mickey Mc Guire

Order this book online at www.trafford.com
or email orders@trafford.com

Most Trafford titles are also available at major online book retailers.

Printed in Victoria, BC, Canada.

ISBN: 978-1-4269-2361-6 (Soft)

Library of Congress Control Number: 2009914034

*We at Trafford believe that it is the responsibility of us all, as both individuals
and corporations, to make choices that are environmentally and socially sound.
You, in turn, are supporting this responsible conduct each time you purchase a
Trafford book, or make use of our publishing services. To find out how you are
helping, please visit www.trafford.com/responsiblepublishing.html*

*Our mission is to efficiently provide the world's finest, most comprehensive
book publishing service, enabling every author to experience success.
To find out how to publish your book, your way, and have it available
worldwide, visit us online at www.trafford.com*

Trafford rev. 01/06/2010

 www.trafford.com

North America & international
toll-free: 1 888 232 4444 (USA & Canada)
phone: 250 383 6864 ♦ fax: 812 355 4082 ♦ email: info@trafford.com

For Linda, thanks for all of your help,
and for keeping me on track.
For Butch and Serena who's encouragement lifted me.
For my sister Darleen just because.

**To the men and women of our Armed
Forces who keep us safe.**

PROLOGUE

March 21, 1931

Dave Chadwick and his new bride Joan took off from Palm Beach Florida, in a Bi-plane, left over from World War I. They headed for a three day Honeymoon in Key West. All was well until Dave flew into a large white cloud some where North of Miami out over the Caribbean. Upon entering the Cloud a strong wind caught the plane and Dave by surprise.

Dave fought the wind, and kept the small plane on course, he thought, but as time passed he could tell there was something wrong. As they came out of the cloud the compass was spinning wildly and Dave could see the ocean, but it didn't look right. Dave dropped to within 100 feet, above the water trying to find some kind of marker, but found nothing.

The Bi-plane was modified for land on water, but Dave felt he could still make Key West. He figured he was East of the Keys, so he banked the plane to the West and keep flying. After two hours on this course he thought he should be some where in the Keys, but saw no land.

He judged they had been flying for four hours, but had no idea where they were, nor how to get back to Palm Beach.

Dave looked at the fuel gauge and saw, to his disbelief, the plane was about to run out of fuel. He had Joan looking out the right side of plane for a spot of land. Shortly he spotted a small dot of land off to his left. Turning the plane toward the dot he quickly saw it was an extremely large Island.

Dave circled the island looking for a place to land the Bi-plane. The only open area was the beach, and it was small, so he made his approach from the sea.

The small plane dropped to the surface of the water and glided on to a sandy beach. As the floats touched the beach the engine, sputtered and stopped.

The two newlyweds got out of the plane and dragged it on shore, so the waves wouldn't pull it out to sea. High tide aided them in getting it farther on the beach.

Dave couldn't understand how he had gotten so far off course. They were safe and sound, setting on a sandy beach, but the daylight was fading quickly.

Taking everything out of the plane they made they way into the tree-line not far from the beach. He and his wife of a few hours made their Honeymoon bed under the stars.

On Dave's fly over of the island he could see it was large, and would take some time to gather enough wood to build a big fire, so a passing ship could spot the island and know people were on it.

The next morning Dave was up early ready to explore the island. Joan wasn't in that much of a hurry to see, what was on the island. Dave explained they had to find food of some kind. His thinking was fruit, and nuts.

They walked farther into the trees watching the lay of the land. The ground started to rise the farther they walked. Before long the pair could hear a thundering sound.

They had no idea what the sound was, but could tell where it was coming from. Walking on, they came to a high water fall. The water was cascading down the side of a tree covered high mountain, forming a small lake.

Checking out the area, Dave found foot prints of birds, and four footed beast. He had done some hiking, and hunting, in the woods around his Grandfathers farm, but didn't recognize the prints.

The Chadwicks camped near the lake for a few days, but Dave wanted to get back to the beach, in case a ship, or boat would happen by. He hadn't resigned himself to being on the island for very long.

Shortly after the Chadwicks were stranded, a storm blow in, on their side of the island.

With the abundance of trees, Dave knew he needed to build a shelter for his wife. There was only one problem, no tools. His first task would be to make tools to cut down the trees.

Using parts of the plane he was able to fashion a saw, to cut and trim the trees. He then to put up a lean-to, which covered them from the weather.

His next problem was food. At first they gathered fruit, but after a few days, they wanted other things to eat. He scouted around the lake, but couldn't trap any of the animals, who came to drink from the lake. He even tried fishing, from the lake, but caught nothing.

One morning, when the couple awoke, there were baskets of food. They didn't know where the food came from, but were very happy to receive it.

Every morning, there would be enough food for the day. The Chadwicks didn't know who was feeding them, but they were thankful.

Dave continued to work on his house...day in, and day out. He would cut trees, drag them back to the beach. Every morning there would be food, and water for them.

After about two weeks, of the food, being set out for them, Dave decided, he would stay awake all night, to catch sight, of the one who was leaving the food, but somehow, he never could stay awake long enough to see their benefactor.

It seemed to them, a year or more had passed. They decided to build a raft out the floats on the plane. Dave worked hard at building the raft, and before long they were ready to put to sea.

After a good night sleep, he woke Joan to get ready to leave. As he opened the door to their cabin, Dave found 5 baskets of food, and 10 jugs of water. Dave couldn't believe, everything left by their benefactor, but gave thanks, loaded the food, and water on the raft.

They launched the raft, and were on their way, having no reason to think, they would ever, make it back home. Dave knew his wife wanted to leave, their island home. He thought to himself, the island was something like heaven, would be.

Days later as they slept, the little raft floated on. Sometime during their rest, the raft began moving faster, and kept to a straight line. When Dave became aware of what was happening to the raft, he found they had floated close to a large ship with men standing on the deck.

Dave started waving, and shouting. The men waved back. Shortly the ship slowed, and a small boat was launched with two men onboard.

The Chadwicks were retrieved, their raft was lifted on board, and carried back to Miami. The authorities questioned them, about where they had been, for the past fifty years. Dave and Joan couldn't believe they had been lost for fifty years.

❧

Years past, and the couple came to grips with the fact they were younger, than all who had known them before they married. They looked, not a day older than the day they left for Key West.

Dave had gone back to the authorities, asking if the government, had found the island. But they gave him the runaround and he knew it. He bought a sail boat, and would spend days, even weeks sailing, around the ocean, trying to locate his island, but to no avail.

The way the world had changed in the time they had been on the island, left the Chadwicks bewildered and wanting to return to their Topic Bay.

CHAPTER ONE
THE INTERVIEW

*"Ahoy, "Windjammer" is there anyone aboard?" I
shouted as I banged on the side of the 38-foot Sailboat with
my hand...*

*"Captain Mike Ryan are you there?" I continued shouting
until I finally got a response.*

*"Yeah, Yeah, I heard---, as the hatch slid open, revealing
a man holding up one hand to shield his eyes, from the
brightness of the early morning sun.*

*He was slender, in his late sixties, his tan skin, set off his
long white hair, not gray, but pure white, with a beard, just
as white, running from ear to ear. His neck and upper lip
were shaven. A light green Tee Shirt, and a pair of tan shorts,
covered his body, but no shoes.*

*"Who are you?" he questioned, moving so the sun was
no longer in his eyes. "What can I do for you, so early in the
morning?"*

*"My name is Mickey Mc Guire." I replied, "I'm a Free
Lance writer. Then quickly added "The Dock Master", Mr.
Jim Chapman, told me, you might give me an interview on
how it was to sail the Triangle." I explained, hoping I had
not gotten him out of the rack.*

1

"*I don't do interviews, son.*" *Was his reply, adding, as he turned to retreat to his hole, "There is no reason to be interviewed."*

"*Please Sir.*" *I begged, stepping closer to the boat, "I would just like to talk with you about, what Mr. Chapman, called "strange happenings at Sea."*

"*I don't know what I can tell you. But, I'm not doing anything today, and I could use the company.*" *He replied, motioning me to come aboard.*

"*I sure want to thank you, Captain.*" *I said, running up the ramp, and followed him through the hatch, down the steps, into the cabin.*

The right side of the cabin, was a good size galley, for a 38-footer. A table sat at the far end with two wooden benches, and on the left side of the cabin was his office. It had a computer with other electronic equipment. I would later find out it was a Gobble Positioning System (G.P.S.) and a Loran Transceiver, plus Radios.

"*Don't get much company now days*"; *the Captain said, reaching the bottom of the steps. "Want a cup of coffee?" he asked, walking to the large urn, setting on the counter next to the sink.*

"*I sure would.*" *I replied, "I left Jacksonville, very early, so I could get here in time to find you, Sir."*

Guess you did. It's only eight-o-clock now." He said, taking two cups to the table. "We can sit over here." He said, sliding in behind the table.

I quickly took out a tape recorder, a note pad and a pen, laying them on the table in front of me.

"*Are you going to record this conversation?*" *Captain Mike asked, taking a long slip of coffee.*

"*If it is alright with you. I really want to get it right the first time.*" *I replied.*

"Sure, I don't know what I can tell you, but I'm all yours." He said, setting his cup down on the table. "So where do we start?" he asked, rolling his hands palms up.

"I have done research on the "Bermuda Triangle*." Your name kept coming up. I understand from the Coast Guard's reports, you had an encounter with the Triangle." I explained.

"I guess, if you go back 20 or 25 years you might say, I had a run in with the government in the area called the "Triangle". He replied reaching for his coffee again.

The following was what Captain Mike Ryan remembered:

The "Windjammer's" white sails snapped tight, and heeled to port, as Mike Ryan brought her up on the wind. It was a beautiful day for sailing, and Mike just had to get away.

He hadn't taken the 38-foot "Hunter" out of her slip at "Buzzard's Roost" since his wife Doreen had became sick with cancer. Now with her death behind him, the "Windjammer" became his only thought. He had loved his wife, with all of his heart, but understood God had other plans for her; at least that was how he was dealing with it.

He had been through a lot in his 39 years. 20 years as an Airborne Ranger, three tours in Vietnam, and a jump into Panama had taught him to deal with almost anything. To some, he was insensitive, and without feelings. Deep down inside, he did care about people.

It was his outlook on life, which he had developed to a point where he kept feelings to himself. He had lost friends, and family through the years. But the loss of his wife was almost more than he could handle. Now he was alone, just him and his boat.

Mike eased off the wind, to let the Main Sail lofted slightly. He winched in on the Jib, and set the auto-steering. Rechecked the rigging, he went below for a cup of coffee.

The main cabin was designed for comfort. Doreen had been the main force in the design and layout, with Mike doing to work. Looking around the cabin brought back many thoughts of his wife. He could even smell her perfume. He made himself a cup of coffee, and went back topside.

The Sun was coming over the horizon. The little bit of fog Mike had sailed through coming out of Charleston Harbor, was slowly burning off. According to the N.O.A.A.D. station at Charleston, the weather to the south was going to be good for the next 36-hours.

He had no place in mind, nor anywhere in particular to go. He just knew he had to get away. He checked the compass heading, and the chart for the area.

He decided the heading he was on, would take him, and the "Windjammer" near the island of Bimimi, just over the "Tongue of the Ocean", and off the east coast of Florida. He had sailed this course many times, but Doreen was with him, and the trips were a lot of fun.

The wind was blowing steady at about 15 knots, so single handling was easy for Mike. He glanced at his watch, he was three hours out of Charleston, and then he looked at the knot meter, which showed the "Windjammer" making a steady 11.5 knots. He judged his position to be 25 miles East of Hilton Head Island, South Carolina. All at once, the marine radio came alive.

"Mayday! Mayday! This is the "Kaysee Rose", a 40-foot Ketch out of Fair Heaven, Maryland, and we have a broken Main Mast, and are without power. Please any vessel hearing this transmission please respond. We are at 33.6 North and 78.4 West, seas are running about 4 to 6 feet with a wind at 15 knots. Please send help." Then the radio went silent.

Mike quickly retrieved the chart, which covered the area. He found the position which had been transmitted. It was only 15 miles southeast of his position. He listened, waiting to see if there was someone closer, but there was no response.

Reaching around inside the hatch, he picked up the radio mike and keyed it, "This is the "Windjammer", out of Charleston and my position is about 18 miles northwest of you."

"I am a 38-foot Sloop, running at about 12 knots. I can be at your location in about 50 minutes. Can you maintain for that long?"

"How much drift do you have at the present time?" "Over."

Again, the high-pitched voice came over the radio. "This is the "Kaysee Rose," since you are the only boat in the area; I guess I have no choose. My drift is South by Southwest at about 3 knots." "Over."

"This is the 'Windjammer' I'll be there as soon as I can." "Over."

"Thanks 'Windjammer'. We'll be watching for you." "Kaysee Rose", Out"

୧୬

CHAPTER TWO

"Wait a minute," I said, interrupting Captain Ryan's story.

"You haven't been out 4 hours, and all ready you have a woman wanting you to come save her from the sea?"

"I guess, at the time it didn't seem like I was saving anyone. Besides there were two woman on board the "Kaysee Rose", one of their names was Kaysee, and the other one was called Rose, thus the name of the boat was "Kaysee Rose"." he replied, and then added, "When I left Charleston, I was really feeling sorry for myself. I think I was even mad at God, for taking my wife, but with that radio call, it made me realize there were still other people out there, who might need my help."

"Anyway, I came down here." he said getting back to his story.

He went to the Global Positioning System, (G.P.S.) Entering the information need to get the course change needed to intercept the "Kaysee Rose".

Back on deck, Mike made the changes in course and adjusted the sails to match the course change, then engaged the auto-steering. He rechecked all of the adjustment.

He rechecked the speed of the "Windjammer", she was now making a little more than 12 knots, and holding on her new course.

Going below again, Mike went to the locker where he had stored his binoculars, and the towline-launching gun. He knew he would need to shoot a line to the "Kaysee Rose", as the seas would slam the two boats together causing more problems.

Back on deck, Mike opened one of the cockpit lockers, pulling out 200 feet of 1 inch line, used for towing, and 200 feet of 1/2 line which he attached to the projectile which had a range of 75 yards.

After arranging all of the lines in the cockpit, so they wouldn't foul, he picked up the glasses, and began scanning the sea for the "Kaysee Rose".

The Sun had burnt off the fog, so it was a bright clear day, with only a few white fluffy clouds in the sky. The wind was holding steady, so the "Windjammer" continued making 12 knots, and the ocean broke over the bow, spraying Mike with water as he continued to look for the "Kaysee Rose".

He looked at his watch seeing it had been 30 minutes since he had talked to the "Kaysee Rose". Mike decided to give her a call. Moving to the radio, Mike reached for the radio mike, but before he could key the mike, the radio came alive.

"Windjammer", "Windjammer", this is the "Kaysee Rose". "Do you have a copy on this station?" "Over."

"Go ahead "Kaysee Rose", "This is the "Windjammer", Mike replied, checking the horizon for the boat.

"Windjammer! Just checking to see if you are on your way." "Over."

"Kaysee Rose," I am still making 12 knots. I should intercept your course in about 20 minutes." "Over."

"I think I have seen your sails, but you look a long way off." "Over."

"I don't see your boat yet, but than your mast is missing, so you would have a low profile. That's why I don't see you yet." "Over."

"I will keep looking, but without the bilge pumps, we are taking on water, and it's filling up below deck. Please keep coming." "Kaysee Rose." "Out."

Mike looked at the horizon, but saw only water. He let out on the main, and readjusted to jib, trying to squeeze a little more speed out of the "Windjammer."

Checking the knot meter, Mike found the "Windjammer" was making a little more than 12 knots. He checked the Loran settings; found the "Windjammer" was still on course.

Mike returned to scanning the ocean for the "Kaysee Rose," but with the raising and falling of the "Windjammer", it was hard for him to see much over four, or five waves ahead. At one point, he thought he caught sight of the boat. As he was raising, and they were on the way down, but he couldn't be sure.

Then suddenly the boat pitched, catching Mike off guard, and with a splash, Mike hit the water.

The coolness of the water stunned him for a minute. Becoming aware of the situation, he now found himself. Mike started to swim to catch the "Windjammer". At this point the safety line attached to the harness, he always wore whenever he went sailing, became taut. He had learned this lesson years before while learning to sail on Lake Huron.

Mike had helped a friend build a 40-foot Ketch, and they had taken it sailing on the lake, before it was completed. One of the things, which weren't installed at the time, were lifelines.

On that trip, there were Mike's wife Dorene, her mother, Ruth Marie, and a friend of Mike's named Delmar.

They had left Port Huron at the mouth of the Black River, out into the St. Clair River, and finally out into Lake Huron. Where they sailed North along the Canadian Shore most of the day. They all had a good time until their return trip.

Mike was checking the design of the boat to see just what it would do under full sail.

The wind was blowing about 20 knots out of the Northeast. Mike brought the boat up on the wind as clean as he could. Everything was going well, until Ruth Marie wouldn't climb back into the cockpit.

Mike tried to explain, with the wind blowing strong, and with the boat heeling, she could slide into the water, if the boat pitched. She was a woman whom you couldn't tell anything. She keep insisting she would be all right.

The little devil on Mike's shoulder caused him to bring the boat up on the wind, just a little more. As the boat responded it caught a wave just right, and in a blink of an eye, Ruth Marie was in the water.

Mike quickly came off the wind, everyone quickly helped to make the sail changes, as Mike brought the boat around to pick up Ruth Marie.

By the time he got the boat back sailing, and could reach Ruth Marie, she had started to panic. Seeing this,

Dorene became impatient, and began to scream at Mike to do "Something!" In a split second, Mike was over the side, and swimming toward Ruth Marie, while trying to calm her down. Getting close to her, she grabbed hold of him trying to keep herself above water, but at the same time, Mike couldn't keep both of them above water. He pushed off from her, otherwise she would have drowned him.

Delmar saw Mike was in trouble. He jumped into the water trying to help Mike, and at the same time calm Ruth Marie down.

With all of the action going on in the water, Dorene found herself alone on board the boat, under full sail. The design of the boat, caused it to find the wind, and the boat began sailing it's self away, leaving the three still in the water.

Mike, and his friend tried to teach Dorene, how to come on, and off the wind, for better than an hour. With her being, so anxious, it was impossible for her to bring the boat close enough for any of them to get back on board. Finally, Del and Ruth Marie, decided to swim for Canada. Mike wouldn't leave his wife.

For the next three hours, Mike calmly talked Dorene into learning how to sail, while he was bobbing around in Lake Huron, like a Channel Marker. She would get close, it just wasn't close enough. With his strength, waning. Mike talked Dorene into sailing right over the top of him.

At first, she refused the idea, but he convinced her, it was the only way he could climb back on board. With dusk setting in, Dorene brought the boat around for another run at Mike. As the bow smashed down on Mike, he grabbed an eighth inch cable, which ran from the bow

10

spire to the water line; holding on for dear life, and with much difficulty, he was able to finally climb on board.

Once on board, and to the relief of Dorene, they sailed to the Canadian shore, where they picked up the other two swimmers. From then on Mike didn't go sailing, without everyone, learning how to handle the sails, and the boat, nor did he leave Port without wearing a safety harness.

With the line becoming taut, it snapped Mike back to his present situation, of being towed behind the "Windjammer" at 12 knots. He was bouncing along the top of the water, like a water skier, who had forgotten to let go of the tow-rope. Shortly, he felt the "Windjammer" begin to slow.

At this point, Mike knew his prior planning was working. Another lesson Mike had learned during his ordeal on Lake Huron.

No mater how good a swimmer you were, you couldn't swim fast enough, to catch a boat under-sail. Mike had designed a system, by which a Sea Anchor would deploy, if he ever fell over-board. Until, now he had never had to use it, but had been sure it would work.

As the sea anchor slowed the "Windjammer", Mike started fighting the water, to roll over on his face, so he would be able to pull himself back on board.

The speed of the boat was still to fast; he was unable to fight his way up the line. With two or three hands full of line, the force of the water caused him to slide back down the line. Even when he rap the line around his hands, the force was so great, it cut into his hands.

Finally he decided to let the boat just drag him along until the speed was reduced to a point where he could climb up the line.

While saving his strength a thought ran through his mind...SHARKS! He knew, he must look like a seal, which will attract Sharks. He fought to hold his head above water, so he could look around checking the area for Sharks. He didn't see fins, but he did see the "Kaysee Rose" crossing some 1000 yards a stern of the "Windjammer".

He could make out two people on deck waving, and jumping up and down. He thought they must be thinking he had missed them, but at the time, he had his own problems to over come.

The "Windjammer" finally slowed enough. He started his 200 feet climb back to the boat. Hand over hand, Mike pulled himself along the line until he reached the ladder on the stern of the "Windjammer". With one hand holding on to the line, and the other on the ladder. Mike paused to catch his breath. It had been a hard fight, but he had won this one.

Climbing the ladder Mike quickly went below, he grabbed a towel, and then went to the radio.

""Kaysee Rose", this is the "Windjammer", "Over." Mike shouted.

Mike waited, but there was no answer from the radio. He tried again, and again, with no response.

He went back out on deck. Looking a stern Mike couldn't see the other boat. He knew it hadn't been very long since he had seen the "Kaysee Rose" cross behind him. He quickly disengaged the auto-steering, and brought in the sea anchor, then swung the "Windjammer" about.

Making the sail changes, and adjusting the course to what he thought should bring him back to the "Kaysee Rose." As the boat came around, Mike began looking for the boat, who had asked for his help.

Within 15 minutes Mike spotted the "Kaysee Rose" just ahead. It looked to be ridding low in the water, with two people on the deck. When they saw the "Windjammer", they started to wave, and jump up and down again.

Mike adjusted the course, so the "Windjammer" would come along the Port side of the other boat. He pooped the Jib, letting it roll up. Then he released the Main Sail, and let it, roll down. He started his Aux. Engine, and eased his way along side of the "Kaysee Rose".

"Hi There;" Mike said, giving the girls on deck a wave. "Sorry it took me a little longer than I thought. I had a little trouble of my own."

"We saw you go sailing by, and thought you hadn't seen us. We didn't know what had happened to you." A beautiful, slim, blonde-haired woman said, giving a smile, which reminded Mike of his wife's. She was wearing a swimsuit, which enhanced her figure. Her friend was a brown-haired woman who looked to be about the same age, with figure to match.

"My name is Mike Ryan, and this is the "Windjammer"." he said, easing his boat along side.

"They call me Kaysee Johnson, and this is my friend Rose Wilson, we're in real trouble." she said, pointing to the water, which covered the cockpit.

"It look's like you have taken on some water. Why haven't the sea-cooks taken it off?" Mike asked, leaning forward, so he could see into the cockpit.

"The seas were rough, and the water just kept breaking over the bow faster than the drains could handle." Kaysee replied, looking over the side.

Well, I guess the first thing we need to do, is to get some of this water pumped out, so your boat will ride higher.

It will make it easier for the "Windjammer" to tow you." Mike said, moving to railing of the "Windjammer."

He placed the bumpers over the side of his boat, so he could tie off the "Windjammer" to the "Kaysee Rose" The seas had calmed enough to where it was possible. Next he tied the "Kaysee Rose" securely to the "Windjammer", and climbed on board.

Going below, Mike wadded through water up to his waist, and made his way to the where the bilge was located. Searching around, he found the wires going to the pump. He pulled out as much wire as he could, and tied them above the water.

Mike returned to the "Windjammer", went to the locker where he kept extra wire. He took out a spool of three-strand wire. Then went to the battery on the "Windjammer", and tied off one end of the wires.

Returning to the "Kaysee Rose", he tried in the power from his boat to the wires on the pump of the "Kaysee Rose".

Within a short time the pump had lowered the water in the cabin of the "Kaysee Rose"

Going back on deck, Mike joined the girls, informing them, most of the water would be pumped out.

"Do you have a place you want me to tow your boat?" Mike asked, the girls, who were now cleaning up the cockpit.

"Not really." Kaysee replied, but I don't think we can get very far the shape we're in." she continued, flashing a smile at Mike.

"We could make Hilton Head, South Carolina, or maybe even Jacksonville, but not much further South." Mike told them, scanning the western horizon.

"Well it doesn't matter, just so it's someplace where we can get the boat fixed. We are to meet a friend in Bimimi, on the 14th, so we need to get it fixed as soon as possible." Kaysee told him.

Mike went forward checking the broken mast. He could see it had broken off just above the deck line. The rear mast was still in tack, but the sail wasn't in place. "Where is the Mizzen Sail?" Mike asked, as he returned aft.

"Oh, we took it down when the Main Mast broke." Rose replied, pointing to a sail bag wedged between the tiller, and the seat locker.

"We'll need to set it, and disconnect the wires to the pump. The Mizzen Sail will help in towing, it will easing the helm." Mike informed them, as he climbed back onto the "Windjammer"

Making fast a line to the stern of his boat, and started the engine, then tossed the line to Kaysee asking her to tie it to the bow of her boat. Mike released the line holding the two boats together. The "Windjammer" began moving out in front of the "Kaysee Rose".

"Will you girls be all right on board by yourself?" he asked, slowing the engine, so he could hear their reply. "Sure, we'll be OK." Kaysee replied, "We sure do appreciate, you coming to our rescue." giving him a wave, and a big smile, showing all of her pure white teeth.

Mike returned their wave as he increased the speed of the engine, and the line to the "Kaysee Rose" became tight. It caused the "Windjammer" to jerk. The engine labored for a short time, than the RPM.s return to normal, and the two boats began to move together.

Mike knew, if he tried to pull the "Kaysee Rose" with just the engine, he wouldn't get very far, as the strain on the engine, would be to great.

He headed the "Windjammer" into the wind, raising the Main Sail, and setting it. Then Mike went to the sheet for the Jib, unfurling it, he adjusted the Jib, and turned on the wind. "The Windjammer" began to sail.

Mike eased the "Windjammer" back on to the course; she had been on before he received the call from the "Kaysee Rose."

Reaching for his chart case, Mike retrieved the chart covering the South Carolina and Georgia coastline. He thought the best place, to tow the "Kaysee Rose", would be Brunswick-Jeryll Island area.

He had put into this area once when he had trouble, with a blown Main Sail, on a trip to the Keys. With in a few hours the Marina at St. Simon Island Light had him a new Main Sail, and he was on his way.

Mike checked the course he had set on the loran, and then entered the information into the Gobble Positioning System, which in turn gave him his present position. He checked the speed of the boat, with the speed he was making, towing the "Kaysee Rose" it would take 29 hours to make St. Simon Light. He decided to put up his spinnaker, hoping it would give the "Windjammer" more speed. As soon as Mike, had the sail in place, and the pole set, he heard a horn blowing.

He could see the two girls, standing on the bow, waving their arms. Mike couldn't see what was wrong, but he knew something must be. Following some choice words, Mike dropped the Spinnaker, secured the pole. Returning to the cockpit, he furled the Jib, and the Main Sail.

Starting the engine, he brought the boat around, so he could come along side the "Kaysee Rose", without crossing the tow-rope. As the "Windjammer" slowed, the "Kaysee Rose" kept moving. As the two boats came close, Mike threw the fenders over the side and shortened the tow-rope until the boats came together.

"What's wrong?" Mike shouted, as he made fast the line.

"Our boat is taking on water!" Rose exclaimed, "It happened when you put up the Spinnaker. The waves came over the bow."

"How much water is in the boat now?" Mike asked.

"Not as much as we had in the beginning, but it wouldn't take long before we would be underwater." Rose replied, stepping back, so Mike could see.

"I'll hook up your pump again, but really there is following seas, so I will put up the Spinnaker, sooner so maybe the seas will not come in over the stern." Mike explained.

"I thought the water was coming in over the bow." Rose said, looking at the water, which now filed the cockpit.

Mike climbed back aboard the "Kaysee Rose", connecting the cable back to the pump. He quickly completing the operation. He moved to the tow-rope where he attached the cable to the tow-rope with wire ties, along the rope, then eased the "Windjammer" back out the full length of the tow-rope.

Once the rope was taunt, Mike proceed to raise the Spinnaker and, the two boats begin moving on the course Mike had set earlier.

For the next few hours, Mike kept an eye on the weather, and the boat he was towing. Everything was going well, slow, but going in the right direction.

"Hey Mike," the voice came from the "Kaysee Rose". He stood up looking to the stern, he could see it was Kaysee, who was standing on the bow of her boat.

"Hey, what's wrong?" Mike asked, expecting another problem.

"No there isn't anything wrong. Just thought you might be lonesome, and want to talk." Kaysee said, climbing out on the bow pulpit.

"You're a long way away, to carry on a conversation." Mike said, leaning forward over the stern rail.

"I can solve that." Kaysee said, jumping to her feet, and headed to the stern of her boat.

Mike watched as she disappeared below deck, only to reappear, within a few minutes, sporting an inflatable raft. She moved to the side of the "Kaysee Rose" and put the raft into the water. She eased over the side into the raft, then made her way to the tow-rope. Hand over hand, she pulled herself, along the rope to the stern of the "Windjammer", where Mike helped her on board.

"See!" Kaysee exclaimed, "I told you I could take care of getting closer, now we can talk without yelling."

"This is a lot better." Mike told her, "I have wanted to know, just how you two, got yourselves into a problem, way out here."

"I guess I have always liked to sail...I have always loved the water, and boating in general was fun. As a young child, my Dad had a boat, and I moved from powerboats to sail through a friend.

"The more I sailed, the more I wondered, what it was like out in the ocean. I knew the water would look the same, but I wondered what it would be like not to have sight of land.

"I couldn't imagine the frame of mind offshore sailing would create. Your entire world, no larger than what you can jump across."

"The idea of being in a monster storm, or sliding down one monster wave, and up the next, in a tiny boat, was more than I could envision." She confessed, moving closer to Mike.

"I know what you mean." Mike uttered, getting up, and heading below.

"Where are you going?" Kaysee asked, as she finished fastening the line to the "Windjammer" from the rubber raft.

"Hope this is the way you like your coffee." He said, sitting down beside her.

"Right now, I'll drink it anyway." she replied, taking the cup.

"You were telling me how you girls ended up, in the middle of the ocean." Mike said, with a smile, and waving to the four winds.

"Well, the opportunity to find out about offshore sailing came more quickly than I had expected, in the form of the "Kaysee Rose". I had been involved in sailing the bays and estuaries around Nantucket, and Cape Cod, where some friends had watched me working on my little Sunfish. Sensing I would like to learn more about sailing, they asked if I would be interested in joining them bring a boat up from the Bahamas, to Annapolis, Maryland. They arranged for the plane tickets. I had to get a sea-bag with a few shirts, shorts and foul weather gear."

"They planed to leave in two weeks. I didn't hesitate in saying yes, but had no idea of what I was getting myself into. The two weeks couldn't go by quick enough, but it did, and we flew to Miami. Then boarded a puddle-jumper over to Nassau, in the Bahamas." "I had an intoxicating night in Nassau, and the next morning, with a massive hangover, I got on the smallest plane, I had ever seen, with no glass in the windows, and a 45-minute fight to Dead Man's Cay."

"We flew over brilliant, light blue water, and pure white beaches, over endless shapes of little islands, and sandy shoals.

You could almost see the ocean current by shape of the sandy shoals, wrapping around the ends, of the islands, leaving the narrowest channels between them."

"Arriving on Dead Man's Cay, we went straight to the boat. It was beautiful then, and I fell in love with her, the first time I saw her. The friends had bought it sight unseen for a very good price."

"Their thoughts were to fly down, pick it up, and sail it back to Annapolis; where they planned to sell it." Kaysee paused, turned around, and took a long hard look at her boat, then shook her head."

Turning back to Mike she continued, "After seeing the boat, I just had to have her. I made them an offer they couldn't refuse. They sold me the "Kaysee Rose", and we sailed back to Nassau, where I called Rose, and had her fly down to meet me."

"Speaking of Rose, she must be wondering what has happened to me." Kaysee said turning to look in the direction of her boat again.

"I should go, get her. She is more than likely starving, not to mention wanting some coffee." Kaysee said, reaching for the line to the dingy.

"No, let me go." Mike insisted. "I'll set up the boat, so we can tow it with out anyone at its' helm." Mike told her, getting to his feet, and untying the line.

Within seconds, he was over the stern of the "Windjammer", and in the dingy, pulling himself along the tow rope to the "Kaysee Rose". Reaching the bow, he eased his way down the Port side, until he saw Rose at the wheel.

"Hi there, can I come aboard?" Mike shouted, as she had not seen him. "Oh! sure, Mike. I didn't see you coming." Rose said, as Mike pulled himself over the side and into the cockpit.

"Kaysee, thought you might like something to eat, and drink. How about coming over to the "Windjammer" with us?" Mike asked, making fast the line to one of the stanchions.

"That sure sounds good. I am hungry, and could use something to drink." She replied, giving Mike a big smile. "But doesn't someone have to keep the boat straight?" She asked, looking at the position of the two boats.

"I can rig your boat, so it will follow the "Windjammer", without you being on board." Mike told her, moving to the Mizzen Sail, where he lowered it, and tied it to the Mizzen Boom.

"There now she will follow, no mater where we go." Mike said, looking over his handy work.

"Great!" Rose exclaimed, "We haven't left yet?"

The two climbed into the dingy, and pulled themselves back to the stern of the "Windjammer".

"Bet you thought I had forgotten about you." Kaysee said as Rose put up her hand for Kaysee to grab.

"Not really, I was lost in a wide awake sleep." Rose confessed.

21

"I knew she was off somewhere. She didn't see me coming along side." Mike said, climbing back on board the "Windjammer".

"It looks like we aren't alone out here." Rose said, pointing over the stern of the "Kaysee Rose".

Kaysee, and Mike both turned to see what Rose was talking about. They could see a black speck in the distance, moving at high speed, in their direction.

"I can't make out who, or what." Mike stated, "But it won't be long before we will know, at the speed, they're traveling."

Turning back to the ridging of the "Windjammer", Mike adjusted the main and rechecked the course. Everything being to his satisfaction he told the girls, "It will take us another two days at this speed. The "Windjammer" is sailing well, but with the "Kaysee Rose" in tow, it is slow going.

Within a matter of a few minutes, the group on the "Windjammer", found out who it was flying across the water, in their direction.

A 109-foot steal hauled vessel slowed along side the "Kaysee Rose", and eased up to the "Windjammer".

Mike saw the boat was one of the Coast Guard's cutters, so he furled the jib and the main sail. He knew the Coast Guard patrolled these waters for drug smugglers. Almost any boat, now days are thought to be smugglers.

"Ahoy, on deck...This is the Coast Guard Cutter "Saskatchewan" out of St. Simon Light. Can we come on board?" the officer of the deck shouted, as the engines on the Cutter, came to an idle.

Cupping his hands about his mouth, Mike shouted back, "You are welcome to come aboard, if you wish."

One of the men standing at the rail tossed a line to Mike, which he quickly attached to one of the cleats of the "Windjammer". With the line secured, the officer had the men, heave on the line until the Cutter was close enough, for the officer, to climb into the cockpit, of the "Windjammer"

"I'm LT. J.R. Blanchard.," the officer said, offering his hand to Mike. "Looks like you ran into some trouble with the other boat."

"Yes, Sir." Mike replied, shaking the officer's hand.

"We've been out on a routine drug run, when the storm came up. It must have been the same one which got your mast." he stated, looking in the direction of the "Kaysee Rose".

"The "Kaysee Rose" belongs to these two ladies." Mike said, gesturing towards the women on the upper deck of the "Windjammer"

"LT. Blanchard, this is Kaysee Johnson, and her friend Rose Wilson. I picked up their radio call yesterday, and sailed to help them.

"We are towing the boat into St. Simon Island for repairs."

"Ladies" the LT replied, nodding his head in their direction.

"What might be your name Captain, and where is your home port?" the LT. ask, turning back to Mike.

"I'm sorry," Mike said, apologetically, "My name is Mike Ryan, and this is the "Windjammer", out of Charleston, South Carolina."

"May I see your papers, and check your boat for Coast Guard Safety Inspection, while I'm on board?"

"Sure!" Mike exclaimed, "I know everything is in order."

"I'm sure it is Captain, but we must earn our money somehow." the LT. quickly replied.

Mike went below, followed closely by the LT. He went to the chart table and retrieved the "Windjammer's" papers. Handing them to the officer, Mike said, "You can check her out down here first. "The fire equipment is in the galley, and on the stern bulkhead. Flotation devices are lashed to the Port bulkhead, forward and up on deck. I have an auto-can dinghy, right up here." Mike said pointing to a can lashed over head.

"I see you use a Loran, for navigation." the LT. commented.

"Yes, but I also use satellite navigation." Mike quickly replied.

LT. Blanchard walked forward, opening the doors to the cabins.

Then made his way to the galley, where he made a quick check of the equipment there. Opening the door to the main cabin, he stuck his head in and looked around, then returned to where Mike was standing.

"Looks first-rate Captain; I guess we can return topside."

Mike followed LT. Blanchard back up on deck, where the LT. began talking to the two girls.

"Where were you girls headed, before the storm hit your boat?" LT. Blanchard asked, moving into the cockpit, and stepping aside, so Mike could join them.

"We were sailing north to Annapolis. We bought the boat in Freeport, outfitted it, and began our trip, when we ran into the storm."

"I had checked the weather" Kaysee said, then turned to face Mike, saying, "If wasn't for Mike Ryan here, I don't know where we would have been by now."

"Our boat was filled with water, and we didn't think we had much time, before it would be on the bottom." Rose added, giving Mike a pat on the back.

"It wasn't much," Mike quickly said, "Nothing more than anyone else would have done if they had been in the area."

"Perhaps," LT. Blanchard said, "but you did come to their aid, and I will see, my log reflects it." There is one other thing, "How did you rigged up the bulge pump to take care of the water?" He asked.

"That was easy," Mike replied, "I ran wires from my battery to the pump on the Kaysee Rose, and the pump did the work."

"Good thinking Captain. You must be Navy," the LT. said, moving towards the rail of the "Windjammer".

"No, Army Airborne." Mike replied.

Turning back, to face Mike, the LT. said "I would never have thought it...a ground ponder on the water. Maybe you missed your calling. At any rate, we are on our way into St. Simon Island; why not let us tow the "Kaysee Rose" into port, and you all can catch up later?"

Turning to Mike, Kaysee asked, "Do you think it will be all right, if the Coast Guard tows the boat in, and we follow?"

"I don't see why not." Mike replied, glancing at the cutter.

"The Cutter will be much faster, and it will give me a chance to show you what the "Windjammer" can do when she isn't towing more than her own weight.," he added, with a smile on his face.

"Good!" LT. Blanchard exclaimed, and began giving orders to the men on the deck of the Cutter.

Within a few minutes, the men had the wires for the bulge pump disconnected, and the tow line switched to the Cutter. Blanchard surveyed the operation as it was reaching completion, he turned to the group saying,

"Well that will take a load off this boat, and we had better get underway. I will have your boat taken to the marina for repairs and will tell them, you will be along in a day or two."

"Thanks LT. Blanchard, for your help." Kaysee said as she jumped down from the deck into the cockpit.

"It's as good as repaired, Miss Johnson, and I will be looking forward to seeing you in port." he replied, climbing back on to the Cutter.

As Mike was casting off the line to the cutter, he saw a Chief Petty Officer looking start at him. Mike thought he recognized him, but couldn't remember from where. As the cutter started to pull away, LT. Blanchard gave them a little salute. "See you at St. Simon Light."

Within minutes the cutter had cleared the "Windjammer", and was getting up to speed, with the "Kaysee Rose" close behind.

"That was nice of him." Rose said, watching the wake caused by the cutter as it got farther away.

"Yes it was," Mike replied, as he made, adjustments to the sails.

"Boy! That was dumb." Kaysee exclaimed, smacking herself on the forehead.

"What was dumb?" Mike and Rose asked in unison.

We should have gotten some of our things, off the boat before we let the Coast Guard tow it away." she replied, putting her head down.

"I have what ever you need, for the next couple of days." Mike replied, giving them both a smile and spreading his arms.

"That's all well, and good, but we had food in the cooler, which will go bad, before we get in."

"Oh well," Mike, said, "There isn't anything we can do about it now. We might as well, sit back, relax, and enjoy the rest of the trip."

"You are right." Kaysee replied, as she took up a place next to the tiller.

"Does this boat sail itself?" Rose asked, looking at the rigging.

"It can, sometimes." Mike replied, "but most of the time you must adjust the sails, the auto-steering helps a lot."

"Why would you like to take over the helm?" he then asked, moving to the auto-steering equipment, which he disengaged and removed.

"Sure, it would feel more like I was doing something around here." Rose replied, putting her hands on the tiller.

"There you go." Mike said moving away, "Now you can feel the boat under your direction." Mike told Rose.

"What do you want me to do?" Kaysee asked, moving out of Rose's way.

"I don't know." Are you girls hungry?" he asked, looking at the two girls.

"I'm not." Rose answered, looking at Kaysee, "Are you?" she asked, pulling on the tiller a little.

"I could use some more coffee, but not food." she replied, glancing over the side of the "Windjammer".

"Hey Mike!" Kaysee exclaimed, "I thought we were going to have good weather until we got to St. Simon

Island." She quickly added, pointing forward over the port bow.

Mike ducked down, so he could see under the Main Sail. "It sure looks like a storm coming up quick." he said, going to the hatchway where he picked up the radio mike.

"Coast Guard Cutter "Saskatchewan", this is the "Windjammer" do you copy this station?" Mike shouted into the radio mike. He waited for a reply, but none came. He tried again and again, receiving no reply.

"What do you think Mike? Are they out of radio range already?" Kaysee vocalized, still looking at the dark clouds gathering ahead of them.

"I don't think so, they have a fast boat, but not that fast."

Mike went down to the cabin, checking the radio, but found nothing wrong.

He turned it to the weather band, and listened to the marine weather forecast, but there was no mention of a storm. They were predicting fair weather for another 24 hours, with winds not to exceed 15 knots.

"I don't know." Mike confessed, "Looks like this is one of those storms which spring up unexpectedly, and the weather radar misses." he told the girls, who by then had their eyes fixed on the coming storm.

Mike climbed up on the upper deck, and walked forward to the jib spare, so he could get a better look.

"What does it look like?" Rose asked, in a nervous voice.

"Looks like one huge electrical storm, but there doesn't seem to be much wind, and the waves don't seem to be growing any. But that cloud formation sure looks funny."

Mike replied, turning, walking back to where the girls were sitting.

"I remember seeing something like that when I was sailing off Bimimi a few years ago, and the clouds looked just like these." Mike announced, but we sailed away from them, because it looked as if the storm would wipe us out. We were in a small Day-Sailor, only 20 foot long. I think we will be all right."

Turning to Kaysee, Mike asked, "How about going below, and getting the slickers. I will reef the jib and Main Sails. We should be OK." Mike said trying to reassure them.

He climbed into the cockpit, moving to a box, and opened it. He flipped a switch, which started a small electric motor, that turned a small hydraulic pump. He engaged one of the two handles, and began lowering the mast.

As the mast came down the Jib, and Main Sails began to furl. The standing rigging were taken up on spools, which kept the cables tight.

With the mast midway down, he released the handle. Using the other handle he raised the mast slightly, just enough to pull the cables tight, and retain the tune of the mast. Completing the reefing, Mike turned the switch off and closed the box.

"That was very impressive." Kaysee said as she handed Mike a slicker. "Why did you reef the main that way?" she asked turning to hand a slicker to Rose.

"It makes the mast more stable in heavy weather. The Main is furled, the mast is shorter, and the shrouds are still tight; plus the boat is still tuned. It's really nice when you are going up a river, or a cut, where the bridges are low, and you must wait for the bridge to open." Mike explained, moving to adjust the Main Sail.

Their attention was drawn back to the storm, which was closing in on them. The clouds seemed to be swirling like a whirlpool in the sky. Where the clouds met the water, it seemed to be nothing but a fog bank.

Mike checked the heading that Rose was sailing. "Looks good." he told her, "try holding this course."

Suddenly, out of nowhere, the clouds roared right into the "Windjammer", rain started falling heavily, and the wind picked up to roughly 50 miles an hour, the wind quickly backed around a full 90 degrees, and was now howling from the other side.

Mike grabbed some line from the locker in the cockpit. He had the girls tie it around their waist, and then tied the other end to the lifeline stanchion, then attached his harness to the sea anchor.

Abruptly, the lighting started. Huge white bolts streaked out of the sky directly into the black water, a quarter of a mile away. The sky lit up, the waves became visible for an instant, and then only the white caps would remain in their sight.

With the lighting streaking across the rigging, the shortened mast was visible. It had a strange green glow, like a dull light off the top of the mast, and the radio antenna.

"Look at that!" Kaysee shouted, pointing at the top of the mast, and rigging.

"It's St. Elmo's fire." Mike shouted back, "It has scared the hell out of sailors, for hundreds of years. Now that we know about electron transfer, everyone understands it is caused by the transfer of negatively charged ions into the air, which is positively charged.

It's a very weak form of electricity; something like lighting, but weaker." Mike explained.

Instantly, the Granddaddy of all lighting bolts broke loose out of the sky, directly in front of the boat. All three ducked, and then Mike looked up to see the lighting split into five fingers, and curve directly toward them.

There were five orange balls leading the bolts. They shot over the top of the mast, illuminating the sky like a football stadium, and then hit the water behind the "Windjammer".

"Wow!" exclaimed Rose, "What was that?" she shouted as if the world was coming to the end.

"I don't have the foggiest idea." Mike replied, watching the balls disappear into the water.

He checked the compass heading to see that the "Windjammer" was still on course. To his surprise the compass was spinning around, and around. There seemed to be a green glow to the entire boat. He quickly looked forward, and saw nothing but fog. It looked as if the fog was so thick he could hardly make out the bow. All of the rigging was glowing green. He had never seen a sight such as this, all the time he had been offshore sailing.

"Mike, come quick!" Rose shouted, "I think we have broke the rudder...There isn't any feel to the tiller anymore. I can't feel the water pushing on it."

Mike moved to the tiller.

Taking it in his hands, he moved it first to the starboard, and then back to port. The "Windjammer" would not answer the helm, no matter what he did. He looked over the stern...he could make out water, but there was no feel to the rudder.

He checked the compass again. It was still spinning, but in the opposite direction. He hadn't noticed before, but the Windjammer was no longer heeling over, and the wind had eased off. It felt as if the boat was floating in mid-air.

He knew better, but the pitching of the waves no longer had an effect on the boat.

"I can't explain it ladies, but we are not in the water. I don't know what is happening, but we are no longer sailing..." Mike shouted.

Kaysee stuck her hand over the side, trying to touch the water. Drawing it back inside the boat, it seemed wet. She put her fingers to her lips..."It's salt water." she remarked, "But it didn't feel like the boat is moving."

"Maybe we are in a dead clam." Mike remarked.

"Dead!" Rose exclaimed, "We're in the Bermuda Triangle."

"That's just an area," Kaysee said, "I don't believe in any of those stories about the Bermuda Triangle. They write them to sell newspapers."

"You might be right." Mike said, "But we are stuck here, until this fog clears.

The compass isn't working. The radar, and GPS are both out." Mike announced.

"I could use some coffee." Kaysee said, getting up from her seat, "Anyone else in?" she asked, moving to the hatch.

"Yeah, I could use some." Mike answered.

"Me too." Rose chimed in, then turned to Mike, "What are we going to do?" she asked in a shaky, and nervous voice.

"There isn't much we can do until, we know where we are, and the wind picks up. I could start the engine, but in this fog, we could run a ground, into a ship, or another boat." Mike informed her. He gave her a smile, hoping it would make her feel better.

"Here's the coffee." Kaysee announced, sticking her head from the hatch. Rose went to help her with the coffee.

"Mike was telling me there isn't anything we can do until the fog lifts." Rose told her, as the two girls rejoined Mike.

"It sure is funny," Kaysee, said, "there are no lights in the cabin. I had to feel my way around. The gas stove works, but nothing electrical."

Mike looked up at the mast. The green light that had glowed from there seemed to be getting weaker.

"It must be the lighting. It must have drawn the charge from the batteries.

We will ride it out, and then see, where we are." Mike informed them.

❧

CHAPTER THREE

"Hey, Mike... Are you on board?" Came a shout from the dock. It stop the interview, as Captain Ryan went up the steps, and stood in the hatch. After a short conversation, a man about the same age as the Captain, but taller. He was wearing shorts, a red tee shirt and a red and blue St. Louis baseball cap, came below, and was introduced as Bert Williams.

Mike told Bert about the interview, and asked if I wanted to hear Bert's story as it was part of his also. I agreed.

"Let me tell you how I came to be involved with Captain Ryan. How his adventure could have coast me my life, and family, but all things work for good for those who believe in Jesus the Christ." Bert said, putting his hand on my shoulder, and asked,

"Do you believe in God, son?"

"Of course!" I exclaimed, "Even satin believes there is a God."

"Good point." said Bert, "but let me tell you, after hearing our story, you will be beyond doubt."

Bert started his story with:

The day was warm and sunny, not uncommon, for South Florida, in mid March. His "Tilled-Green" "Triumph" convertible cruised down I-95. He had been on the road for some 16 hours straight.

He had left Charleston, South Carolina heading for Miami, to visit his sister and her new husband.

She had moved to Florida, following the death of her first husband, and it had been many years since, Bert had seen her.

Now with the death of his wife, and early retirement from the automotive company, in Detroit, he decided to make the most of the time he had on hand.

For years, he made the daily trip of sixty-miles, from the farm into Detroit. Now he planned to travel the country, seeing places he had only read about. Other than the six years, he spent in the Marines, serving in Vietnam, this was the first time, he had been away from the farm.

He had stopped in Charleston to see some friends, he had made while in the service. But the warm sunny beaches were calling him south.

His sister's new husband was in Real Estate, and told Bert of the places in Miami, which were available, if he would only come down for a visit.

The winter had been cold in Michigan, and Bert wanted to have some fun in the sun, before he joined everyone else.

He wrote his sister, asking her to find him a place on Biscayne Bay. He would have stayed with her, but he wanted a place of his own. He had decided it was time for him to start a new life.

Many thoughts, of what his new life, would be like, ran through his mind as he sped South.

Before he knew where he was, he found his way to his sister's house, just off the Inter-State. She had given him very good directions, thus he had little trouble, finding it.

As he pulled the Triumph, into the long horseshoe driveway, Bert caught sight of his sister, running out to meet him.

"Hi kid!" Bert exclaimed, as she came to his car, "I made it, and you thought I was kidding, about coming down."

"No, I knew this time you would make it...it's been to many years since I saw...I wasn't sure this car was yours." Earlene said, throwing her arms around Bert's neck, almost before he had a chance to bring the car to a stop.

"I have a hundred, and one things to tell you." she shouted, "I don't know where to start."

"How about letting me get out of the car, and we can go from there." Bert said, kissing her on the cheek.

"I'm just so excited, you're finally here...I can't wait to show you off to all of my friends. Let's go in the house," she said, taking Bert by the hand, leading him toward the house.

Bert followed his little sister into the large ranch style, with a sunken family room, which over looked the swimming pool, in the back yard.

"Where is your husband?" Bert asked, as she lead him into the kitchen.

"Oh, he's over at your new apartment. Making last minute changes. I know you're going to love it. It's just what you wanted, with a balcony over-looking the bay. You can see for miles from there," she said, throwing her arms around Bert and hugging him again.

"We would rather have you stay with us, but I understand you wanting to have you're own place." she told him, walking to the counter where a pot of coffee stood. "Want some?" Earlene asked, pointing to the pot.

"I sure could use some; I've been on the road a long time. I didn't even stop for coffee, since I left Charleston." Bert told her, as she placed a cup in front of him.

"You should see the view of the city, at night from your balcony, it will take your breath away. It's a good thing it has an elevator...you live on the 17th floor," she said, moving to the stove, where there was something in the oven.

"Hungry?" she asked, opening the oven, sliding out a big roasting pan.

"Just a little," Bert replied, "Bet I can guess what's in the oven," Bert said, getting up, and walking over to make sure he was right.

"You know what I would make for you, the first time I saw you."

"Yip! Roast Pork, with carrots, and potatoes." Bert replied, looking into the pot.

"You do still like it don't you?" Earlene asked, standing up to look him in the face.

"I sure do." Bert said, "But I don't cook it for myself. You know Dad doesn't like pork, so we have beef most of the time."

"How is the old man?" she asked, as she poked the carrots to see if they were done.

"About the same, him and Jill don't go many places now days, the snow has kept them close to the farm. Their are both in good health." Bert stated, as the door opened, and Earlene's husband walked in.

"Hey! You made it." Dale shouted, extending his hand to greet his brother-in-law. "Have any trouble finding the place?" he asked.

"No trouble at all, Earlene gave good directions." Bert replied, moving back to the counter, where his coffee cup sat.

"How long before dinner," Dale asked, moving to a stool beside Bert.

"Not long." Earlene stated, pouring him a cup of coffee.

"Grab your coffee, and I'll show you around. I know your sister didn't take the time. She was so happy to see you that everything else went out of her head." Dale said, as he moved, to the back door.

While Bert, and Dale walked around the back yard, Earlene finished preparing dinner, and a short time later the back door opened, with Earlene hollering at the two "Dinner is on the table.

The dinner was done to perfection. Bert's sister was a "Good Cook"; it was one thing their Grandmother, had insisted on.

"After dinner, we will take you to your apartment. I'm sure you must be tired, and need a good night sleep. Dale told Bert.

"Just a little...it has been a long day." Bert admitted, pushing himself back from the table, "That sure was a good dinner, Earlene, it's one I haven't had in a long time." Bert said, leaning over giving his sister a kiss.

"I'm glad you liked it. We don't have it very often either," she said, giving him a big smile.

After cleaning the table, and putting the dishes in the dishwasher, the threesome left for Bert's apartment. It was only a short drive to the bay. Bert followed Dale into the parking garage, to the forth level, where they parked.

"You could parked on another two levels, but this is the easiest way to get out in the morning." Dale said, as they walked to the elevator.

Once in the apartment, Bert could see just what his sister, had been talking about...the view was breathtaking.

"So? What do you think?" Earlene asked, walking to the balcony.

"Isn't it everything I said, it would be?" she asked.

"It sure is a lot more than I expected." Bert admitted, joining her on the balcony.

The breeze drifted through the apartment, Bert had always wanted to live by the water. His folks had a cottage on Lake Erie, but this was nothing like anything he had seen before.

"We have everything turned on...the phone works, and there is maid service. Dale explained, "We knew you wouldn't want to keep house for yourself."

"I don't know how I can ever thank you enough. This is just what I needed." Bert told them.

"Hey! What are sisters for?"

"Come on I'll help you get your things out of the car." Dale said walking to the door.

"I don't have, all that much." Bert confessed. "I told Dad to send me the rest, once I got here, and saw what I would need."

"That's good thinking." Earlene said, patting Bert on the back,

"One thing for sure you don't need, is Winter cloths."

"Call me in the morning." Earlene said, as they were leaving. "I'll show you around the city."

"OK, but it won't be very early, I think I will sleep in." Bert informed her.

Bert thanked, Dale for all he had done, in getting the apartment ready for him, and for having him for dinner.

"You know you are always welcome, at our house, Bert." Dale said, "Just don't forget, where we live...I'm glad you are in Florida."

Bert closed the door behind his sister, and brother-in-law Then walked out on the balcony, to look at the skyline one more time, before starting to unpack.

After two hours of unpacking, Bert decided it was time for a break. He went to kitchen, and made himself, a cup of coffee. Then took it out on the balcony, where he looked down, into the marina, and out at the bay.

"This sure is better than Winter in Michigan." he thought to himself, "but I should get some sleep." he thought, trying to convince himself to go to bed.

"What the hell." He said to himself. "You can sleep when your dead."

Turning to go back in side, Bert could hear what sounded like a party, somewhere in the marina, just below him. He walked back to the railing, trying see who, was partying, but couldn't.

Going back inside, he closed the door behind him. Setting his coffee cup on the bar, he walked to the front door, and entered the hallway, leading to the elevator. Where he met a couple coming toward him.

"Hi there, you must be Dale Coat's brother-in-law. We heard you would be moving in next door." The shout, gray haired man said, adding "I'm Doctor John Billings, and this is my wife Janet. We live right next door to you."

"I'm glad to meet you, and yes, I am Dale's brother-in-law. My name is Bert Williams." Bert replied, extending his hand to the man. "I'm just moving in tonight."

"We are sure glad, to have someone next door, that we can get to know…it is so hard down here, to meet decent people now a days." the woman said, giving Bert a smile. "I hope we will be seeing you around" she added, as they started walking toward their apartment.

"Oh, you will." Bert replied, as he walked to the elevator, they had just exited.

As the door to the elevator closed, Bert pushed the button for the first floor. He decided to walk down to the marina, to see just what kind of party, he was missing.

He walked out of the parking garage, down the walkway, and across a parking lot, before entering the gate, leading to the marina.

At the entrance, there were three docks with boats… big boats…on either side. Bert took the center dock, and started down, looking at the yachts on both sides. He had gone only a few feet, when he heard the sounds of a party, coming from a yacht four slips down.

As he approached a tall, slander woman, climbed down the steps onto the dock, in front of him. As she turned she caught sight of Bert.

"Hi there coming to the party?" she asked, as she straitened her dress, walking toward Bert.

"No, I've just moved down here, so I don't know, who is giving the party." Bert confessed, "In fact I don't know anyone at all."

"I was that way when I moved here from Iowa…My name is Linda Carrie," the woman said, extending her hand, for Bert to take.

"Hi, my name is Bert Williams, and I live just up there." Bert replied, taking her hand, and pointing over his shoulder.

"Up where?" the woman asked, looking first at Bert, and then at the building directly in front of her.

"Up there, on the 17th floor." Bert said, pointing to his balcony, "See the balcony in the middle of the 17th floor...that's the one I just moved into tonight."

"That's a nice apartment complex," she said, "I had a friend who lived there, but she lived, on the third floor. I'll bet the view from up there would be great. In my friends apartment, you could only see the marina."

"Yeah, the view is great. I can see the lights of the city, and almost the whole bay." Bert told her.

"Hey, if you just moved in, why not come to the party with me. I'm on my way to get some more beer, but you sure would be welcome. The guy who owns the boat is a friend on mine, and his motto is "The more the merrier the party." Doesn't that sound like fun?" she asked, coming closer to Bert.

"Yes it does... sound like fun, but are you sure it would be all right?" he asked, in a somewhat shy voice.

"Sure it will be all right." she replied, taking Bert by the arm, "Come with me...we will get the beer, and then it's right back here, to the party."

"Sounds great to me," Bert said, letting her lead him back up the dock toward the parking lot.

"My car is parked right up here. We won't be very long. The store is just three blocks down. she said, pointing to a bright red Camero.

"A pretty car," Bert stated, getting in, and closing the door.

"I like it, and it gets me where I want to go." she replied, giving him a smile, and flipping her red hair, back from her face.

"Where did you say you were from?" Bert asked, as she started the car.

"I'm from Sioux City, Iowa, and I've been down here for the past two Winters," she answered, turning in her seat, to see out the back window.

"Two winters." Bert repeated, "Does that mean you go back to Sioux City in the summer?" he then asked, without taking his eyes off of her.

"Well, the first Summer I did. But this last year, I stayed down here, and just loved it. Besides there isn't anything back there, for me anymore." she said, shifting into first gear, and they headed out of the parking lot.

"Where are you from?" she asked, as she turned right on Highway A1A.

"I just left Michigan, where I have a 380 acre farm, it was my Grandfather's. With death of my wife, and an early retirement, I decided to move down here." Bert told her, trying not to bore her with past history.

"Looks like we have a lot in common." she said, as the car turned into the parking lot of a 7/11 store.

When it came to a stop, she told Bert, "I will be right out, all I have to get is some beer." she paused, turning to Bert, "You do drink beer, don't you?"

"Yeah, and I like water too." he replied, opening the door on his side.

As they met at the front of the car, Linda asked, "How about red heads?"

"I don't know you are the first one I have met." Bert replied, giving her a big smile.

"OK! We must make it a good impression for all red heads, in America," she said, taking his arm, as they entered the store.

"They sent me for Miller Lite. Is that Ok with you?, or do you drink some other kind of beer?" she asked, walking to the cooler with cases in it.

"Miller Lite is fine," Bert said, opening the cooler door, and extracting two cases.

"Do we need anything else?" Bert asked, as he carried the beer to the counter, at the front of the store.

"No, this should be all we need." Linda replied, reaching for her purse.

"I'll get it." Bert said, setting the cases on the counter.

"You don't need to do that!" she exclaimed, "the guys gave me money for the beer. So save it, you might want to take me out to dinner, or something."

"Since you put it that way," Bert said, turning to the young blonde behind the counter, "The lady will pay."

"It must be Miller Time," she said, as she punched in the price of the beer.

Linda paid for the beer, and Bert carried them to the car. Setting them in the back seat.

As he slid into the front seat, Linda got in and started the car.

"Now let's go party!" she exclaimed, putting her hand to Bert's face, and giving it a little pat.

"I guess, I should worn you, when we get back to the boat, everyone will give you the third degree. I'm like their sister. So they are going to want to know everything about you. If you become uneasy with it, just give me a sign, and I will get them off your case." Linda said, as she pulled the car to a halt, in the parking lot of the marina.

"I'll get the beer." Bert said, as he got out of the car.

"For some reason, I was sure you would." Linda responded, as she locked the car doors, and started down the dock-way, towards the boat.

Approaching the boat, Linda climbed aboard, and told Bert to hand her, the cases of beer. "It will be easier for you to climb aboard." she said, taking the beer for him.

With Bert on board, she handed the beer back to him. They walked the few steps, to the sliding door of the main salon. Linda sledded the door open, announcing her return with, "Knock, knock, I'm back."

A man with white hair turned, and upon seeing Linda, said, "Good here is our girl with the beer."

Bert handed the beer to the man, as Linda said, "This is Bert Williams, everyone." "He has just moved down here from Michigan, and I thought we might have him over for a party. That way he will get to know some people around here."

"Glad to have you here, Bert" the white haired man said, "My name is John O' Malley, and this is my boat." then turned to Linda saying, introduce him around, and I will be right back, I'll put this beer on ice."

Linda did as she was told. Taking Bert by the hand she went from group to group, introducing him to the 20 some people, at the party.

Approaching the last set of four people, Linda said, "Jim Butler, my friend, Bert Williams. He has just moved into those new apartments on the other side of the parking lot." the man extend his hand to Bert, saying, "Glad to met you, Bert. What do you think of the apartments?" he asked, shaking Bert's hand.

"I've only been here for a few hours, but everything looks great. I real like the balcony. You can see the entire harbor from there."

The man thought for a mount and said, "There are only two apartments which, over look this side of building. There is one my partner owns, and the other, my Real Estate broker has, for his wife's brother. You must be Earlene's brother, Right?"

"You know my sister, and brother-in-law?" Bert asked, with a suppressed, look on his face.

"I sure do...Your Brother-in-law, has been a God sent. He has almost all of the apartments sold, or leased." Jim said, then added,

"I don't know how he has done it, but I have been able to start another project, as soon as I had this one completed."

Jim turned, and walked to the sliding door, which Bert, and Linda had entered a short time earlier saying,

"Everyone, can I have your attention. The man you have all just met as Bert Williams, is none other than Earlene's brother. A small world, or what?"

"Here, here!" everyone chained in at once."

Linda squeezed Bert's arm saying, "I know your sister really well. We are close friends. We go shopping, and to the club together. I knew there was something about you I liked, the first moment our eyes met. Want a beer? I'll go get it for you."

"Sure, I could use one. Little did I know my sister, and her husband were so, well known. I'll go with you to get that beer." Bert replied, following Linda to the galley area, where she opened the cooler, and retrieved a can of Miller Lit, handing it to Bert.

"Oh, yes your family is well known around here." "In fact, your sister told me yesterday, you were coming down. She said, she would introduce us. She said, she was sure I would like you. I saw you, and you know what? She was right." Linda said, leaning over and giving Bert a kiss, on the cheek.

"I don't know how to take all of this." Bert confessed, looking around at all of the people, he had just met, and at the girl who had picked him up on the dock, just an hour ago.

"Things around here move fast don't they," He said, giving Linda a smile. Taking him by the hand, she leaded him back into the main salon, where John O'Malley was standing.

"How on earth, did you meet Bert here, so soon?" John asked, taking Bert's hand, and giving it a shake.

"I was just talking to your sister, this morning. She was telling how she was looking forward, to seeing you. It has been sometime since you two have been together." he told Bert.

"Yes, it has been quite a while...what with the service, and the farm in Michigan. She didn't get back home much, and I couldn't leave, but now our father is taking care of the farm, and I am here." Bert replied.

"Well, you have a good time, but you must excuse me I must check the tide. This boat can be more work, than I had planed. It's like a woman, you can't leave them along, for very long." John said, as he hurried to the sliding door.

Opening it, he shouted, "OK! Now the party is complete!", stepping a side to let a woman, and man enter.

As the light of the salon shown the faces, everyone could see, it was Earlene, and Dale. John gave Earlene a kiss on the cheek, and shook Dale's hand saying, load enough for everyone to hear.

"I'm glad you guys showed up. I was beginning to think you weren't coming, what with your brother, just getting into town."

"You know we wouldn't miss a party on your boat, John." Earlene said, stepping into the salon.

"Hi Sis, Bet you guys, never expected to see me here." Bert said, as he approached the two newcomers.

"Well! No wonder you didn't answer the phone. How on earth did you find this place?" Earlene exclaimed, throwing her arms around his neck.

"Have you been here very long?" She asked, giving him a kiss. She turned to the rest of the group, who had gathered around.

"Has everyone met my big brother, Bert? He has just moved down from Michigan, to be with his sister."

"Yes, I have introduced him to everyone." Linda said, coming to Bert's side.

"How did Bert met you?" Earlene asked, giving Linda a strange look.

"He is the brother you wanted me to meet, right?" Linda asked, moving closer to Bert.

"Yeah, but I thought I would introduce you to him. Where did you pick him up?" she asked, cunningly.

"I don't think I picked him up, as much as he struck me as someone who was lonely, and needed a friend." Linda explained, giving Bert's arm a squeeze.

"The truth is sister; I heard music from my balcony, and thought I would find out where the party was. I didn't think I would be going to the party. I just wanted to see where it was. Then I met Linda, and she invited me to come along." Bert explained, and then went on to say, "I had no idea, that everyone here would be friends of my little sister."

"Well, I'm glade, you found the right party to attend. It sure would have been nice, if you would have let me know, but I can see how it would have been hard." Earlene told Bert.

"Ok, enough, where is the beer. I sure could use one." Dale said, as he looked around the solon, to see where they had put the cooler.

"I know where they are, I will get you one." Bert said, moving from his sister, to where he had seen John put the beer.

As he returned with the beer, John told Dale, and Earlene that there was snacks on the counter, they should help their selves.

Everyone on the boat, went back to conversing, about everything under the sun. Bert and Linda walked out on the deck, for some fresh air, and so they could be alone.

"The sky, the stars look, and feel so close down here." Bert said, putting his back to the rail, taking in the sky.

"This time of year, they do seem like you could reach up, and pick them, like oranges." Linda replied, joining him in his upward gaze.

Bert directed his look to the girl, standing beside him, saying "I'm glad we met, before my sister introduced us."

"I hope she's not mad at me, but there was something about the way you said, Hi, made me want to know you better. I hope you don't think, I do that all the time. Any other time, I might have returned your Hi, but I would have kept walking. Hoping we would be introduced by someone."

"Well, that would work sometimes, but I'm sure am glad, you asked me to accompany you to the party. My sister, has been known to introduce me to the wrong people. So, through the years, I've become leery of the girls, she has tried to fix me up with." Bert confessed, looking back up at the night sky.

"So, does that mean you wouldn't have liked me, if your sister would have introduced us?" Linda asked, giving Bert a cold look, which he caught quickly.

"No, No, that's not what I'm saying, but I might have tried to get out of meeting you at all. I'm glade we met the way we did. It looks like I would have missed out, on meeting a terrific girl."

"I'm glad you feel that way." Linda replied, accepting the complement, and taking Bert by the arm.

Bert turned to face her, and was about to kiss her, when a voice came over his shoulder.

"This is where you two went." Earlene said, as she approached the couple.

"Yeah, I thought we should get to know each other better. Sis" Bert said, steeping back to face his sister.

"Everyone thought you two had left. I told them I would find you, and drag, you back to the party," she said, taking Bert's arm easing him back to the solon.

"I know you can use another beer. Besides, there is someone else, I want you to meet." Earlene said, giving Linda a sly look, as the three moved back down the side of the boat.

"Do I know them?" Linda asked holding Bert's other arm.

"Oh Linda, you know everyone." Earlene replied, not giving her time to ask who it was.

As the threesome entered the solon, Dale met them at the door saying, "I see you found them."

"Yeah, they were just up on deck." Earlene said, moving to the cooler with the beer in it.

"Bert I would like you to meet, Bill Davis, he is our local "Dock Master". He knows everything going on around here." Dale said, moving to the side of the tall middle-aged man.

"I'm glad to meet you." Bert said, taking the hand extended to him.

"Hi, Boss," Linda said, sticking her head around Bert's back.

"Not paying much attention to Linda, Bill went on saying, "Dale was just telling me, you like the water, and have sailed the Great Lakes." Davis said, taking back his hand, in time to fill it with the beer, Earlene handed him.

"Yes, I like sailing very much. I find it more relaxing than power. That is, as long as you are not in a hurry." Bert replied, giving a smile to his brother-in-law, who himself like boats, but he was a power-man.

"I have been trying to convene Bert that Power Boating is the only way to go. You control where, and when you get there, rather than being at the mercy of Mother Nature." Dale interjected, as Bert turned to listen to Linda, who was tugging at his arm.

"I want to go back up on deck. Do you want to come along?" she asked, giving him a big smile, letting go of his arm.

"I'll be along in minute. If that is all right with you." Bert replied, feeling like he was dropping her attention.

"Sure, if you would rather be with these, gentleman. I'll be on deck," she told him, as she walked to the sliding door.

"I can see where power down here, would be better than sail. If you wanted to go around the bay. But if you wanted to go out in the ocean, I think sail; would be the only way to go." Bert said, turning back to the conversation with Bill Davis, and Dale.

"There just happens to be a boat, which has been docked here for a long time. It's arrival in the marina was under other than favorable conduction. It seams, that the ordinal owner disappeared off her decks just out side the harbor. In fact, it was the father of a friend of Linda's. I don't know if she has heard from him lately, but I know he was some place in Europe, the last time I heard." Bill told Bert. Going on to say "I think he gave Linda the boat, but she has done nothing with it."

"Maybe I will ask her about it. By the way, she is waiting for me up on deck. I think, I have kept her waiting long enough. If you guys don't mind, I will go join her." Bert said, turning to leave, but was stop by his sister.

"Where do you think you are going?" Earlene asked, as she took hold of Bert's arm.

"I was going to join Linda, up on the forward deck. Why, do you need something Sis?" Bert asked, giving his sister a big smile

"No, I just thought you might be lonesome, but I guess not. I will go over by Dale." Earlene said, as she gave Bert, a pat on the cheek.

"Linda is a nice person. I'm glad you met her on your own. I was going to introduce you to her in the morning. But now if something goes wrong you can't, blame me."

Bert gave his sister, a kiss on the cheek. Then walked toward the sliding door, leading to the upper deck, where he found Linda, pacing the deck, and looking at the stars.

Bert coughed slightly, as he approached, thinking he wouldn't startle her, but she jumped anyway.

"Wasn't sure you were going to come up here. I guess it was hard to get away from the guys, talking about boats." she said, giving him a glance, and then went back to looking up at the night sky.

"Yeah, Dale, and Bill wanted me to stay, and talk boating. I think they wanted to keep me from being with you." Bert said, in a laughing voice.

"Oh, they were just trying, to make you feel part of the group. They haven't had anyone new, in the gathering in a long time. I'm sure they want to see, just how you're going to fit in."

"All of them seem to like you. Your sister, has told me so much about you, I almost think I have known you for years." Linda said, looking back at Bert; who had steeped closer, looking in the same direction as she had been.

She slipped her hand in his, as they both stared out into space. She could feel the warmth of his hand, and knew she was getting close.

She liked the man, she found standing next to her. It had been a long time, since she had felt anything, for any man. This one wasn't only fun to be around, but was also a friend's brother.

Her own life, hadn't been going very well. With the divorce, and her ex-husband, still around. She didn't know, just how much Bert's sister, had told him about her. She hoped Earlene, would have given her a good endorsement, but she wasn't sure. Everyone had liked Peter Fox.

He had been a nice guy on the surface, but had problems dealing with life in general. His mood swings, weren't bad in the beginning, but after they had been married, a few months, things began to fall apart. She wanted, to tell Bert, about her marriage, but was afraid of running him off, before he had a chance to get to know her.

Linda turned the conversation back to water, and being in Florida, a topic that would be safer.

"Do you like to swim?" Linda asked, looking over the side of the boat, and than back at Bert.

"Sure!" Bert replied, quickly giving her a smile, and a squeeze to her arm.

"Well, let's go swimming now." she said, looking back at the stars in the night sky.

"Would you like to swim in salt water, or would the pool be better?" He asked, turning to face her, looking her straight in her deep blue eyes.

"I was thinking, more like just going over the side, right here, and now." she replied, leaning forward, giving him a kiss on the cheek, followed with a big smile.

Bert had heard, Miami was fast and loose, but he didn't expect to run into it at a party, where his sister's friends were. But than all things change over the years, and this wasn't Michigan, he thought to himself.

"OK!" Bert replied, as he started to unbutton his shirt.

"I was only kidding," she said, taking hold of his hands from his shirt, and putting them around her neck.

"Well, if you don't want to go swimming here. What do you want to do?" Bert asked, steeping back a steep.

"I just wanted to see, just how far you would go with your sister down stairs." she told him, moving closer, sliding her arms around his neck, pulling him to her lips.

The kiss lasted a long time. Bert was sure someone, was going to come up, to see what the two had been doing on the upper deck.

Thoughts of his sister, coming to check on him, ran through his mind. What's with this woman? What's she after? Why is she coming on so strong?

As the kiss ended, Linda pushed Bert back a little, and looked him straight in the eyes, saying, "Wow! You are some kisser. Where have you been all of my life?"

"Just hiding out, on the farm." Bert replied, giving her a little smile.

"Hey you two." a voice shouted from the lower deck. "Come on back to the party. Everyone is beginning to wonder where you have been hiding."

`It was a voice that both recognize. It was the voice of Bert's sister.

"Guess we had better get back down stairs." Linda said, taking Bert by the arm, and moved toward the steeps.

"We will get away from here as soon as we can." Bert said, as they walked down the steeps.

Earlene was standing at the bottom waiting for them. "Everyone thought you two had left, without saying a word," she said, taking Bert by his other arm; leading him back into the main cabin.

As they entered, Bert could hear voices say, "There they are. They didn't leave yet."

Dale came over to Bert saying as he approached, "I thought you two had left. Bert come over here, I want you to get in on this conversation with Bill and Dr. O' Malley. They seem to think you might have a point about sailing, verses motor boating."

Bert turned to say something to Linda, but his sister had dragged her off to a group of people, who were in a discussion over what was going on over the weekend. Linda glanced back at him, and glared over her shoulder. He gave her a smile, and followed Dale.

"Now tell my brother-in-law what you two, were saying about sailing. He is really into sailing. myself I like power." Dale instructed as they approached.

"Hi, Bert, we thought you, and my secretary had left. She has a way of capturing the attention." Bill said, patting Bert on the back.

"No, we were just up on deck looking at the stars." he explained.

"I'm sure you were just looking at the stars, all that time. Dr. O' Malley added, giving Bert a smile.

"You guys don't think I'm going to kiss, and tell, do you?" Bert said, in a sheepish voice.

"We wouldn't think of it." But, that's a nice shade of lipstick. Dale interjected, as all three laughed.

"Have you talked to Linda about the boat?" Bill asked, changing the conversation.

"No, not yet. We were talking about other things, but I will. What kind of boat does she have?" Bert asked, turning to look in Linda's direction.

"She had better tell you about it. There was some surreptitious surrounding the boat." Bill explained, as he turned back to Dale, and the Doctor.

With Bill's words, Bert walked toward Linda, wondering how he was going to bring up, the subject of the boat, without getting personnel. Until he asked her, he wouldn't know what the, guys, were talking about.

Linda saw Bert start towards her. Moving away from the group of women, she had been talking to, meeting him in the middle of the cabin.

"Want to get out of here?" she asked, as Bert came face to face with her.

"I was thinking about it."

"But how do we do it without being to conspicuous?" He asked, giving a look around the cabin. "You know what they will think, if we say we're leaving."

"Yeah right, your sister will want to know where we are going. She will think, I am taking you away from her. I have never seen her act so presumptive." Linda said, turning to look over her shoulder.

"Well, I am her big brother. I guess she just wants to keep me safe, since this is the first time I've been in Florida." Bert said, giving Linda a little smile, as he took her by the arm, and headed for the door.

"Hey Bert, where are you going," Earlene hollered, as Bert, and Linda paused to open the door.

"Linda is going to show me her boat." Bert stated, sliding the door open. He then turned back to the group of people, who had gathered at the doorway. "We will be right back, if not; thanks for the party, and we will see you all tomorrow."

The couple steeped out the door, quickly closed it behind them, before anyone could say another word.

"I don't know if that will work or not, but at least we are out of there." Bert said, as he helped Linda down over the side of the boat, and onto the dock.

"I hope no one will be to upset with us, especially your sister." Linda confessed, straightening her dress, once she had reached the dock.

Bert quickly joined her on the dock. They were half way to the parking lot, when they heard a voice they both knew, and was half expecting.

"Hold up you two. Wait until I get to you. I have something to say." Earlene shouted, waving her hands in the air.

Bert, and Linda stopped, turned around and waited.

"I had a feeling she would come after us." Linda said, taking Bert's arm, and holding on to it tightly.

"Are you two going over to that old boat, tonight?" she asked, when she was close to the couple.

"Not really. We just wanted to get away from the party. We wanted to talk, and everyone, wanted us to talk to them. We want to talk to each other." Bert said, quickly, knowing that his statement might surprise his sister, and didn't want to hurt her, or mad.

"Oh, Ok! I'll see you tomorrow, right?" she asked, with a withdrawn voice, and drooping her head, as if to say, I don't mean to interfere.

"Sure Sis. I call you in the morning. Don't worry, I'll be all right." Bert reassured her, as he leaned over kissing her on the cheek.

"I know, but I still want us to be friends. I haven't seen you in so long." Earlene said, giving him a big childish smile.

"I will take good care of him." Linda said, patting Earlene on the arm.

"Oh, I'm sure of that," she replied, "That is what I'm worried about." Then they all laughed.

"Go on, get out of here you two. I'll talk to you in the morning." Earlene said, as she turned, and started back to the party.

"Well that was easier than I thought, it would be." Linda said, easing Bert on up the dock.

They had only taken a few steps, when Linda turned to Bert, asking, "How did you know about the "Witchcraft"? I don't remember telling you about it."

"You didn't. Dale, Bill, and Doc. were talking about it. They said, you would tell me about it, when you were ready." Bert replied, giving her a little understanding smile.

"We could always go up to my new apartment, if you would rather." Bert said, opening the gate to the parking lot for her.

"Yeah, we could, but I know this place called "The Shipwreck".

"It is a nice quit little place, and the decor is more along the line of the story, I am going to tell you." Linda said, easing him toward her car.

The drive to the lounge was a short one, and Bert didn't have a chance to ask her about her boat. He thought to himself, as they proceeded to the parking lot, of a small lounge on highway 1A1.

As they entered the bar, Bert could see what Linda meant by quite. There was only one other couple, sitting in a booth, back in corner.

Linda, lead the way to a table, a short way for the bar, where they took up seats. They had just sat down, when the Bar Maid, approached asking if she could take their order.

"What would you like?" she asked, looking across the table at Linda.

"I'll have a Screwdriver." She stated, giving a smile to the young blonde, standing at the table.

"Ok, I'll have a Johnny Walker "Red", and Water." Bert said, arranging the napkins, the waitress had place in front of him.

"Fine." the waitress said, "I'll be right back with you drinks." Turned, and walked to the bar to place the orders.

"I don't know how to start my story." Linda confessed, looking Bert in the eye.

"Have you ever heard of the Bermuda Triangle?" she asked, as the waitress placed their drinks in front of them.

"I've heard of it." Bert said, "But I don't know much about it. Other than it is someplace, out in the Atlantic Ocean."

"Well, it is out in the Atlantic, but the Atlantic, is just out there." Linda said, pointing out the window, just to his right.

"That's where my story is." Linda said, looking into his eyes.

As she turned to look, out the window, she began to tell him about the "Witchcraft"".

"A few years ago, my mother, and her friend went out by buoy #7, which is just out side the bay, to see the lights of Miami, and that was the last time anyone has heard anything of them, to this day."

"Oh Harold, had made a call to the Coast Guard, about some trouble with the boat, but by the time the Coast Guard arrived at the buoy, there was no sign of them. The boat was riding at anchor, but there was no one on board. The Coast Guard towed the boat back into marina, and ran a search for my mother and Harold, but there wasn't anything to go on."

"According to the Coast Guard, they must have tried to swim to shore, and had drown. But their bodies have never turned up. They went so far as to say, that Mom and Harold's bodies could have been devoured by sharks. Isn't that a horrible thought." She asked, brushing a tear from her right eye.

"Yes it is!" Bert exclaimed, "The Coast Guard hasn't done anything else to find them?"

"No not at all. They say it is just another unexplained disappearance in the area known as the Bermuda Triangle." Linda replied, taking a sip from her glass.

"So what have you done with the boat?" Bert asked, trying to gently get her away from the thoughts of her mother, and friend who had gone missing.

"Nothing." she said, placing the glass back on her napkin. "It has been to hard to even go down the dock to where the boat is tied up. Let alone go on board," she said, brushing another tear from her eye.

"Are you going to take me to see it?" Bert asked, setting his glass back on the table.

"I guess, we could go see it tomorrow, or sometime. I should check on it. Someone, was telling me, it's in bad shape. But like I said, I haven't been there in a long time." she replied, looking around the lounge.

The Waitress approached the table, asking if they wanted another drink, as the lounge was going to close shortly.

"Thanks." Bert said, "But we are going right after we finish this one." he told her holding up his glass.

"Yeah, we should get going." Linda said, as she reached for her handbag, which she had placed under the table, on the floor.

"Will you take me home?" Bert asked, sliding his chair back, and getting to his feet.

"I had planned on it." Linda replied, putting her glass on the table, getting to her feet.

Bert went to the bar, and paid his bill, leaving the waitress a tip. They thanked the bartender, and the waitress as they walked from the lounge.

It was only a short trip from the lounge to Bert's apartment. When they had arrived in the parking lot. "Will I see you tomorrow?" Bert asked, as he was getting out of the car.

"Sure! If you want. I really enjoyed being with you I'm looking forward to seeing you tomorrow. What time would you like me to pick you up?" Linda asked, after Bert had closed the car door.

"What ever time is good for you." He replied, bending down so he could speak through the window.

"I'll be here about 7:30." Linda said, giving him a smile as she eased the car forward, and headed out of the lot.

Bert watched as she drove away. Wondering just where this encounter was going to lead. Then he turned, and walked the 17 flights to his apartment.

ᔇ

CHAPTER FOUR

Bert's story was interrupted, by the sound of women's voices, on the upper deck of the "Windjammer".

"Hey Mike are you going to give us a hand, moving all this stuff on the boat?" a woman's voice came through the hatch.

"Not right this minute." Mike replied, in a loud voice.

Bert stood up, and walked the short distance to the ladder, leading to the upper deck, saying "We are being interviewed by a writer."

"A writer, what on earth is he writing about?" came a reply from the woman.

"We are telling him, how we found the island, for the Chadwicks" Bert answered.

In the next second, a woman dressed in a one piece swimsuit, started to descend the steeps, telling Bert to get out of her way.

Mike Ryan stood saying "This is Mickey Mc Guire, and he is doing a story on what we went through in the "Bermuda Triangle", thirty years ago."

"Kaysee, this is Mickey Mc Guire. Mickey this is my loving wife, Kaysee."

I got up, and extended my hand, which she took quickly, saying I'm glad to meet you, but why would you want to write about us old fogies?"

"I was doing some reach on the Triangle, and ran across Captain Mike's name in a number of the Coast Guard's reports, and thought I might get some good information from him." I replied, setting back down at the table.

"I supposes he told you how I chased him down here, after he saved us from the clutches of the sea." Kaysee said, with a big smile, sliding down, and sitting on the bench beside me.

"Captain Mike, told me about how he met you and Rose at sea, and gave you a lift to the marina in Georgia." I replied, looking at my notes.

"We haven't got to that part of the story yet." Mike said, taking a sip of his coffee.

Kaysee got up from the bench, and headed to the hatch, where she shouted through the hatch, "Hey! Rose, come down here, there is someone who wants to meet you."

Turning back to me she said, "You must meet Rose, she is the one who can confirm what I am about to tell you… if you want to here our story, which took place after Mike, came to our rescues."

"Oh, sure, I like to hear your story." I replied, not knowing what all she would tell me.

Rose descend the steps, and came to the table beside Kaysee. I stood the best I could sneezed into the bulkhead as I was. She was short, and was wearing a two-piece swimsuit, that showed a good figurer, for her age. Her salt and pepper hair was cut short, and tapered on the back of her neck.

"This is Mickey." Kaysee said, as Rose stuck out her hand for me to take.

"Hey, I'm glad to meet you." I said, and then sat back down.

"Rose is the one who got me to sail the boat down here. I wanted to go back North, but she insisted we come to Miami." Kaysee said, moving over to give Rose room, at the end of the bench.

"Now, you know that's not true Kaysee, you were the one who, wanted to come South, after the boat was fixed." Rose stated, with a frown on her face.

"Well, maybe a little." Kaysee said, reaching over, and patting Mike's hand. "Where would you like me to start our story?" Kaysee asked.

"How about where you two arrived in Miami." I said going back to my notes.

☙

The sun was high in the clear blue sky over Biscayne Bay, as the "Kaysee-Rose" entered the choppy waters, of the Miami basin. It had been a long trip for the two girls, following the repair of their boat in Georgia. They had stopped in Melbourne, just long enough to get supplies, for the rest of the trip south.

Now Kaysee Jackson had her shipmate, and friend lower the Main Sail, so she could handle the boat, in the channel of the Bay. She quickly started the Diesel engine, engaged to transmission, gaining control of the boat, and headed it around the channel markers, on the east side of the bay.

"Wow! Look how big Miami is from the water." Rose exclaimed, handing Kaysee a cup of coffee. "Do you think we will ever find Mike down here?"

"I sure hope so." Kaysee replied, taking the cup, "I would hate to think, we came this far, not to find him."

"Look at all of the sailboats. Where on earth, do we start looking?" Rose asked, shaking her dark brown hair in the breeze.

"All we can do is check all of the marinas, on this side of the bay, and if he's not here, we will check the other side." Kaysee replied, taking a sip of coffee, then gesturing to the right with her cup hand, "See that sign. The Marina Del Ray is just on the right."

"We'll put in there. I don't know, how much fuel we have in the tank. I want to stretch my legs, it has been a long trip." Kaysee said, drinking the last of her coffee.

Kaysee guided the boat along the main channel of the marina, until she saw a sign stating that all visitors should tie up at the main fuel dock, and sign in at the office.

"Maybe the marina office, will have some idea where we could start looking for Mike." Kaysee said, pointing to the sign.

Kaysee followed the signs to the main fuel dock. She eased the boat into the dock, next to the fuel pumps.

Coming close to the pier, she backed off the throttle, with the chugging of the engine, slowed the boat's drift into the dock.

Rose jumped from the boat with a line in her hand. She tied it to one of the cleats on the dock. First she tide the bow, then ran to the stern catching the line Kaysee throw her. Rose pulled on the line bringing the stern of the boat to the dock.

"There that will hold it for awhile." Rose said, as she stood up looking in the direction of the office,

"Great." Kaysee replied, as she steeped off the boat, and headed for the marina office.

It was only a short walk to the office. As the girls entered, they saw a long counter with two men, and a woman setting at their desks.

One of the men looked up. Seeing the girls, he moved to the counter, giving them a big smile, and asking if he could help them.

"Well first," Kaysee responded, "We have sailed down from St. Simon Island Georgia. We are looking for a place to dock our boat, and we are looking for a friend."

"Is there anyway you could tell us, if a friend of ours, is staying here?" Kaysee asked, letting her eyes drift to the floor.

"If they are staying on their boat I can tell you, if you tell me, what their name is." The man replied.

"His name is Mike Ryan, and the name of his boat, is the Windjammer." Kaysee stated, looking at Rose, giving her a smile.

"Hmm...I don't remember leasing a slip to anyone by that name." he said, adding "But maybe someone else did."

The man, turned to the woman, who was looking in his direction, "Linda, can you help me? Please."

"I will try, Bill." the woman said, walking up to the counter.

"This is Kaysee, and Rose." Bill said, gesturing to the two girls; "They are looking for a Mike Ryan, a friend who just came down from South Carolina. They think he would be staying on his boat." Bill added, as the girls acknowledged his introduction.

"Let me look in the log. I think I remember, leasing a slip to someone by that name." Linda said, as she walked to a large ledger on the counter.

"Yes, I did, lease a slip, (9-17) on the third. Which was four days ago," she told the girls, turning back to them.

"Great!" Kaysee exclaimed, and went on to ask, "Where can I find that slip? Is it far from here?"

"No, it just two piers down from where your boat will be." Bill replied, giving Linda a big smile, and saying "Thanks Linda."

"What kind, and size boat do you have?" Bill asked, giving Rose his biggest smile, then looked back at Kaysee.

"It is a 40 foot Ketch." Kaysee said, "It is right out there." Rose added, pointing to the boat at the fuel dock.

"Hey, nice looking boat." He said, as he pulled out papers from under the counter, and handed them to Kaysee.

"Need to fill these out, and I will be right back." he said, turning, and going to a cabinet, hanging on the wall. Then returned to the counter.

"It's at pier 17, slip 23. You can't miss the slip it's right beside an old boat called the "Witchcraft." It's in need of repairs badly," he stated, looking over the papers, Kaysee had just filled out.

"Everything looks good here. It will cost you twenty-one dollars a day, which includes the electric, and water at the slip. There are showers just over there." he said, pointing to a small building, out the window, behind the counter. "They are open 24 hours, so you can use them when ever you like."

"Thanks." Kaysee said, "I think we will be staying for about three days. Do we pay now?" she asked, reaching in her pocket, and bring out some folding money.

"Yeah, we require a deposit of one hundred dollars." he replied.

"Ok." Kaysee said, "We get back what ever we don't use, right?"

"Oh sure." he replied, handing a key to Kaysee. Then stated, "This key opens the locker, at the slip. In it is the electrical cord and a hose pipe." "By the way, my name is Bill Davies. If there is anything I can do to make your stay better, please let me know."

"Thanks, Bill." Rose said, returning his smile, adding how she hoped to be see him around.

"Thanks for all of your help." Kaysee said, "I guess we had better find our slip and get settled."

The two girls walked down the pier to their boat. Rose untied the lines holding the boat in place, while Kaysee started the engine, she was ready by the time Rose had the boat free.

"Go head, push us off." Kaysee shouted.

With a big heavy push, Rose got the boat moving, and jumped aboard. Kaysee swing the bow of the boat around, heading back out to the main channel. Made a right turn, and eased the boat forward until she saw the pier 17. She turned up the cut until she came to slip 23. Slowing the engine as she turned into the slip, Rose was ready to jump off to keep the boat from hitting the dock. Then she tied off the boat front, and back.

"I guess this is the slip we were told about." Rose said, as she walked forward to meet Kaysee just stepping off.

Looking around Kaysee took notice of the boat in the slip next to theirs.

"Someone doesn't think much of that boat." Kaysee said, pointing to the big "Chris-Craft" "Cabin Cruiser".

"Yeah, the paint and everything is pealing off. It looks like, in another month, it will be on the bottom." Rose added, as they moved up the dock.

"I wonder where Mike's boat is." Kaysee stated, looking around the marina.

"You're really hung-up on this guy, aren't you?" Rose asked, looking her friend in the eye.

"Well, not really, I would like to see what he has been doing since he left us." Kaysee replied, with a huge smile.

"Yeah; right!" Rose said, turning, and walking the rest of the way up the dock.

"I don't know what difference it makes." Kaysee said, running to catch up. "You're still in love with your Ex." she added, coming along side.

"I was hoping this trip would get him out of your mind. I thought maybe you would find someone, who would love you for yourself. You have spent the pass 10 years, doing everything, that man wanted.

Then what did he do? He didn't find another woman, but was afraid you would get everything he owned. Now that is dumb, and you aren't in your right mind, to still think, he will want you back." Kaysee didn't like spouting off at Rose, but she had been holding it back for the entire trip.

She had known Rose, and her ex-husband for years, but could never understand why Rose, keep wanting him back. The guy was never home, so Rose would go out to dinner with her, and Jill. The conversation would always drift to Rose's ex. Why Rose didn't ditch him, from her mind, was beyond Kaysee's understanding.

"You are probably right." Rose said, and then added, "I just haven't found the right guy."

"What was wrong with the guy in the marina office?" Kaysee asked, putting her arm around Rose's neck.

"Nothing that I could see, but I'm not as out going as you are." Rose replied, "You have always, been able to have a conversation, with just about anyone."

"You're right. Now let's go find Mike. Maybe he has a friend down here, that would be good for you." Kaysee said, giving Rose's neck a squeeze.

"Ok." Rose replied, her voice sounding artificial.

The two walked on, following the dock until they came to pier, which read 09. It was only a few slips down to 17.

"This is the slip we were told was Mike's. He must be out sailing, or something." Kaysee said, hanging her head as they stood in front of the slip. "Guess we'll come back later."

"You can come back later. I'm hungry; I want to get some real food." Rose said, turning around, heading back toward the office.

"Hang on Rose. I want to leave a note for Mike." Kaysee shouted, as Rose turned the corner.

She quickly scribbled a note on the back of the slip receipt, and attached it to the pole by the electric box. Then she ran to catch up with Rose.

"You sound out of breathe." Rose said, as Kaysee settled into her stride. "I guess I am." she replied,

"It's been weeks since I've done any running. I think we need to start working out, while we're in port. Otherwise we won't be able to handle the boat, in rough weather." Kaysee added.

The two girls walked down the boardwalk until they came to the restaurant. It was in the same building as the office.

The building was open in the center, with the office on one side, the restaurant on the other. On the outside bulletin board, were newspaper clippings, showing local fisherman, with their catches, as well as ads for fishing tournaments.

The two entered the front door, and looked for a table. Kaysee saw one toward the back, over looked the water.

"How about that one?" Kaysee asked, pointing a table that was empty. "Sure, it looks good." Rose said, starting to walk to it. When a voice startled them, from behind.

"Haven't I seen you two, somewhere before? Somewhere like the middle of the Atlantic Ocean. "The voice asks.

The girls instantly recognized the voice, and turned together, screaming in unison, "Mike!"

Kaysee was the first to get to him, throwing her arms around his neck, and giving him a kiss on the cheek. Rose was close behind, and squeezed in, added her kiss to the other cheek.

"Well what a reception." Mike said, as he recovers his composure. "I didn't know you girls were coming to Florida. How long have you been here, and where are you staying?" he quickly asked.

Rose was the one to answer first. "We just got here a little while ago, and our boat is in a slip right here in the marina."

"We are getting something to eat. Why don't you come set with us, and fill us in on what's happening in your life?" Kaysee asked, taking his arm and moving toward the table.

"Ok, but there isn't much." Mike replied, holding the chair for Kaysee, and then for Rose, before taking the chair between them.

"Where is the Windjammer?" Kaysee asked, settling back in her chair.

"I have a slip here, but the hull needed cleaning. There is this guy across the bay that does a real good job, and doesn't charge an arm or leg."

"I'm stay in a motel just down the street, and I'll have my boat back tomorrow." Mike explained. "So what is happening with you two girls?" he asked, turning from side to side, looking for the waiter.

"We got the boat fixed in Georgia, and decided the weather would be better down this way, than trying to go up north." Kaysee stated, giving a smile, and brushing her hair back from her face.

"Actually Mike, Kaysee wanted to come south to see, if she could find you." Rose stated, giving Kaysee a glair.

"Well, she's done that. Now what?" Mike asked, looking Kaysee in the eyes.

"Rose, has missed the point." Kaysee quickly stated, "I wanted to come down here for the weather, but since we have found you, or rather you found us. I guess we could just hang around, and see what happens." Kaysee stated, as her face flushed as she put her hand on Mike's arm.

"Sound good, but I don't have any plans for the near further. I thought I might sail down to the Keys when I get the "Windjammer" back, but that's not written in stone." Mike replied, motioning for the waiter to come to the table.

"Yes, Mr. Ryan, something I can do for you?" the waiter asked as he came to the table.

"I think these girls would like something to eat. Why don't we start with menus, and three cups of coffee," Mike told him.

"We are quite hungry." Rose stated, "We only had coffee, and toast for breakfast."

"You two, sure look good. Is everything all right with the boat?" Mike asked, glancing out the window, as a small tugboat, was pulling an old "Chris-Craft" "Cabin Cruiser."

"Excuse me Mr. Ryan," the waiter said, drawing Mike's attention back to the table. "You had a phone call from the marina office. The Dock Master would like you to come over as soon as you can."

"Thanks," Mike replied, "Order me a bucket of boiled shrimp, and I will be right back," he added, sliding his chair away from the table. "You girls go ahead, and order what ever you want. The food is better than the sign might lead you to believe." Mike said, pointing to the sign over the bar. Which read, "Fast Jake's, the Home of Lousy Food and Warm Beer"?

☙

CHAPTER FIVE

At this point Mike broke into Kaysee's story, to explain why he had to go to the marina office.

Mike headed for the front door. He walked across the breezeway, and into the marina office. "Is the Dock Master in?" Mike asked, looking around the office.

"Yeah, he's in his office Mr. Ryan. I think he wanted to talk to you. I will tell him you are here," the clerk said, then disappeared into one of the rooms behind the counter.

Shortly a man in a blue uniform appeared at the doorway, and motioned for Mike to come in.

"This way, Mr. Ryan." the clerk instructed opening the gate through the counter.

"Bill Davies, "Dock Master", Mr. Ryan." the tall man stated, extending his hand for Mike to take.

"You know my last name." Mike replied, griping the man's hand, "But call me Mike."

"All right Mike," he replied, taking back his hand, and motioning to a chair for Mike to have a seat.

"The reason I asked you to come in, is because I have received a quire from the State Department. They're wanting to know if you keep your boat in our marina."

"Why would the State Department want to know anything about me, or my boat?" Mike asked, with a puzzled look on his face.

"They said it had to do with something about your encounter with the Coast Guard, and a boat you had in tow." Bill Davies, replied, handing Mike a copy of a letter.

"I did answer a distress call from two girls, who had loss their mast in a storm. The Coast Guard came along, and took their boat into Georgia, but I have no idea what that has to do with me." Mike stated, flipping the letter back on to the desk.

"I don't know anymore than what is in the letter. What do you want me to tell the government?" Bill asked, leaning forward on the desk.

"It is up to you. I don't understand, but my boat isn't in the marina right now. Of course, I should have it back tomorrow. I'm having the bottom cleaned." Mike stated, scathing his head. "In fact the girls I helped are next door right now." Mike continued.

"I don't think there is any problem, but it does seem strange that the government would make a request like this." Bill said, pointing to the letter on the desk.

"I'll take my time answering it. We'll just see what happens." he stated getting up and extending his hand. "I'll keep you posted."

"Thanks for letting me know about the letter." Mike said, shaking the man's hand before leaving the office.

Mike walked back into the restaurant, to the table where the girls were just receiving their food.

"Good timing." Kaysee said, as Mike slipped back into his chair.

"We were wounding if you were going to make it back before your food got cool." Rose added, "Let's give Thanks for our food, and for Mike coming to our aid, in the middle of the ocean."

After the prayer all three said, "Amen."

"Not being noise, but is there a problem with the "Dock Master"?" Kaysee asked, as she took a sip of coffee.

"He told me about the government wanting to know, if I was keeping my boat here in the marina." Mike explained, gazing out the window. "I don't understand why, they would be checking on me."

"Are you in some kind of a jam?" Rose asked, in a soft whisper.

"Not that I am aware of, but you know our government. They can dream up reasons to check on people."

"Do you think it's serious, Mike?" Kaysee asked, putting her hand on his arm, and giving a little pat. "You know if there is anything I, we can do, just say so. We owe you more than anyone in this world."

"Thanks girls, but I have no idea what is going on." Mike replied, giving each a big smile.

"Are you two staying on the boat, tonight?" Mike asked, wiping his chain with his napkin.

"No, I thought we would get a motel room. We have been on the boat for weeks. I think it's time for a break." Kaysee replied, looking over at Rose, who was watching a couple entering the restaurant.

"I think, I know those people coming this way." Rose stated, leaning forward, and in a low voice.

Kaysee looked up, and nodded to the couple as they sat down at the table a cross from theirs. "Aren't they the ones we talked to in Melbourne? When we put in for supplies the other day."

"I think so." Rose replied, getting up, she walked over to their table.

"Sometimes, that girl surprises me." Kaysee said, looking at Mike with a grin.

"Hey Mike." Rose shouted, in a loud wispier, motioning for him to join her.

"Wonder what she wants?" Mike said, getting up from the table.

"Excuse me." Mike said, moving to where Rose was standing.

Mike stood next to Rose, as she said, "Mike, these are the people we met in Melbourne. They have been looking for you. You're becoming a very popular person."

Dave Chadwick, stood up and extended his hand to Mike. He looked to be in his thirties and his wife show about the same age.

"We have come a long way to find you. Do you have time to talk with us? We have a predicament, and I think you can help."

"I guess." Mike replied, with skepticism in his voice.

"Well sit down, can we talk right now? If it is all right. This is my wife Joan." Dave said, gesturing, to the woman seated at the table.

"Why don't we slide our tables together we'll have more room." Mike said, sliding out a chair, so the table would fit.

The waiter, who had just seated another couple by the window, came over, and helped arrange the tables. Then asked Dave, "Can I take your order?"

"I'll have what ever these folks are having, and my wife wants a steak, with a baked potato." Dave replied, taking his seat at the table.

After everyone were settled, Dave began telling Mike his problem.

જી

CHAPTER SIX

"Wait a minute." I said, looking around at the group who had gathered in the cabin of the "Windjammer".

"How did Chadwick know about you finding the girls adrift in the Atlantic? And than knew to look for you down here." I asked.

"Well according to Dave it all started:

With the sound of breaking glass. Dave Chadwick, went racing into the kitchen where he found his wife of 60 years standing at the sink in tears, rubbing her hands. Glancing at his wife, he saw a broken drinking glass at her feet.

"What happened?" he asked, with deep concern in his voice. "Are you all right? Did you cut your hand?" he queried, moving to her side, and looking at her hand.

"Yes, I'm OK." she replied, in a disgusting voice. "My hand just quit. I couldn't hold on to the glass, and it fall to the floor. I wish I knew what is wrong."

"I guess we've put off going to a doctor long enough." She stated, turning to face her husband, as he put his arms around her, trying to comfort her.

"We'll keep the appointment for tomorrow. I have been trying to get you to go for the past six months," he said, hugging her, and then kissing her on the neck.

"I know." she said, lifting her head. "We both need a check up, but you know what they are going to say. "We are just getting old." she stated, giving a little chuckle. "We have out lived all the people who knew us before we were married."

"I know Sweetheart. I wish we could find our island. We wouldn't worry about life." Dave said, giving her another kiss on her neck

Dave helped his wife into the living room of their apartment, which over looked the ocean. He walked to the sliding door, eased it open, and steeped out onto the balcony. He stared out into the vastness of the night. "I know it is out there somewhere." he said, half to himself, and yet loud enough, for his wife to here.

"Come back in here." She said, motioning for him to come by her on the cough. "It's just so frustrating, not being able to find it. You would think the government could locate the island. They have ships sailing across that part of the ocean everyday, and after 10 years, they still don't know anymore now, than they did when we came back." Dave said, put his head on her chest.

Joan began rubbing his hair, than gave him a kiss on the top of his head. "I know sweetheart. We would still be on our island if I hadn't wanted to get back to cultivation so bad. Had I known then, what I know now, we never would have left that beautiful island."

"It's not all your fault," he said, pulling his head back, so he could look into her eyes, which were glazed over. "I wanted to come back too. You never know what you have until you loose it."

"I was reading a book called, "The Bermuda Triangle" by Charles Berlitz, where he was saying something about Time-Space Warps.

I didn't understand it, but than I don't understand, how this country can put people on the moon, and have sent spaceship to the plants. It sounds like Buck Rogers of our time. Hell! When we left on our honeymoon, people said, we would get lost in that plane we had." "Boy! Were they right. We sure had a long honeymoon didn't we?"

"Yes we have. I thank the Lord everyday that I married you." she said, pulling his head back to her chest. "Can I go to bed now? I don't feel to well."

"Sure Honey! I'll be in shortly; I want to read the newspaper before I come to bed." Dave said, helping his wife to her feet.

Dave walked into the kitchen, laid the paper on the table, and went to the microwave to make himself a cup of coffee. Returning to the table, he began leafing through the paper. Not really read the article, but scanning the headlines, when he came across one reading: 38-FOOT SAIL BOAT ARRIVES 30 HOURS EARLY. He quickly read the rest of the article.

Dave rushed into the bedroom, with the newspaper in hand, turned on the overhead light, saying "Honey, Honey, you must see this article."

"Sweetheart, can't it wait until morning? I'm really tried." she replied, turning over, pulling the covers over her head.

"Yeah, sure it will keep until morning." Dave said, turning out the lights, and closing the door behind him.

He walked back into the kitchen, sat down at the table, and read the article again:

ST. SIMON'S ISLAND, GA. (WN)--According to authorities here a 38 foot sailboat arrived in port some 30 hours before a U.S. Coast Guard Cutter.

The sailboat, was boarded by the Coast Guard on the high seas, and had taken in tow another sailboat, that had been damaged during a storm last Tuesday.

The 38 foot "Windjammer" out of Charleston, South Carolina, owned by Mike Ryan, was sailing south some sixty miles off the coast, when he receive a distress call from a 40-foot Ketch, who had lost all of her sails and was taking on water.

Ryan sailed his boat to their rescue, and later was overtaken by the Coast Guard Cutter, "Saskatchewan", Commanded by LT. G. R. Blanchard.

The "Saskatchewan", a 109 foot, patrol cutter, was on a routine drug search, when they came across the two boats, and offered to tow the "Kaysee-Rose," into port.

The Coast Guard Cutter, a much faster boat arrived at St. Simon's Light after the "Windjammer".

When asked, how this could happen. The Coast Guard declined to answer. Saying only, "they would look into the report."

Captain Ryan, reported that his boat sailed into a cloud-bank. When he cleared the fog, he had arrived at St. Simon's Island, before the Cutter.

"I don't know what the cloud-bank was, nor how we arrived before the Cutter." Captain Ryan stated, "but it was like being in Limbo." The two women on board the "Windjammer" are the owners of the "Kaysee-Rose."

All three on the "Windjammer" are in good shape, following the ordeal, but are bewildered by the fact of their arrival. Captain Ryan, plans to sail on to Miami as soon as his shipmates have their boat repaired.

୧୬

Dave took a piece of paper from the note pad, and began to write the name of the Captain and the sailboat's name.

I wonder, Dave thought to himself. Could this guy, help me answer the question about time-space warps?

He quickly went to the bookshelf, and retrieved the book he had been reading about the Bermuda Triangle.

He opened the book and began reading the chapter on Time-Space Warps and Other Worlds:

"OK, so what is the Bermuda Triangle anyway?" Dave asked himself, as he turned the pages of the book. He came across the answer to his question: "The Bermuda Triangle" a line which runs from Florida's East Coast, North to the island of Bermuda, from there back to the South to just off Puerto Rico, West almost to the coast of Cuba and then back to South's Florida Coast line, forming the shape of a triangle.

As Dave read the book, he couldn't understand, why if there has been so much going on in this area, for so long. Why hasn't someone come up with an answer?

"Are you going to stay up all night?" a voice, came from behind him as he sat at the table.

Turning he replied, "No Dear, I was going to come to bed. But since you are up; why don't you take a look at this article in the newspaper?"

"All right, if that will make you sleep better." She said, taking the paper in her hand.

After she had glanced at the article, she asked, "What does this have to do with finding our island?"

"Well, I was thinking, this guy, who was sailing through the "Bermuda Triangle," might have more information on where he was, and how he got there." and then added.

"I think it maybe the same "Cloud" we flew through, when we left Palm Beach on the way to Key West." Dave told her.

"Perhaps, but I don't think we will ever find that island again, or if we do it will be too late to do any good." Joan said, putting her hand on his shoulder, "Let's go back to bed. We can sort it out in the morning." She said, turning and starting for the bedroom. Dave was right behind her, after turning out the lights and checking the doors.

"I was reading in the book I found, the "Bermuda Triangle" has been around since Columbus's time. No one has ever found out what has causes all of the disappearance of ships, and planes." Dave recounted as he climbed into bed.

"If no one has found out anything about this area. What makes you think this guy who got lost in it, knows anymore?" his wife asked, turning over to hug him as he made himself conformable.

"Well, I'm not sure he does, but it sure can't hurt. Maybe he will tell me something that will give us a clue as to how to get into this "Cloud" again, and then we can find our island." Dave replied, giving her a kiss.

After a moment, Joan said, "I'm not sure I want to get lost in the "Bermuda Triangle" It doesn't sound like a good place to be."

"That may be true, but it may be the only way we can find our island." Dave responded.

"I'm tried, Sweetheart, Let's talk about this in the morning."

"Sure." Dave said, rolling on to his back staring up at the dark ceiling.

Sleep didn't come to Dave that easy. He laid for what seemed like hours wondering if the "Bermuda Triangle" had anything to do with his lost island.

Lying there, he made up his mind to contact the man who had the experience in the Triangle. Perhaps, he could help him find the lost island.

Dave knew the trip to the doctor in the morning, was going to be hard on his wife. He had a good idea what the doctor was going to tell her. He could feel much the same problems growing within in himself.

"Hell" he thought, we've out lived most of the people we knew and went to school with, or knew when we were married, back in 1931.

Just because we looked like we're only in our late twenties, he knew they were pushing eighty hard, and being away from their island, these past ten years, was starting to take it toll on them.

Maybe we were caught in the "Bermuda Triangle". We sure flew though a cloud, much as the one recounted in the newspaper.

He didn't want to tell his wife; he knew what was wrong with her, but he knew it was only a matter of time. Joan would be hard to live with if she knew, she was getting older by the day.

Dave finally fell asleep, but it was a restless sleep. His mind was working overtime. His dreams went from the weird to the bazaar, and back again.

He would wake up enough to see what time it was, then he would fall back asleep, only to dream, and wake up again. The last time he woke up, he looked at the clock, it read Six o' clock. He decided to get up make coffee, and let his wife continue to sleep.

As he sat at the table looking over the newspaper, he had read the night before. He made notes of where Mike Ryan was from, and how he had described the cloud that he had sailed into.

Dave Chadwick was convinced in his mind, Mike Ryan could help him, and his wife find their island in the Sun.

"Good Morning." his wife said, has she entered the dinning room. "Have you been up all night?" she asked, walking to the coffee pot, and pouring herself a cup, returned to the table.

"No, I got up about six, but I let you sleep in." he replied.

"You know I have to be at the doctor's office by nine." she stated, "And you know it takes me an hour to get ready."

"I know my dear. I was going to come wake you up, but thought you could use a little more sleep." he replied, giving her a smile, lifting his cup, as if it were a toast.

"What are you reading?" she asked, leaning over trying to read the paper backwards.

"I was just going over what we talked about last night, before we went to bed." he answer.

"I know you think this guy can help, but how on earth are we going to find him? Let alone talk him into helping us." Joan said, patting Dave on the arm.

"I know it isn't going to be easy, but we must try something.

We sure haven't had any luck with the government, and we never will. Those guys in Washington don't care about us anymore than the man in the moon." Dave replied, with a deceased voice.

"Now you know, they would help us if there was anyway to know for sure where it was, and how to get to it." Joan stated, setting her cup back on the table.

"It is time for us to get ready," she said, get up from the table, heading for the bathroom.

"I don't believe the government about anything." Dave said, setting the paper back on the table.

He looked at his notes, thinking to himself...right after we get out of the doctors office we're heading south.

Within a few minutes, Joan returned dressed ready to go.

"Are you ready?" she asked, coming to Dave's side.

"Yeah, I'm ready." Dave replied, adding, "We need to pack an over-night bag."

"Oh, Dave, I don't feel like taking a trip. Not today, I didn't sleep well last night, and I'm worried about what the doctor will find." she pleated.

"I know you may not feel like the trip, but I have this feeling, if we don't find the island soon, we may not live to find it at all." Dave confessed, getting up from the table.

"Very well." she replied, "I just hope the doctor can give some reason for the way I have been acting, lately."

Joan slowly walked to the bedroom, put some cloths in an overnight bag, and return to the dinning room where Dave was waiting.

"Let's go before I change my mind." Joan said, walking to the door. Dave followed her out to the car. Where he opened the car door for her, then walked around, and got in.

It was only a short drive to the doctor's office. Dave let Joan out in front of the office, and drove on down the block until he found a parking place.

Walking back to the doctor's office, Dave wondered just where all the doctor visits were going to lead. They sure hadn't done any good so far, and he wasn't sure they every would.

"Good Morning, Mr. Chadwick." the girl at the reception deck said, as Dave entered the office.

"Your wife is already in with the doctor. Just have a seat I'm sure she won't be very long."

Dave went to the table picked a magazine on sailing and sat down. He had only turned a few pages when a door open to the waiting room opened, and a nurse steeped around the door, so she could see who was waiting.

"Mr. Chadwick? Mr. David Chadwick?" she asked, looking around. "Yes." Dave said, getting up from his chair, taking a few steeps toward the nurse.

"Will you come this way? The doctor would like to talk to you."

"Sure." he replied.

She led him down a hallway, stopping at the doctor's office. She knocked, opened the door, and stepped aside letting Dave enter the office.

The doctor stood up saying "Mr. Chadwick?" Extending his hand Dave took it, giving it a firm shake, and replying "Yes."

"Please take a seat next to your wife." the doctor said, as he sat down behind his desk.

"I have been talking to your wife about the problems she has been having. I have checked her for everything I can think of to check, but there is just nothing wrong. She has told me about your extended honeymoon."

"There is a doctor in Miami, who could help. I know he has been doing research on ageing. The cause, and effect."

"The bottom line is, I'm recommending you take her to see him. He may be able to help." the doctor instructed, as he made notes in Joan's medical file.

"I'll have the nurse make copies of this file. You can take it with you, so Dr. John O'Malley will know everything we've checked up here. The nurse will give you his address and telephone number. I suggest you get in touch with him as soon as you can." the doctor told them.

The doctor gave instruction to the nurse. The couple left his office, and went back into the waiting room.

"See it's a good thing, I had you pack, before we came down here." Dave said, with a grin on his face.

"I know, I know," Joan chimed, "At first I thought you had talked to the doctor, before I got to his office." she confessed.

"Now you know I wouldn't do anything like that Dear." Dave replied, putting his arm around her waist.

"Yes, but it sure is turning out as thro you did." Joan replied, leaning her head on his shoulder.

Shortly the nurse appeared at the window, saying "Mrs. Chadwick, I have the information the doctor wanted you to take with you to Dr. O'Malley."

Joan walked to the window, pickup the large enveloped, thanked the girl for her trouble. Then headed for the outside door, with her husband right behind.

They quickly got to the car, and were on their way to Miami, about a four-hour drive.

For a long time both were silent, then Joan spoke up. "Do you think we will every find out what is going on with me?"

"Sure honey, this new doctor will know just what is wrong. He will be able to fix it." Dave replied, without taking his eyes off the road.

"I hope so, I'm tried of feeling this way."

"I know you're tried of hearing me complain about it." Joan said, with tears coming to her eyes.

"Now look, there is no reason to feel so bad about it. Maybe we are just getting old. Maybe time is catching up with us. Remember we have out lived all of friends and family. What more could we ask." Dave reassured her.

"We could find our island, and this would go away." Joan said, sharply.

The Chadwicks had been on the road for about three hours, when Joan told her husband, she needed to stop at the next rest area.

"There is one in about 10 miles. I'll stop then." Dave said, looking at his odometer.

"That will be fine." Joan replied, giving her husband a smile, then going back looking at the file the doctor had sent with her.

Within a few minutes, Dave pulled the car into the rest area. His wife could use the little girl's room, and he could stitch his legs. Traveling three hours, they were only fifty miles from Miami.

Dave knew a motel were they would stay. It was one of the nicer ones on the bay. Most of the motels around the airport were owned, and operated by foreigners.

You couldn't understand them, and they always cooking something that smiled as if it had just washed up on shore.

Dave had only walked a short way from the car, when he saw two men, looking like they were from the government. The car was black and had no extras.

The men seamed to be watching him, but he could not be sure. As soon as his wife came back, they were on their way again.

Dave keep a close eye on his rear view mirror. He couldn't tell if the black car was following him, but he wasn't slowing down to find out.

Within an hour and a half, the couple pulled into the motel parking lot. Dave went in registered, and was in their room before anyone knew they were even there.

"Why don't you call the doctor's office, and make an appointment for tomorrow morning?" Dave asked, setting the bag on the little stand by the television. "We can go see the doctor, then we will look for Mike Ryan." Dave went on.

Joan did as her husband ask, and after a couple of rings, Joan made the appointment.

"The appointment is for Nine A.M." Joan said, as she hung up the phone. "Will that be early enough?"

"Yes, that will do nicely." Dave answered, reaching for the remote to turn on the TV.

"Just how do you plan on finding this Mike Ryan?" Joan asked, making room to set down on the bed.

"I guess I will just go to each marina in the area, and asked them if there is anyone staying there. If they say "Yes". Then we will just walk over to the slip he has his boat, and we will surprise him." Dave explained, flipping from one channel to an other.

&

CHAPTER SEVEN

"That tells me why he was looking for you, but how did he and his wife end up on the island in the first place?" I asked.

"Here again, according to Dave, as we all were sitting, hanging on his every word he said."

"I guess I should start at the beginning." Dave said, taking a sip of his coffee.

"It was March back in 1931, when Joan and I got married. We planned to fly to Key West for our Honeymoon. I had this bi-plane left over from the Great War, the one they now call WWI."

"Anyway, we took off from West Palm Beach. I stayed close to the coastline most of the way, but some where around here I got feather out. I flew into a cloudbank, much like the one I heard you and these girls sailed into, not so very long ago."

"It didn't seem as if we were in the cloud very long, but when I came out, I had no idea where we were."

"My compass had went crazy as we entered the cloud. When we came out it acted like it was working, so I flew west thinking I would find land, and get my bearings."

"But the longer I flew the more confessed I became. Fuel was getting low I had to find some place to set down."

"Off in the distance I saw what look like an island. I kept flying straight for it. Just about the time the engine gave out, we were over the island, and I set the plane down on the beach." Dave explained taking a bit of the food he had order.

Then continued, "Anyway time pasted, we didn't know just how much time, but we stayed on the island thinking maybe a ship would come by. But nothing, so we built a raft, loaded it with food, water, and what little cloths we had, and set sail.

We were on the raft for eight days, I know because we had enough water for 10 days. At any rate, sometime during that last night we must have sailed or floated through a fog because everything felt wet.

"When the sun came up the next morning, the sea around us looked different, I can't explain just how it was different, but it was, and by afternoon a ship picked us up, and took us back to Miami."

"We were glad to get back, but when we understood just how long we had been gone, and how everything had changed. We decided we wanted to go back. By this time, we were very very well off.

I bought a boat, and tried to find our island, but to no avail.

The government even got into the act, but they tell us there is no such island, but we are living proof. At lease for awhile." Dave concluded, patting his wife on the shoulder.

༚

CHAPTER EIGHT

I interrupted Mike's telling of Dave's story saying, "That is unbelievable. So did you help him find the island?

"I am getting to it, but there was a lot that went on during this first meeting." Mike explained.

"Wow!" Mike exclaimed, shaking his head, "That is some story, but I don't see how I can help. We didn't see an island. We just got to Georgia before the Coast Guard. I don't understand how we did even that."

"I understand, but the thing is you all have been through it. Maybe not as long as we were, but you know strange things can happen out there." Dave replied, with a serious tone in his voice. He went on, "I have a theory about the cloud."

"There have been many boats, planes, and people that have disappeared out there, over many many years. But the government, and anyone who has not been there, say we're all crazy."

A red haired woman, saying, "I couldn't help over hearing your story, and it sounds like what happened to my mother." interrupting the disquisition. She went on, "They were just out side the harbor right by a channel marker, and they haven't been seen, or heard from since."

"See Mike, there is another, who believes, but can't do anything about it." Dave said, taking another sip of his coffee.

"I'm sorry, what is your name?" Dave asked, getting up from his chair.

"My name is Linda Carrie, and this is Bert Williams a friend of mine." she replied, motioning for Bert to join her at the table.

Bert nodded as he approached the table. "I'm a farm boy from Michigan, but Linda has been telling me about the ordeal with her mother. It's a wonder that the Navy or Coast Guard, or someone hasn't found something."

"This is the whole point," Dave continued, "We have been trying to find our island. The government keeps saying there is no island. We know there really is an island, and I need to find it real soon." Dave paused, and looked at his wife, giving her a smile.

"My wife is getting sicker by the day. I need to get her back on our island. If we could only find it, she would be well in no time. I'm sure the island has healing air or something."

"We were on the island, and never got sick." Dave told the group.

"That's great, but I don't see how I can help. I wouldn't have any idea where to start looking." Mike confessed, stretching his arms out in front of him.

"I know the feeling," Dave said, putting his hand on Mike's shoulder, "I have been there, but if I could explain my theory about the door. I believe it is the answer to the mystery of the Bermuda Triangle." Dave said, looking around the room, to see whom else might be listening.

"A door?" Mike asked, with a surprised look on his face. "What kind of a door?"

"Well, I say a door, but only because I have no other way to explain it. When ships, or planes get lost, it is as if a door is opened, and they go through. Then it closes. No one is seen again. Except in rare cases like ours, and yours." Dave explained.

"I guess I could see how it might appear like a door opening and then closing." Mike stated, "How do we find this door?" He asked, and then went on "If we find it, what do we do with it? Do you think we can hold it open?"

"To tell you the truth, I hadn't given that part much thought. But I do know, if we could find it once, I know we could find it again. Providing of course we knew what we were looking for." Dave stated, setting back down beside his wife.

"Wow!" Rose said, taking a drink of coffee, "That is a lot to think about."

ᴄ⌒ɔ

CHAPTER NINE

With the sound of another female voice at the open hatch, the interview was interrupted again.

"That sounds like Linda." Kaysee said, getting up, and go to the hatch.

"We are all down here." she hollowed, to the person on the upper deck.

"Who is this?" I asked as a pretty red head started down the steeps.

"Oh this is my wife Linda." Bert said, putting an arm around her.

I smiled, and told her my name, and explained I was interviewing Mike, Bert, Kaysee, and Rose about all what happened to them in their search for Chadwick's Island.

"Great!" she said, turning to Bert asking, "Have you told Mickey how I came up with the idea to plot all of the missing planes, and boats, by having Esther Easterday, write the program to find the Door?"

"No!" I said, "But you could pick up the story, at that point."

"Sure." Linda said, as she explained how they were all with Dave Chadwick in the restaurant.

"There may be a way you could periodically tell where the door would open. It would take a lot of work, but I have a friend who writes computer program, that could give you a general idea, where the next opening might be." Linda explained, moving closer to Bert.

"You may have a point." Mike replied, giving Linda a smile.

"Do you think your friend could meet with us, to discuss the information he would need to write the program?" Dave asked, and than added, "I would make it well, worth his while."

"I could ask, but it's not a him. He's a she. Linda, told Dave, giving him a big smile. "I beg your pardon, and I stand corrected. If she would help us?" Dave replied, giving Linda a big grin and a nod.

"I could call, and ask her to meet you somewhere tomorrow. If she doesn't have other plans that is." Linda said, giving Bert a push in the direction of their table.

"Please." Dave said, as he saw the couple moving back to their table, "Come join us. We do, so need your help." He pleaded.

Linda looked a Bert, as if to say what do we do. "Ok," Bert said, pulling Linda back to the tables where the group sat.

"Great!" Dave exclaimed, setting back down. "And what about you Mr. Ryan? Will you join our search? Money will not hinder your search. Joan, and I have more money than we will ever use, even if we live to be a hundred years old. Which we're pushing it very hard." Dave stated, giving Mike a very serious look.

"I don't know why you think I can find this island. But if we can come up with a plan, I guess I can try. If nothing else we can sail around the Atlantic, looking into all the cloudbanks. Hoping one of them will be the right one." Mike replied, with a laughing tone to his voice.

"Now that is the sprit." Dave said, giving Mike a pat on the back.

"Thank you very much, Mike Ryan." Joan Chadwick said, putting her arm around her husband, "Dave can be very pushy, when he wants something."

"Not at all, my dear. I just know Mike will find our island. I know it deep down in my heart."

"I would like to know if finding the island will save you." Dave responded, and then turn back to the group saying

"Now! Let's have some food, and we can go over what we are going to need for our search."

છ૭

"Alright" I said, looking back at my notes. I turned to Bert and asked "What happened after Linda drove away after the party?"

He started in on his story again….

Bert was awaken to his phone ringing. At first, he didn't realize his telephone was ringing off the hook. He didn't know how long it had been ringing. He bounced out of bed and ran to answer the phone.

"It's 7:35 the voice on the other end said. Bert looked out the sliding door and the sun was barely casting a shadow over the apartment building, he knew it had to be early in the morning. "I thought you meant 7:30 PM, not AM" he said, before the voice could say another word. He recognized the voice.

He paused to catch his breath, when the voice broke in "Bert, I was calling to tell you I was running late, and it would be a half hour, before I can pick you up."

The vision of the Redhead flashed to his mind as she continued, "I guess you're not up yet. Get dressed, and I will be there shortly." Then the line went silent.

Hanging up the phone, he starched his head, and rubbed his eyes before heading for the Bathroom. He quickly showed, and dressed, then made himself a cup of coffee. He sat at the table by the sliding door looking out over the marina.

The sun hadn't reached much of it, but he could see people moving about. They must be getting ready to take their boats out. He quickly drank his coffee, and went to the front door, and set it ajar, so Linda could come in while he finished shaving.

"Hello, Bert are you here?" Linda asked, walking into the apartment. She took a second to look around, heard Bert humming in the bathroom. She walked to the sliding door opened it, and walked out on the balcony. She looked out over Biscayne Bay. She could see her office, and could see boats coming, and going from the marina. She knew the day would be busy, as the weekends, always had many people coming into the office needing something.

Without turning to see, Linda knew Bert had finished shaving. She could smell his after shave. A second later Bert coughed softly. He didn't want to startle her, as he approached the sliding door.

"Have you been here long." He asked, as she turned to look him straight in the eyes.

"No, but you shouldn't leave your front door open. You never know who will walk in.," she told him, widening her smile.

"Sorry I'm so late. Are you ready to go look at the boat?" she asked, pointing in the direction they would be going."

"Sure, but I thought you were talking about 7:30 PM. "I'm awake now, and ready for anything." Bert said, heading for the front door.

Going down in the Elevator, Bert told her how great she look in her shorts and Tee shirt. "You look like you live in Florida."

They walked across the parking lot, and out onto the pier where the "Witchcraft" was docked. Approaching the slip Bert noticed a single mast sailboat, being tied up in the next slip, by a man in his forties, with sandy brown hair. He waved as the two passed.

"It sure needs a lot of work," Linda said, as they came to the gangway. I don't know if I want to go on board, or not."

"Is it because of what happened to your mother, or because the boat is in such bad shape?" Bert asked, stepping up on the gangway.

"Maybe a little of both." She replied, putting her hand in the middle of his back.

Bert leaded the way onto the boat. He could see it was a well build, and a beautiful boat, when it was new.

The teat wood was still in good shape. Some of the deck boards needed to be replaced, and the railings, would need to be painted, but the stauncher look like it was still sound. The windows, which lined the cabin, needed cleaning, and one or two replaced. He wondered, what shape the power units would be in. He was sure the saltwater had done its damage.

Linda stepped up to the solon door. She rubbed the window, and peered in. She couldn't see much, so she opened it, and stepped in side, with Bert right behind her. "Wow!" Linda exclaimed, "Things haven't changed since I was in here, right after my mother went missing." She walked to the table, "The plates are just as they left them." She said, brushing off the dust from the tablecloth.

Bert stepped pass her, up into the control station. He saw the keys where still in the switch, and everything was in the off position. "Maybe this boat will be able to be repaired. I know Chris-craft was built in Michigan, and it was designed to last a good long time." He said turning back to Linda, who had been silent.

"Let's get out of here. It feels strange knowing this is where my mother was last. I sure wish I could find out what happened, and where she went." Linda said, wiping away a tear, from her eye.

Bert could feel her pain. He didn't know what had happened, but he knew, he wanted to be part of the answer.

This woman was different then any he had met during his life. One thing for sure, he like the way she carried herself. The conference she showed last night at the party. The way people around her accepted her for herself. Even his sister must have thought, Bert and this woman would be drawn to each other.

"Let's take a look at the hull. That'll tell us how much work we have to do." Bert said, walking out on the deck.

"Hi there, you going to fix up this cruiser?" a voice asked, causing Bert to turn to see the man who had waved to them, as they walked up to the "Witchcraft". "Are you the owners?" he asked, moving closer to the boat.

"It belongs to my friend Linda. We are look at getting it back seaworthy." Bert replied, walking down the gangway closing the distance between the two men."

"My name is Mike Ryan, this is my boat the "Windjammer", he said, extending his hand to Bert.

Taking the extended hand say, "I'm Bert Williams. I have moved down here from Michigan." He explained, "That sure is a beautiful sailboat. Bigger than any, I have seen on Lake St.Clair. How big is it?" Bert asked, to keep the conversation going.

"38-feet," Mike replied, walking down the pier checking the hull on the "Witchcraft". "Looks like you are going to need a bottom job." Mike stated, "I had mind done yesterday." He explained. The people who did it are really good, and they don't charge an arm, and a leg to repaint it with fungal retardant paint."

Linda joined Bert on the pier, and Bert introduced her to Mike Ryan. "I met you the day you rented the slip. I must not have made an imprecation on you at the time." Linda said, turning to look at the "Witchcraft"

"Your friend Bert told me, you were thinking about fixing up this old Chris-Craft." Mike said, taking a steep toward the boat, then added, "I knew, I had seen you someplace before, but I didn't think it was the Dock Master's Office." giving the couple a big smile. "I heard there was a story behind this boat. Can you tell me about it?" Mike asked, and then saw his question brought hurt to Linda's face. "I'm sorry I didn't know it would bring back bad memories." He quickly added.

"My mother was lost off this boat a few years ago. The Coast Guard looked into it, but never found anything. Today is the first time I've been down, to the boat." Linda explained, taking Bert's arm.

After saying their goodbyes to Mike, the couple headed for Linda's office, and shortly Linda had a company on the way to fix the hull of the "Witchcraft".

"Now that's taken care of. Let's go get something to eat at the restaurant. " Linda said, with the return of her humor.

❦

CHAPTER TEN

"After getting the boat fix, and meeting up with Mike, and the rest. Linda, and I got involved looking for the island...and here we are." Bert told me.

"I know there is more to the story. Did you find the island, and did Chadwick get to go to his island?" I asked, trying to get more information.

Mike jumped here saying "Let me tell you about the run-in we had with the government. A man named Heilman...I had dealings with him in Vietnam. I never thought I would have to deal with him again." Mike said, looking around at the others. "He told me how he, and Big Bill got started on the case."

It was a cold, and windy day when Paul Heilman, a tall dark haired man, in his early forties, was told to report to the Director of Operations Office. He had been working on a missing Persons Case, which had taken him, and his partner, all over the Caribbean. Checking areas he, and Big Bill Boyd, thought the person might have taken up hiding. It was a straight-forward case; according to the reports, they had been given.

Now he was standing in front of the Director's office door, not knowing why he had been called. He thought back across all of the time he had spent looking for John De Long, and his daughter. Really, it was his steep-daughter. The mother kept insisting that they were loss at sea; but Heilman, and the Director had been through many of these kinds of cases. They were quit sure the man had just left, with a younger woman.

Paul entered the Director's outer-office where he was greeted by Emily Teeter, the Director's Girl Friday. She answered the phone, when you called in, and handled the day-to-day business dealings, seldom did you ever talk directly with the Director.

"Good morning, Mr. Heilman, How are you this fine day," was her greeting as Paul closed the door behind him.

"Great Emily, What is up with the Director? He's not mad about all the time Big Bill, and I have spent on the De Long case, is he?" Paul asked, stepping forward to the desk.

"No, it's nothing like that, but I'm not real sure what it's about. He has been keeping things to himself lately. It must have to do with something, which took place down in Georgia, the other day."

"But I'm not sure. Let me tell him you are here." she told Paul, pushing her chair back, and disappeared into the door behind her.

Paul glanced around the office. It had been awhile since the Director had called him to his office for a briefing. "There must be something a foot." Paul thought, continuing his observation of the office, when Emily reappeared, behind her desk, saying, "He will see you now."

Paul stepped around the desk, and entered the Director's office were he was greeted with, "How are you doing my boy? It has been awhile since we last talked. Come in, and set down. We have some things to go over about the case you, and Big Bill, are working on. Something that might be connected to the De Long case.

"Here's a fill on a Dave Chadwick's, it might help you with the De Long case. The man keeps asking about some island. He and his wife had been on for over fifty years. The Navy, says there isn't an island, or a piece of land in the Caribbean, they don't have on the map. Then there is this one, on a Captain who left Charleston, SC., and helped a couple of girls who had bought a boat someplace in the Caribbean. They were on their way north, when they ran into a storm, ripping off their mast, leaving them a drift. This Captain helped them out. The Coast Guard has gotten involved. Now they want us to tell them what has happened." the director explained, stacking the folder on his desk.

"I know it sounds like a tall order, but I'm sure you, and Big Bill will come up with an answer. You two always do." the director told Paul.

"Yes Sir." Paul replied, "Do you want us to stick to the standard reply, or do we really want to know what has happened?"

"We really want to know, but it's for our use only, not for the General Public," the director instructed.

"Very well, sir. Big Bill, and I will get right on it. Do you have a place you would like us to start? Or can I handle it the way, I think best?" Paul asked, picking up the Chadwick fill from the desk.

"You guys handle it the way you want. Just keep me informed on your progress." the director replied, leaning back in his chair, starring at the ceiling.

Paul took this as a good point to leave. "Will that do it, Sir?" he asked, getting to his feet.

"Yeah, you guys get out there, and find out what is going on, as soon as you can." He lowered head starring straight at Paul saying, "What ever you do, keep us out of the papers. Those News Boys will have a field day with this story."

"We'll do our best, Sir." Paul said, as he turned, and headed for the door.

"If you need any help, or information, get it from Emily. I will let her know what you are doing." the director said, as Paul opened the door.

Back in the outer office, Paul told Emily, as he was ready to leave. "I will be in touch. The man will clue you in on what I'm going to be working on. So you will be hearing from me soon."

Paul exited the building heading to the car, he had parked in a lot down the street. He knew it was easier to get in, and out of the city from that lot, rather then trying to find a parking spot, closer to the building.

It was a short drive to the apartment where he had left Big Bill. He would pick him up, and they would head for Georgia.

Paul thought about flying, but knew Big Bill didn't like to fly. He decided they would drive. With both of them driving, it would only take two days. This would give him a chance to go over the files, he had received from the director.

Paul, and Big Bill had been on the De Long case for months, and hadn't made much progress. It wasn't because they hadn't covered the ground. They covered it, and then covered it again, but there just seemed to be something they were missing. Something just didn't gel. He had been in Vietnam where nothing made any sense; but he always seemed to come up with the right answers. Other cases of missing people were easy, compared to this one.

Within minutes Paul was in front of the apartment building. Big Bill was packed, and they were on their way out of the door, when they were met by the Landlady.

"You boys off on another assignment?" she asked, giving them, the once over and seeing suitcases in their hands.

"Yes, Ms. Brown. We will be gone for a few days." Paul said, giving her a big smile.

"You always say you will only be gone for a few days. Then I don't see you for months on end." she said, putting her hands on her hips.

"I know." Paul said, "But our work keeps on the go. We will see you get the check for the apartment, on the first of the month."

"It's not the rent I'm worried about." She said, putting her hands into her pockets, and retrieving a note.

"This is a note from my niece. She wants to meet you, Paul. She's a good looking girl, I think you would like her, if you were ever around to meet her," the landlady said, handing it to Paul.

He took it, glancing at the note, and a picture, which was with it.

"You are right; she is a good looking girl." Paul replied, handing the picture to Big Bill.

"Yeah, she sure is a looker." Big Bill said, handing it back to Paul.

"I will try to let you know when we'll be back." Paul said, trying to ease his way to the car. "Maybe I'll have a few days off when we get back. I'll call your niece then." Paul told her.

"Ok, but don't be gone to long. You know the old saying, "Time and Tide…" she said turning, and walking down the hallway.

Outside, they put their bags in the trunk of the car. "You want me to drive?" Big Bill asked, taking the keys out of the trunk lid.

"Ok, you can drive, and I will go over the papers the director gave me. It will give me a chance to see just what we're going to be doing in Georgia." Paul replied, getting in on the passenger's side.

It didn't take Big Bill very long to dive through the city, and have them heading down I-95 South. The traffic was light for that time of the day… Normally the traffic was backed up for miles around DC.

Paul settled back, and began to go through the papers he had receive earlier. There were all the notes on the Chadwick's case. As he read, he began to see, they weren't going to be back in DC, for awhile.

"Boy here's another one." Paul said, looking out the window.

"What's that?" Bill asked, turning his head to look at Paul.

"Another one of these people, who thinks there is something going on in the Atlantic Ocean." Paul replied, looking back at the papers.

"What do they think is going on?" Bill asked, staring back at the road.

"The "Bermuda Triangle" you know the place where Atlantis is thought to be." Paul said, not looking up from the papers.

"Hey!" Paul exclaimed, "I think I know this guy. I think, I remember him from Vietnam. I remember the name anyway."

"What is his name," Bill asked, glancing over at the guy setting next to him.

"Mike Ryan." Paul replied, "Mean anything to you?" he asked.

"I don't think so." Bill replied, "But than I know a lot of people, but I don't remember their names. I can remember face and places, but not names," Bill told Paul.

"Well if this is the same guy, I hope he doesn't remember me. Our last meeting wasn't the best."

"Were you working for the company back then?" Bill asked, taking an exit ramp.

"Yes, I was. The mission we were on didn't turn out the way Ryan thought it should have." Paul explained, as Bill brought the car to a stop in a gas station

While Bill was gassing up the car, Paul put in a phone call to Emily. He asked her to send a fax to all marinas on the eastern seaboard from Washington to Miami, asking for information on Mike Ryan, where he kept his boat, and if his boat was in port at this time.

They were back on the road, and they were crossing the Virginia, North Carolina line, when Big Bill asked, "Were do you want to stop for the night?"

Paul looked at his watch, then at the map lying on the seat beside him. "I think we can make Charleston, South Carolina, before dark. I'll call the Knights Inn there by the airport. We can spend the night, and tomorrow we

113

go out to Folly Beach, and check out this Mike Ryan. He probably won't be there, but the marina might know where he was going. According to these papers, he was in Georgia, a month ago, but maybe he came back this way.

"That will be good. We can stop at that little bar there in North Charleston, where the girl, with the big chow dogs works. I don't remember her name, but she was fun to drink with, most of the time."

Big Bill stated, taking a drink from the coffee mug on the dash.

"Be careful Bill, as I remember she was living some guy with fussy hair. He didn't like guys hanging around his woman." Paul warmed.

"Yeah, your right, maybe I should stay clear of that place. I would hate to hurt someone." Big Bill replied, rubbing his chin.

"You know, I have a better idea. Maybe we should just drive right out to the island, and stay at the Holiday Inn. That way we will all ready be close to the marina. And we won't lose much time in the morning." Paul said, closing file on Mike Ryan.

The trip to Foley Beach was slow going. The two-line road was busy, due to the fine weather.

Paul looked out the side window as they passed miles of swampland and small canals, wondering what it would be like to live on an Island.

Crossing the last humpback bridge, Big Bill made his way to the parking lot at the Holiday Inn. The building looked well keep. At the front entrance stood a Bellman waiting to load a car, which had pulled up.

The Green Triumph had only one person in it. The man was younger than Paul, but was the same height, with Brown Hair almost to his shoulders

As Paul and Big Bill walked passed the bellman, Bill made a comment to the driver, "Nice car, how fast will it go on the open road,"

"I don't know." was the man's reply, "I haven't opened it up."

Bill joined Paul at the Front Desk signing the card the clerk handed him.

"You're in room 402; it is on the ocean side of the building." she told them.

Walking to the elevator Paul took notice of the fountain in the middle of the lobby. It looked as if it had been an after thought, but the sound of the running water brought peaceful thoughts to his mind.

Traveling by car always tensed him up. Not that Bill's driving was bad, just unnerving.

Entering the room, Paul laid his bag on the bed closest to the sliding door that opened on to the balcony. It over looked the beach, with waves breaking on it. His mind jumped back to his days in Vietnam and the last days of the war. He hated to remember those days as many good men lost their lives for nothing.

We should have won that one, but the government kept changing the orders. No one knew what was coming next. He thought about the young Captain in the 101st Airborne who had taken his men through the jungle in hopes of capturing a Vietcong General.

Only to have the government change the orders without telling Ryan. It had been Paul Heilman who was responsible for alerting the General of the planned capture. It left Ryan's men high and dry, as the General made his way to a meeting at another compound.

The General's men were waiting for them. It cost many lives and when Paul had last talked to Ryan in

Saigon, he was not a happy camper. In fact, he told Paul if he ever crossed paths again, things, would be different.

Paul wasn't sure what the Captain meant, but he was not looking forward to seeing Ryan.

Paul was jerked back to the present, when Big Bill joining him on the balcony. "Want to get some food?" Bill asked, walking to the other end of the railing. "It's been awhile, since I had anything."

"Yea, sounds good. There must be a restaurant close, maybe there is one here in the motel." Paul replied, still looking out over the ocean.

"I saw a Bar & Grill on our way in. I think it was back up the street about two blocks. We could try there."

"We need to change cloths before we head out. We don't want the locals to think we're feds." Paul told Big Bill.

"I have beach cloths in my bag. It will only take a minute. How about you? Are you alright?" Bill asked, as he walked back into the room.

"Go ahead I'll be right in." Paul said, looking over the railing, to the sidewalk below.

A girl in her late twenties was entering the beach door. She had short red hair or maybe, it was a reflection from the sunburn she sported. His pondered the idea of meeting the Landlady's Niece. From the picture, she gave him, the girl looked cute, but could she put up with Paul's work hours.

He turned as Big Bill walked to the Sliding Door. "I'm really hungry. Can we go now?" he asked, moving, so Paul could get back into the room.

"Let me put on another shirt, and I will be ready to walk out the door." Paul replied.

The two men walked up the street leading from the Beach area. Paul glanced at the building along the street. They looked as if they were left over from the Civil War era. Paint would work wonders he thought. This part of the beach area must not have been hit by a Hurricane lately.

The Bar & Grill stood three stories tall. The front looked like a barn, if it hadn't had so many seafaring articles standing by the door.

A couple came out the door as Bill was reaching for the handle. "Oh, Sorry, the man said, as he passed them.

"Paul, you think anyone around here knows this Mike Ryan?" Bill asked, holding the door.

"I doubt it, but we can ask. Ryan might come in here when he is in town." Paul said, sliding pass Big Bill.

Paul gave the place the once over. He thought he saw someone he knew from an interview he had when he was working the De Long Case, but he didn't remember her name. "Must be getting old." He said, setting down at a table a few feet from the bar.

The server, a dark haired girl came to their table. She was dressed in a Yellow swim suite, and could have worked "Hooter's", if there had been one in the area. Giving Big Bill a smile to match his size asked, what they wanted to drink.

Bill caught the smile, and stated he wanted a cold beer.

Watch brought the question from her "What kind?"

Bill told her he didn't care, but she insisted he make a choice. "Alright make it a Blue Ribbon. Turning to Paul, she asked "For you Sir." "I'll have a Bud, if it's cold." Paul replied, to Big Bill's joy.

"She called you SIR." You must be getting old." Big Bill said, turning to watch the waitress walk to the bar, where she place their drink order.

Returning with the drinks, she inquired if they were going to want something from the Grill. Bill was the first to answer. "I'm dying of hunger, sweet thing. Do you live around here?"

She went through the entire menu while Bill looked her up and down. He finial picked a Shrimp Dinner, and Paul order Roast Beef.

"Not a seafood lover?" she asked, writing the order on a pad, she had on the tray, she held in one hand. Yes, I like seafood, but I'll have it in Florida.

"You're going to Florida?" she asked, in Sweeny sounding voice. Paul saw an opening to ask about Ryan. "Yes, we were to meet a guy from here, but we haven't been able to find him yet. You might know him. His name is Mike Ryan."

"I sure do. He keeps his sailboat over at the marina just up this street, about three blocks. He and his wife came in almost every weekend, but than she got sick, and I didn't see him for about a year.

A month or two ago, he started coming everyday. He said, he was fixing up his boat. It's been a couple of weeks since, I talked to him last." She stated, turning to look at a couple, who had hailed her for their check.

"I'll be right back." She said, walking to the couple's table.

"Sounds like we are on another wild Grosse Chase." Bill whispered, picking up his beer.

"I had a feeling we wouldn't find him here, but maybe we can find out what his state of mind was, and why he left." Paul responded.

The waitress returned with their food. As she set it on their table, she picked up the conversation where she had left off. "The last time Mike was in, he said he planned to sail the Caribbean, but no place special. That's all I know." She said, walking away.

"Let's eat, and we can check the marina in the morning." Big Bill said, picking up a fork full of cold slaw.

୶

Early the next morning, Paul and Big Bill checked out of the motel and headed for the marina.

"Brazed Roast Marina" a sign read over a dirt road which lead back to the intercostals waterway.

"This must be it." Bill said, turning on the road. It was filled dips and valleys, so the car rocked back, and forth till Paul said, "You know it takes a good driver to hit everyone of those dips." To which Big Bill said, "Thank you very much," then Paul added "But it takes a better driver to miss one or two."

"You want to drive?" Bill asked, turning into a parking spot.

"Maybe when we leave. Right now let's see what we can find out here." Paul answered.

Exiting the car, they walked around the building with the office in it, then out to the docks. "What are we looking for?" Big Bill asked.

There were many boats coming and going. Paul felt the warmth of the raising sun on his body. He wasn't sure what the boat would look like. He knew it was a 38-foot Hunter, but other than the type of boat, Paul had no other information.

"Let's go to the office. Maybe they can tell us what the boat looks like, or at least the name." Bill said, moving toward the building.

Climbing the stairs to the office, they entered to find an old man standing behind a desk covered with papers.

"Can I help you?" the man asked, when Paul was still a few feet from him.

"We need some information on Mike Ryan." I hope you can supply it." Paul went on to identify himself as working for the government. It's our belief Mike Ryan keeps his boat docked here."

"I have over 200 slips out there. I don't remember everyone who rents one from me." The man said, closing the distance between them.

"You must keep a record of who has a boat in the slips. I need to know if his boat is in a slip, or if he has left." Paul said, extending his hand.

"If you put it that way, I can look to see if he has one."

The man said, shaking Paul's hand. "In fact I think I got a letter, or something from the government asking the same question.

"Our office has put out a request for information." Paul replied, moving to the counter in the middle of the office.

"I know I have the letter here somewhere," the man said, moving papers around on his desk. I was going to fill it out, and send it back, but I haven't had the time."

"Check your fills. Just tell us what you know." Paul told the man

The man went to a file cabinet, retrieving a folder bring it to where Paul was standing.

"There isn't much in here." He said, showing it to Paul. "Let's see," Paul, said, glancing at the file. "It shows Mike Ryan has had his boat docked here for five years. Yet you don't know him.

"I may know him, but I don't know him by name." the man replied, let me look at the papers."

The man took the folder. He spent a few minutes looking through the file, then told Paul, "Oh Yeah, Ryan's wife had died a few months earlier, and he had taken the boat out, but hadn't told him, where he was going.

"In fact," the man said, "The day Mike Ryan left, he thought he might sail South to warmer weather."

"What is the name of his boat?" Paul asked, headed for the door.

"It listed here as the "Windjammer"." The man said, closing the file, laying it on the desk.

"Thanks." Paul said, opening the door and letting Big Bill walk down the stairs first. At the bottom, Bill asked, if Paul wanted to drive. Paul told him, he could drive, if he would miss some of the ruts in the road.

Paul instructed Big Bill to head for I-95 South. Then told him the road he needs to take, to get them out to the Interstate, without going back into Charleston. Before long Big Bill had their Big Black Ford motoring South on I-95.

Paul settled back and began going through the file, he had in his hand. He flipped the papers trying to find any information, to help him, decided where Mike Ryan would have gone.

He found a fax from the Coast Guard stating they had towed a boat into St. Simons Island two weeks earlier.

Breaking the silence Paul said, "We need to stop at Savanna to check out this report."

"We are close to Savanna." Big Bill replied, pointing to a sign stating the next three exits for Savanna Georgia.

Taking out the map, Paul explained, the roads needed to guide the car to the Coast Guard Station on St. Simons Island. With only one missed turn, Big Bill was able to find the station.

"Good job." Paul told, Bill as pulled up to the gate guard. After showing their ID. The guard told them "Follow this road for two blocks. and it will be the building on your left."

Paul didn't know how much more information the Coast Guard could give them, but he and Big Bill had to check out every possibility. Even at the cost of time. He knew they would catch up with Ryan, some where down the road.

Entering the building, Paul saw a Master Chief Petty Officer he had known from the days in Vietnam. He tried to remember the chief's name, but like Bill, it would not come to mind.

Master Chief, Paul Heilman here. Can we get some information on a Coast Guard Cutter Named "Saskatchewan"?" I believe it's commanded by a LT. Blanchard.

The Master Chief strolled to the counter with all the military decorum required for his office. "Sir, can I see your ID, and why you need the Officer in question?"

As the Master Chief looked over Paul and Big Bill's cards he asked, "Don't I know you Mr. Heilman? Weren't you in Nam back in the Sixties?"

"Yes I was. I knew, I have met you before, but I don't remember your name Chief I'm sorry." Paul confessed, turning to see Big Bill smiling.

"That's alright Sir, it is Browning I was Navy then, and not as much rank."

"Well Chief Browning, is LT. Blanchard around? Can I speak to him?" Paul asked, looking around the office.

"He is on leave right now Sir, but he'll be back in a week. Can I help you with something?"

"Perhaps; what do you know about a boat, the "Saskatchewan" took in tow, and brought here for repairs." Paul explained, shifting his weight from one leg to the other.

"You must be talking about the boat called "Kaysee Rose". We brought it back here without any problems. The women who owned the boat had it repaired at the marina, and sailed off." The Chief told the two. "What else you need?" the Chief asked.

"I have a fax from D.C. stating there was another boat involved." Paul said, looking the Chief in the eye.

"Yes, there was another boat. Let me get the file." He said, moving a to cabinet to his left.

After thumbing through the file folders the Chief removed one, opening it, as he walked back to Paul, and Big Bill. 'Yeah, the boat the "Windjammer" out of Charleston SC and owned by a Mike Ryan, had answered a distress call from the "Kaysee Rose". Ryan was towing their boat when we came upon them, and took over the tow. The "Windjammer" brought the women here. I was on the cutter at the time, so I know what I am talking about." The Chief said, shutting the folder.

"I have a report that the "Windjammer" arrived in port before the cutter." Paul said, watching the Chief's face show the rage growing up inside him, adding "Over day ahead of you.

"Yes they did." the Chief confessed, "but they must have been running with the wind, or something. I know after we started towing the disabled boat, we came straight to port. In fact, we were concerned we wouldn't have enough fuel to reach port, because of towing the boat."

"Lt. Blanchard did the fuel consumption rate telling me, we had enough." Turning to answer the phone, Paul over heard him take a report that a Deep Sea fishing boat had lost power."

The Chief, returned, and told Paul, he had to get a Cutter out to help a fishing boat, but would be back as soon as he had them underway.

Paul and Big Bill thanked the Chief, for his information, but they had to get back on the road. Stating he wanted to be in Miami, before days end.

Leaving the office Paul told Big Bill "He's not telling us all he knows, but we don't have time to set around, and dig it out of him.

As soon as the Chief had a Cutter on its way to the disabled fishing boat, he took out his wallet, and thumbed through it, until he found a slip of paper. He glanced at the door, to make sure the agents, had left. Picking up the phone he dialed the number on the paper.

&

"It's going to be a fast trip to make South Florida by dark.

"I know.' Paul said, "But I had to give him some reason for us leaving so fast. I didn't want him to think, we were out to get Mike Ryan. I vitally remember the Chief being with Ryan, on a boat in Vietnam. A boat that was shoot out from underneath them, on the Mien Cong.

"I thought you told me this Ryan was in the Army, what was he doing on a boat in the war zone?" Big Bill asked, as he was speeding down the Inter-state once again.

"Ryan was in the Army, the 101st Airborne Division, but he had been assigned to the River Patrol. This was before our run in up at Hue."

"I don't remember all of the details, but I'm sure the Chief does, and I think, he has been in touch with Ryan. If not, he will be shortly." Paul explained. "There is one thing that gets me about this job; we are always a day late, and a dollar short. We are always running behind. For once I wish we could be on time." Paul said, venting his fasciations."

"I'm driving as fast as I can, without getting the local police involved." Big Bill replied, checking his speed."

"I know, Bill, we are making good time. Let's take a break. I need to stretch my legs, and I'm sure you do also." Paul said, picking up the map. He checked the next rest area, telling Bill the next area was forty miles ahead. "We can stop there, get some coffee, and go over what we know right now. All the cases, seam to be about the same area of the ocean."

The black Ford pulled into the rest area at Hollywood Florida. Bill was eager to get out of the car. Paul walked a short distance to the coffee machine. He noticed many people walking their dogs, or headed for the Restrooms some almost running.

One couple Paul saw, looked at him as if they knew who he was, but didn't speak. He shrugged it off walking back to the car where he waited for Big Bill to return.

☙

CHAPTER ELEVEN

"Hold on a minute." I said, "Let me get this straight in my mind." This is where you found out who in the government was looking for you Mike, and they were looking for the Chadwicks also?"

"Yes, I had received a call for a Master Chief who had been in the Navy when I was in Vietnam. After the war he had switched to the Coast Guard. He was there when I got this Crucifix from his Boat Commander, when he died in my arms. We had been patrolling on the river, and the VC blow the boat out of the water. This was before I had the run in with Heilman, up at Hue." Mike said, looking at the group.

"That the most I've ever heard you tell about your action in Vietnam." Bert said, putting his hand on Mike's shoulder.

"I'm proud of what we did over there, but I didn't do as much as a lot of guys who didn't make it back." Mike replied.

"Ok, let's get back to the story. What happened next?" I asked try to get the group back on track.

"There was a lot of things going on at the same time."
Mike told me, then turned to Bert and said, "Why not tell
Mickey about what happen after Linda got the "Witchcraft"
back from being repaired?

The sun was high in the sky when Bert's telephone rang.
A sound he had been expecting, but it still caught him
off guard. Getting up from the chair on the balcony, he
headed for the telephone, which he had moved closer to
the sliding door.

Putting phone to his ear, he heard the voice say, "It's
me, and the "Witchcraft" is back," Bert knew the voice
instantly, as she went on to say, "I'm in the office. Do you
want to come down? We will go look at it. I would like to
see what the hull repairs are like."

The vision of the redhead on the other end of the line
brought thoughts of the first night Bert had met her.

"Bert are you there?" Linda asked, snapping Bert back
to the conversation.

"Yes, I'm here." He replied, shaking his head, adding,
"I will meet you in your office. I'll be right there."

"Great, I'll wait for you...I missed you all day. See
you in a minute.

A second was all it would take him to close up the
apartment, and be on his way to the dock below. He
was looking forward to having time with Linda, and the
"Witchcraft" was a good reason for him to be quick to
meet her.

The office was a busy place. People coming in for
information or whatever else they thought they needed.
Bert had only known Linda a few days, but already she
was becoming the important spot in his life.

He could hardly believe how fast everything had happened. He knew his sister wasn't happy about all of the time he was spending with Linda. But than she had always wanted all of Bert's attention. Over the years, he had learned to live with it. He just hoped Linda would understand.

Linda didn't have family alive, so it might be hard. The request for them to come for dinner at least once a week, was how he could keep peace. Bert like it because he didn't know many places to take Linda out for dinner. He also knew Linda didn't like to cook.

"That didn't take very long." Linda said, as Bert walked into the office.

Bill Davis was standing in the doorway to his office, seeing Bert, he waved, asking, "You going down by the "Witchcraft" are you?" "It should look better, than before, it went across the bay."

"I sure hope so,' Bert responded.

"Are you ready?" Linda asked, taking Bret's arm, and waving with other hand, "See you in the morning." She told him.

"Alright, but be careful; you know we need you around here." Bill told her as they closed the door behind them.

"I had the boat people move the "Witchcraft" up by Mike Ryan's "Windjammer". It is closer to the storage shade. We may need something from there. The marina keeps a lot of junk in there. It may come in handy for the "Witchcraft", Linda told Bert.

They walked hand in hand the short distance to the new slip.

"There she sets." Bert said, as they rounded the prier. "She sure looks better, with the haul repainted."

As the couple walked closer, they could see the "Witchcraft" was returned to her vintage shape.

"Now that's what a "Chris-Craft" should look like." Bert said, as he climbed aboard. He pulled the gangway down onto the prier, so Linda could get aboard.

Linda walked to the bow, bouncing and checking the deck boards as she went. "Look's like they have done a good job on the deck. Made it shine like brand new." She said, turning back to see Bert opening the door to the salon.

"Nothing has changed in here." Bert said, as Linda appeared in the doorway.

"I told them, we would clean up the inside. I didn't want my mother's things moved. I don't understand, how she could've been lost at sea, for so long." Linda said, as tears started welling up in her eyes.

Bert moved close to her, putting his arms around her neck. "I know this is hard on you, but we must clean it up. I need to check out the power plant. We need to be ready when Dave Chadwick, and Mike Ryan are ready to go looking for Dave's island. Maybe we will get lucky, and find your mother in the process."

"I know you're right." Linda replied, putting her head on his chest, kissing him, just below his Adam's apple.

They stood holding each other for a long while. "You had better take a look at the motors, or we will never make it out of the Harbor." Linda told, him moving to the desk, setting on the other side of the salon.

"Since you put it that way. I guess I'd better get busy." Bert replied, heading aft to where the power plants was located.

He had no trouble telling what powered the boat. A quick look told him, they were twin Chrysler 300 F gasoline engine. He had worked on many of the same engines while working in Detroit. His memory went back to High School, when Bert and his Grandfather had built a Dragster with the same motors.

They had spent many hours getting the motors to pull together, and had won many trophies in the "D" gas class, on the Drag Strip.

Bert went right to work checking the gas lines from the tank to the motors. They looked to be in good shape, up to the filters.

Then he checked the fuel pumps, and the filters on the carbonators, all seemed to be in good conduction. He checked the spark plugs. Pulling each one, he checked the gap. Some he reset, and others only needed the carbon, brushed from them.

Bert had saved the air cleaners for last. As he pulled the filter from the right motor, he head a load scream from Linda. He straitened up so quickly, hitting his on the deck above. He back out of the engine compartment, holding the top of his head, with his left hand. He hurried to the main salon where he had left Linda, going through the desk.

As he entered. Bert saw Linda by the desk holding a picture in one hand, the other covered her mouth.

"What is wrong?" Bert asked, as he moved to her side. He saw a strange look on her face, as if she had seen a ghost.

"Look! It's a picture of my mother." She said, with tears streaming from her eyes. "It was taken the summer she disappeared."

"Wow! She sure looks good. She wasn't very old, was she?" Bert commented taking her in to his arms, and kissing her on the top of her head.

"No she was only forty, but now she would be fifty." Linda told him, as she looked up into his dark brown eyes. Then noticed blood trickling down the left side of his face.

"Oh, Bert what happened? You have blood running down your face!" she exclaimed, pushing him away, so she could get a better look, at his wound.

"It's nothing." He said, putting his hand back on his head. He could feel where he had bumped it. "I'll be alright. I just banged my head when I heard you scream. I moved to quick. It will stop in a minute." He added taking his hand away.

"So how are the motors?" Linda asked, as she was blotting the blood from Bert's face.

"Not bad." was his reply, "Not bad at all. I'm about to clean the air filters, then we can try to start them. There's plenty of gas in the tank. The guys you had repair the haul, must have put some gas in when they brought it home."

"Yes, I had them put in 50 gallons, at the pump by the office." Linda responded, "They told me they had checked and repacked all of the propeller shafts. They said, the propellers are good to go."

Going back to finish up with the air filters, Bert found a tag on the transmission shaft stating it had been serviced the day before. He quickly cleaned and replaced the air filters. Putting the tools back in the toolbox, he had found in the engine compartment, he was ready to test the engines.

Going forward he found the key, and tried it to start the engines, but nothing happened. He went aft, and checked the battery compartment.

The batteries had been disconnected. They look to be in good shape, not corroded, so he reconnected the cables. Then went forward.

As he passed Linda, who was hard at work, cleaning the windows in the salon, Bert, smiled as she seemed to be having fun. If cleaning windows could be fun. He wanted to go over to give her a kiss, but thought better.

Once more, he tried to start the engines of the "Witchcraft". This time they began to turn over. He pulled out the choke…the engines coughed and sprang to life. Bert pushed in the choke, and the engines began to purer, as only a Chris-Craft inboard could sound.

Linda came running to where Bert was standing, throw her arms around his waist saying, "You did it… Buckwheat, you did it…we are out of the woods."

Her outburst caught Bert by surprise, he almost turned the key off, thinking there was something wrong.

"Ye Haw," Bert hollowed, turning to grab Linda around her neck with his arm. He drew her to him, holding her close for a long time. "They sound great," he finally said, giving her a kiss on her forehead.

"Hey buddy," Linda said, taking his head in her hands, "Let's do this right." as she pressed her lips to his. They held the kiss, for a long time, while the "Witchcraft" sat idling.

They were startled by the sound of the salon door sliding open. "Hey guys, it sounds like you got her running." Bill Davis, said coming to where they stood. "Are you ready for sea trails yet?" he asked, with a big smile.

"Not yet. I still have a lot of cleaning to do. I've only cleaned some of the windows." Linda confessed, turning and walking back the desk.

She picked up the picture of her mother. Turning to where Bill stood, said, "Take a look at this Bill."

Davis, walked to where she stood, glancing down at the picture. "Your mother; she always did take a good picture." He said.

He walked over to a chart table, looking down at the chart, with pushpins, stuck all around the ocean, many of them close to the bay.

"What is this?" he asked, looking at Bert, who had walked closer to Linda.

"I don't know, we haven't got that far yet." Linda said, looking around his body.

"It looks like someone has plotted points around the ocean and bay. I wonder what they had in mind when they placed the pins." Bill pondered, continuing to look at the chart.

While they were looking at the chart table the "Witchcraft" rolled to it's Port side, from the wake of a passing boat. As the boat rolled in the other direction, a loud bang sounded, as a book fell to the deck.

"That is strange." Linda said, walking to pick up the book.

"You must have moved it, when you were cleaning." Bill said, turning back to the chart.

"Wow!" Linda said, "Look at the title of this book." handing it to Bert.

"Limbo of the Lost" Bert read out loud.

"What do you make of it?" Linda asked, looking at Bill Davies.

"Don't know." he replied taking the book from Bert's hand.

"Looks like a book on ship that have disappeared around Caribbean. He stated, leafing through the book.

"Pick one, and let's see if it matches any of the pins on the board." Bert said.

Bill stopped at a page, and began reading about a ship which had vanished just out side the harbor. In the text it gave the longitude and latitude.

Bill took the numbers, and ran his finger to the intersection and sure enough there was a pin at the spot.

"Well, it looks like, someone was plotted the coordinates, of missing ship, in this area." Bill said, going to another disappearance. It also, had a pin at the intersection.

"Guess ,we solved, this mystery." Bert said, taking Linda's hand.

"It sure is funny, how just the right book, fell from the bookshelf." Linda said, looking around the cabin.

"Maybe someone or something, is trying to help us." Bill said, closing the book, and handing back to Linda.

"Hey Guys I came down to remind you about the meeting with Dave Chadwick in the restaurant." Bill, told them.

"I almost forgot." Linda replied, as she took Bert's hand and started for the door. "I'll take this book, along to show, Mike and the others.

∾

"Is everyone here?" Dave Chadwick asked, as the group gathered at the restaurant.

"Looks like everyone, except for Linda and Bert. They will be right along, Linda was cleaning her boat. Rose stated, as she seated herself next to Mike, and Kaysee, leaving room, for Bert, and Linda next to her.

"Here they come." Rose stated, sliding her chair closer to the table.

"Sorry we're late, but we found something, on the "Witchcraft" that might give us a lead to the "Triangle's Door", you were talking about the last time, we were here." Bert told, Dave.

"Yeah, I have it right here." Bill said, taking the chair next to Rose, passing the book to Dave.

"What does this book have to do with our island?" Dave asked, picking up the book.

The title of the book was "Limbo of the Lost", by John Wallace Spencer, Bill explained, He went on saying, "It tells about the ships, and planes lost in the "Bermuda Triangle". We found a chart, on the "Witchcraft", that plotted out most of the ships which have been lost. Bert, Linda, and I think, who ever plotted the last known positions, of these ships, found a pattern to these positions, and may have found the door, you have been telling us about." "What we need now is to find out where and when the door will open. How long before, it will open in the same area. I'm not sure once you enter the door, you would be able to exit it in the same spot, nor how long, before you could get out."

"I will call Ester Easterday right away." Linda said, sliding her chair to get up. "I'll be right back."

While Linda left to call her friend, the rest of the group started making a list of what they thought they might need for the trip to find Dave's Island.

According to Mike, the Chadwicks wanted to be sure everyone would be safe in the search.

Dave wanted to use everyone's boat. The "Windjammer", the "Kaysee Rose", and the "Witchcraft",

H. Mickey Mc Guire

so he had each owner make a list of the things, each one would need, to out-fit their own boats.

By the time the list had been complied, Linda had retuned with the answer they wanted.

Her friend Esther, would meet with Linda, and go over what the group needed to know, to find the Door. Linda told them Esther had sounded very positive, about being able, to locate the common point.

After the meeting Mike, Kaysee and Bert went shopping for the items needed.

CHAPTER TWELVE

OK, while everyone went shopping; you went to see your friend Esther Easterday? I asked, turning to Linda.

Yes, Linda replied, then went on to tell me how she had thought someone was following her. She didn't know who, but there was a car behind her most of the way, to the University of South Florida. Then she started her story.

Linda had retrieved the chart and book from the "Witchcraft", and was on her way, to meet with Esther. She worked in the University's Computer Lab. Her job was creating computer programs, to do all sorts of things. One was comparing various land masses to that of other planets in our Galactic neighborhood.

As Linda parked, and got out of the car, the hair on the back of her neck seemed to stand on end.

She glanced around, as carefully as she could. She didn't want it to look like, she was aware of anything. There was a lot of cars in the parking lot, but there wasn't any movement, in the bushes.

To be on the safe side, she entered the building beside the one where Esther worked. She went down to the basement, walked across a corridor, to the right building. Up the stairs to the Lab, where Esther had her office.

She knocked on the door-jam, as Esther look up. She was talking on the phone, and Linda heard her say, "No I don't know anyone by that name." then Esther, paused, looking straight at Linda, and said, "Yes, I know her. She is a very close friend. I don't understand, why you want, all this information. What did you say your name was?" Esther looked at the phone, as if it would bit her. Shaking her head she replaced the phone in it's cradle.

"Linda," Esther said, getting up from her desk, she extended her hand to Linda, then said "Have a seat."

Linda handed the rolled up chart to Esther, saying "This the chart I told you about. This book seems to have something to do with the chart." she then added, "It may have something to do with my mother. It was on the "Witchcraft". Perhaps Harold, was the one who plotted the missing boats and ships."

Esther unrolled the chart and glanced at the markings on it.

"These marks by the pin holes, are those spots were the ships have been thought, to have disappeared?" she asked, picking up the book.

"Yeah, and I brought that book a long, just in case, there was something in it you could use." Linda replied, shifting in her chair.

"Why don't I make a copy of this chart. I sure would hate to have something happen to it." Esther said, standing up, and moving to the copying machine in the corner.

"How long, do you think it will take you to have the program to help us find the point where all these disappearances come together?" Linda asked, getting up from her chair.

"I was going to ask you what you wanted me to look for." Esther said, turning toward Linda.

"Do you think there is a single spot, where all these ship were lost?' Esther asked, taking the chart from the copier.

"That's what my friends, seem to think." Linda replied, stepping back by her chair.

"Give me a couple of days, to see what I can come up with." "There you go." Esther said, handing the chart back to Linda.

"Thanks, for all your help." Linda said, rolling up the chart.

"I hate to be nosy, but can I ask a question, and not make you mad?" Linda asked with a smile.

"Sure, we have been friends for years. What's on your mind?" Esther replied.

"Who was on the phone?" she asked, setting back down in the chair across the desk from Esther.

"I don't know. He said, his name was Paul something, and he worked for the government." She replied, setting down. "He wanted to know, if I knew a Mike Ryan." "Do you know this Mike Ryan?" Esther asked, pushing her phone to the side of her desk.

"Yes I do, but I just met him, an hour or so, before I called you." she answered. "I don't understand, how this agent, could have connected, me to Mike Ryan, and you, so quick."

"I don't know, but I answered the phone, just before you stepped to the doorway.

"It sure is strange." Linda said, "But I had a feeling I was being followed on my way over here."

"Let me do some checking and I will get back to you." Esther replied, patting the top of her computer.

"Great! You can call me at the Marina Office" Linda said, getting up and heading for the door.

"I'll call you as soon as I have anything." Esther said, as Linda walked out of the office.

Linda left the building and made her way to her car. She was continually looking around trying to see who was watching her. Starting her car, she saw two men getting out of a big black car and headed her way. She quickly put the car in gear, making her way out of the parking lot.

As Linda made a right turn out of the lot, she looked back and could see the two men getting back in their car. She went three blocks making a right turn on to a side street, and parked where she could see the street she had just came off.

She sat there watching, for a short time. Then she saw the black car go speeding by. She smiled to her self, knowing she had out smarted who ever was in the black car.

After waiting a few more minutes, she made her way back to the marina office, where she called Bert. Telling him to meet her in his parking garage.

As Bert came close to her car, she got out running to him. She took his arm, and moved him to the stairway, saying frantically, "There are two guys trying to follow me. They were at Esther's office when I came out. They tried to catch me before I got to my car, but I gave them the slip. I don't think they are here yet, but they will be.

Some guy named Paul something, already talked to Esther just as I walked into her office." She said, tightening her grip on his arm.

"What did they look like?" Bert asked, prying her hand from his arm.

"Oh, sorry," she said, moving her hand, to her pockets. "I don't know. They were big and walked like they owned the world." than added, "They frightened the Hell out of me. I could just see them pulling a gun, and blowing me away." Linda said, putting her head on his shoulder.

Bert put his arm around her, holding her to his side. "I think we need to contact Mike, and see what he thinks. These guys must be from the government. But I don't understand what they want from you."

"When I was in Esther's office, she told me, the guy on the phone, asked if she knew Mike Ryan, and me. Just what is the deal.?" Linda asked, in a strained voice.

"Let's go up to my apartment, and see if we can contact Mike or the Chadwicks." Bert said giving her a smile.

They took the elevator, to the 17th floor. As they exited, Doc. Billings was coming down the hallway.

"Hi, Bert, everything's going well I see." Doc. Billings said, giving Bert a big smile. "By the way, there was a guy in a dark suit, who wanted to know which was your apartment. I told him you weren't in, but he said, he just needed the number. I told him. I hope it was alright." Billings added.

"Sure Doc., it's Ok." Bert said, as he put his key in the lock, then stopped. "Maybe this isn't a good idea." Bert said, withdrawing the key.

"Why? What are you thinking?" Linda asked, looking around.

"If someone in a dark suit has been here, there's a good chance they have bugged my apartment." Bert replied, taking Linda by the arm, heading back to the garage, telling her "We'll take my car. I'll stop by the motel, see if Mike and the girls are there. If not, we will go over to Earlene's, and hide out until, we can contact Mike."

"What is with this Cape and Sword deal?" Linda asked, walking to Bert's car.

∽

CHAPTER THIRTEEN

Captain Mike jumped in the story saying, "This is where we ran into someone giving the government information on where we were and what we were planning. You know it's one thing for people to be concerned for your well being and another to just out and out lie to your face."

"That's true Mike, but when they sell you out for money. It just shows you friends aren't always friends." Bert interjected.

So where does the rest of the story go from here? I asked, looking around at everyone looking like they had eat the cat.

I could tell what ever happened it still had a heart wrenching effect on each and everyone of them.

"Well, I guess we should pick it up when I had the run in with Paul Heilman and Big Bill Boyd." Mike said, refilling his cup. "Why not let me tell, Mickey how we ended up knowing who was rating us out?" Linda asked, starting the rest of the story.

At the time Kaysee, Rose and Mike were spending a couple of nights in a motel, down the street from the marina. Bert knock on the motel room with Linda right behind him.

"Hi guys. What up?" Rose said, as she opened the door.

Bert moved into the room quickly.

Linda closing the door behind them. "Where is Mike?" he asked, moving to the window over looking the parking lot.

"Him and Kaysee went out for something to eat." Rose replied, "What's wrong? What's going on, Bert?" she queried, stepping back from the door.

"I'm not sure, but I need to talk to Mike right away." he told her.

"They should be back shortly. You and Linda want something to drink?" she asked, heading for kitchenette in the back of the room.

"No thanks." Bert said, turning to Linda "You want something?"

"Just a glass of water." she replied.

Rose got a glass of water and handed it to Linda. "Now what is going on with you two? You act like a killer is following you." Rose told them.

"You might be closer to the truth than you think. We can't talk here." Bert said, moving away from the window, adding, "Get your bag and come with us."

"Where are we going?" Rose asked, without moving.

Bert steeped close to Rose, whispering in her ear. "This place may have bugs."

"Oh, Ok, Let's get going if your in that big of a hurry. I only need this, pointing to a oversize hand bag. It has everything in it." she explained, heading for the door.

"Wait, Where are the Chadwicks staying?" Bert asked in a whisper.

"In room 101, on the ground floor." Rose answered, in the same low voice.

"Do you know where Mike took Kaysee?" Rose nodded, pointing to a pad of paper.

Bert took the pen and wrote: *That's alright, you and Linda take my car. See if you can get in touch with Mike. Linda you know where they need to go. I will take the Chadwicks to the same place. We need to do this as fast as we can.*

Bert handed his keys to Linda. Looked out the door to see if there was anyone lurking in the parking lot. Not seeing anyone, he beckoned the girls out the door.

While the girls went one way, Bert went in the other direction and down the stairs. He quickly found Room 101, looked around and knocked.

Dave Chadwick came to the door. "Hey Bert; right? What can I do for you?" he asked, stepping a side so Bert could enter.

"I think we have a problem with the government." Bert mouthed.

"What are you talking about" Dave asked, with a stunned look on his face.

"I think your room may be wired for sound." Bert replied. "We can't talk here. Can we go to your car? I have a place that should be safe." Bert explained.

"I don't understand. But, yes we can go." Dave replied, turning to the bathroom, he walked in telling his wife, to get her purse.

"Why?" questioned, Joan coming into the main room.

"Don't talk so loud." Dave said. "Just get it, and come with us."

The trio left the motel room and headed for Dave's car. Bert open the door for Joan, then got in the back seat.

Once the car was moving, Bert leaned forward, telling the Chadwicks about what had taken place when Linda had gone to see her friend Esther.

"I don't know why the government would be so interested in any of us. We aren't doing nothing illegal." Dave said, getting ready to enter the Interstate.

"Let's not go on the Interstate. There should be side streets we can take to get to my sister's." Bert said, looking behind them.

"I know Miami quite well. Just give me her address and I will get us there." Dave told Bert, changing lanes heading north.

Bert gave him the address. With a lot of turns, Dave navigated his car to Earlene's house.

Pulling into the drive Bert saw his car was already there. Earlene was standing in the driveway, with her arms folded across her chest.

"Not a good sign." Bert said, getting out of Dave's car. He then told the Chadwicks, his sister would want to help, her big brother.

As Bert walked to where his sister was standing. She greeted him with, "Alright, what have you got yourself into now? Linda said you would tell me, when you got here. Now your here. What's going on?" she asked. Seeing the Chadwicks come her way. "Who are these people?" She asked, dropping her arms to her side.

"Dave Chadwick, this my sister Earlene." Bert said, turning to Dave. Then said, "Earlene this is Dave Chadwick, and his wife Joan."

"Nice to meet you." Earlene said, in her most formal voice.

"Can we go in your house? I will explain every thing." Bert said, giving his sister a kiss on the cheek. "Has anyone been here?" He asked, as they entered the house.

"Not until Linda and Rose came knocking on my door." Earlene stated, giving her brother a questioning look.

"No, I mean someone like a service man, or telephone man." Bert explained.

"Not that I know of, and I have been here all morning. Dale is out showing some apartments, and won't be back until evening." she replied, moving everyone into the kitchen.

Linda and Rose met Bert at the coffee pot. Bert drew himself a cup of coffee, then asked if anyone else wanted a cup.

Earlene told everyone to set down at the dining table.

"Alright." she said, pulling up a stool, next to Bert, and asked, "What is going on?"

Bert started explaining about how Linda had been followed when she went to see Esther, and had came back to meet up with Bert. Then how he had gone looking for Mike. Found out Rose was by herself. He went on to tell, how he had got the Chadwicks, finishing with. "And here we are." Bert said, taking a sip of coffee.

"That explains how you got here. Why is the government following all of you?" Earlene asked looking around the table.

147

"The answer to that is the big question of the hour." Bert replied, giving her a big smile.

"We need to get in contact with Mike." Bert said, looking around for an answer.

"Where are they?" Earlene asked, going to the bread box, asking anyone want some cake?"

She had no takers, and returned to the stool.

"They were going to get something to eat." Rose replied, then went on, "Linda and I stopped where they said they were going, but they weren't there. Then we came straight here."

"Mike isn't from around here, so there can't be to many places, they could go." Rose said, to the group.

"True." Bert replied.

"Maybe they went to his boat or our boat." Rose interjected.

"How can we get word to him?" Bert asked, rubbing his forehead.

Earlene turned to Linda saying, "Why don't you call Bill Davis? He could see if this Mike is on his boat, or Rose's boat.

"That's a great idea, Sis" Bert said, patting her on the head.

"What are sisters for?" she told him, pointing to the phone on the counter.

Linda went to the counter, pick up the phone and dialed the number.

Everyone heard Linda's conversation. She asked if they would check the "Windjammer" and the "Kaysee Rose" to see if Mike Ryan, or Kaysee was around. "Their not? Are you sure? Ok. Then would you check the apartment parking garage, and see if there's a new red Mustang, with rental stickers on the bumper. It'll be parked on the fourth level. Ok. If it is, will you leave a note on the windshield, with this number?" She gave Earlene's phone number.

"Ok, also put on it, they need to call using a pay phone. Thanks Bill. Yeah it's Earlene's number. Thanks again Bill. I'll see you in the morning." she said goodbye, and hung up the phone, saying, that was Bill, he told me he was sure they weren't on the boats. They may have gone to Bert's apartment. Maybe their rental car will be in the parking garage.

"Let's hope that'll work." Bert said, drinking from his coffee cup.

"Now explain what is going on." Earlene said, looking around the table, again.

"I'm looking to find an island, which my wife, and I were on for fifty years. Bert and the rest have been gracious enough to help." Dave said, and then went on.

"You never know what you have, until you loss it. We had paradise. But didn't realize how good we had it. We wanted to come back here. Only to find out we don't fit in and can't stay. Joan is sick.

We've been to Doctor John O' Malley. He's telling us, because of being on the island, our bodies are starting to shut down. He couldn't tell us how long we had left. Only God knows when your time is up. So we must find the island as soon as we can." Dave said, putting his arm around his wife's neck.

"What story!" Earlene said, watching the Chadwicks. "What ever we can do to help, Dale and I will." she added.

Dave explained they were staying in a motel room, but he had a 48 foot Schooner in a marina in Melbourne; he would like to bring it down. He needed to contact a friend, who would sail it down, if Dave could call him.

Earlene told him to use her phone. Stating Dale calls over the world, a call to Melbourne would be nothing.

Dave made the call and told everyone, his boat would be on it's way in the morning. He had told the friend to meet him at the marina Del Ray.

"Then that is it." Bert said. "We just have to wait for Mike and Kaysee to call."

"Yeah, if they get the message." Linda said, moving closer.

"In the mean time. Everyone is staying for dinner." Earlene said, getting up from the table. "It will only take a little bit to get it going." she added, going to the stove.

All the women said they would help. Dave told Earlene that he didn't want to impose, but Earlene wouldn't hear it. Saying she had to make dinner for Dale and a few more wasn't a problem.

☙

CHAPTER FOURTEEN

"According to Heilman." Mike said, then went on to explain. "He had a man on the inside. The guy was a friend of ours, or at least we thought he was a friend. He had been in on most of the meeting, in the beginning, but when we found out who he was and that he was feeding Heilman information. We changed how we went about getting ready to look for the door."

"How did all this come about?" I asked, looking around the cabin. Then Captain Mike pick up the story stating the following as best he could remember:

"We are in Miami, but as yet haven't found out where Ryan, nor Chadwick are hanging out." Paul said, talking to Emily on the phone.

"I have received word from our man down there. He is telling us Ryan has his boat the "Windjammer" docked in the Marina Del Ray. The slip number is 9-17. The guy says Ryan has a group of people around him. Probably four to six people. One of which is your man Chadwick. According to the guy another one of the group is a Linda Carrie, who works in the Dock Master's office. He goes on to say this Linda has a friend who works at the University of South Florida as a computer programmer. Her name is Esther Easterday. According to her profile, she is one smart cookie.

"Why do they need a programmer? Any ideas?" Paul asked, interrupting Emily.

"Yeah, if you will hold on I'm getting to the best part." she says, going on with her information, "What the guy is telling his Department; all these people are trying to find a door in a cloud of some kind. I don't truly understand, what he means by a door. But he says, if they can find this door, it will lead Chadwick back to his island. You getting all of this?" she asked, waiting for Paul's answer.

"I got it. Don't completely understand it. I'll figure it out, as we go along." Paul replied.

'Ok, there is more. The Director is telling me, you must stop Ryan, or anyone else from looking for this lost island. He doesn't want these people sailing around dangerous waters. He told me to tell you to do what ever it takes. Stop them at all cost."

"What does he want me to do? Sink their boats. Kill them? My God Emily, these people are Americans."

"They haven't broken an laws. What am I to do?" Paul asked, shaking his head.

"I don't know Paul. The Director just said, "At all cost." "This information is coming through DEA." she replied, and then the phone went dead.

Paul couldn't believe what he had just been told. He knew if he ran into Ryan there would be problems, but he had his orders. Just like last time. They are making him the goat. "Boy I hate it, when they put me in the middle." Paul said out loud.

"What is wrong?" Big Bill asked, walking up to Paul with two cups of coffee.

"You aren't going to believe, what they want us to do." Paul told him.

"What do they want?" Big Bill asked, looking at the phone Paul still held in his hand.

"They want us to stop Ryan, and Chadwick from sailing out in the Atlantic."

"How are we going to do that? We don't even know where they are right now." Big Bill replied, watching Paul hang up the receiver.

"Emily told me how we're going to find Ryan, and the rest. I know where Ryan is keeping his boat." Paul said, heading for the car.

"Where are we going?" Big Bill asked, getting in on the driver's side.

"Let's just set here and drink our coffee. I'll fill you in on the phone conversation, I just had with Emily." Paul said, getting in on the other side.

After talking with Big Bill, Heilman decided their best course of action, was to go to the marina, and stake it out. They might get lucky. They might actually see Ryan face to face.

He tells Big Bill, "I think we need more help, there is no way we can be six places at once."

"Your right about that." Big Bill replied, drinking the last of his coffee. Then asked, "So what do you want to do?" looking over at Paul.

"Let me call Emily back. Maybe we can get some help down here. There may be guys from DEA who can help us." Paul told him getting out of the car, heading for the pay phone.

153

Big Bill watched while Paul went to the phone. Twenty minutes later, Paul returned to the car, "saying, "We have help. We need to go to DEA headquarters. They have six guys all ready on the group. I need to talk to them, before Ryan gets wind of these DEA guys."

"So, you want me to drive to DEA headquarters?" Bill asked, starting the car, and checking traffic.

"No, first I think we should go to the "Marina Del Ray." Paul told him checking his notes.

"Ok, tell me where it is, and we'll be on our way." Big Bill replied, checking behind him again.

Paul gave him the direction, and with in a few minutes, they were pulling into the parking lot, at the marina. Paul got out, and headed for the dock office, with Big Bill following him, into the office.

ॐ

Two men entered the Club, where Mike and Kaysee stopped to eat. They were dress in dark suits and were well over six foot. They walked as if they knew where they were going, and Mike could tell, they were headed straight for him.

"I know it must be Heilman." Mike said, as he pulled Kaysee from the stool, she had been sitting on, at a tall table, eating a ham sandwich.

"How do you know?" she asked, catching her footing, as Mike towed her to the back of the building.

"Come on we needed to get out of here, I'll explain latter." Mike replied, as he opened the back door, making their way, through the back alley to the parking lot.

Once they were in the car he started the engine, ready to drive off. A big black car pulled into the alley, behind his Mustang, blocking his way.

"Duck down in the seat." Mike yelled, as he locked the doors. He looked around for a way to escape. He knew the car blocking him from backing out, was a government issue. Mike couldn't believe he had put himself, and Kaysee in a place where they could be seized so easily.

The parking lot had filled up with cars, parked in every direction. He had parked, so he could pull straight ahead. Now there was a little Japanese model, parked in front of him. The only way out, was to push the little car out of his way.

Mike looked in the side mirror. He could see a guy dressed in a dark suit, getting out of the drivers side, with what looked like a gun in his hand.

"Hold on!" Mike shouted, as he pulled the Mustang in first gear, easing it to the bumper of the car in front. The car moved, as Mike looked back seeing the guy in black, start running toward him. Mike gunned the Mustang harder. He was able to get by the car in front of him, before the man coming from the rear, could reach his car.

Quickly Mike made the street. Went three blocks, then made a hard left turn. He hoped if the black car was going to follow him, they would have to wait for traffic to clear, before taking up the chase again.

"It's a long shoot, but maybe I can lose these guys." Mike explained, "We'll head for the water front, and the boats. Then hide out until they give up, and go someplace else." Mike told Kaysee, as she got back up in the seat, fastening her seat belt.

"How did they know we had this car?" Kaysee asked, shifting around, so she could see out the back window.

"Don't know." Mike replied, keeping his eyes on the road ahead. "Must have been watching us for some time."

It was a half hour before Mike, and Kaysee pulled into the parking building, where Bert kept his car. They made their way to the marina, and headed for the "Windjammer".

"Don't you think we should go to the "Kaysee Rose" Kaysee said, as they were going through the gate.

"No." Mike replied, "I don't want Heilman, or anyone else, to connect your boat, or the 'Witchcraft" to me. We will hide out on the "Windjammer" maybe they haven't found it yet."

Mike checked behind them, as they made their way around the boat slips, and headed down the dock, to the "Windjammer".

As they neared the boat, Mike heard the sound of a speedboat coming into the marina. It pulled up to the fuel pump. He could see there were two men dressed in black. Mike couldn't make out their faces, but in his gut, he felt they had to be working for Heilman.

"Quick, get on board, and below, before they see us." Mike said, crouching along side his boat.

Kaysee did as instructed with out a word. Quietly they entered the gangway. Mike reached for the small flashlight which he kept by the hatch. Turning it on, a red glow lit compartment.

Mike went to the air vent above the navigation desk, opening it just slightly. He could hear voices, but couldn't make out what was being said. He stayed by the vent trying to see, if the men were coming his way.

He decided to make the "Windjammer" look more like there was no one on board. He went to the bow, opening the front hatch. He stuck his head out and looked around. He could see there was a guard at the gas pumps. He was talking to someone, but Mike couldn't see who it was. He guessed it was the two guys, who had arrived in the small boat.

He crawled out the hatch, making his way to the main gangway. He slipped the latch in place and lock the pad lock.

Making his way back to the front hatch, he could hear the guard shouting, "You can't go down there." Then he heard a splash, and someone running. Mike slip back through the hatch, closing it behind him.

"Turn out the flashlight." Mike whispered, just loud enough for Kaysee to hear.

He eased his way to where Kaysee was sitting. He told her to stay still. "We don't need the boat rocking if those guys come this way."

The time seemed to stop. To Mike it seemed like hours, since they had boarded the "Windjammer". He look at his watch, and saw it had only been a few minutes. It was hard to tell, if the guys were still on the dock.

Just when Mike thought they might have left. He felt the boat rock, telling him they had just stepped on board. He made a hand sign for Kaysee to remain still.

More time passed slowly. Mike heard someone, trying the lock at the gangway. One of the men telling the other, "It looks like no one's on board." The boat rocked again, giving the feeling, the men were leaving.

Mike waited for five minutes. Not feeling any movement from the men on deck, he move to Kaysee's side, saying "I think we are safe for awhile. I have a feeling they will be back. We need to get word to the others, as soon as we can."

Again Mike went to the front hatch. He slowly open it, just enough to see the dock along side the "Windjammer". Seeing no one around, he slide out laying flat on the deck. He waited a few minutes before going to the main gangway. He unlocked the lock sliding the gangway open. He could see Kaysee looking up at him with a knife in her hand.

"It's just me." Mike whispered, and motioned for her to come up on deck. "I think they've left. We'll go up to the dock office." Mike explained, closing the hatch and relocked it.

Making their way toward the dock office. Mike check in the direction of the gas pumps, didn't see the guard, nor the men. But the boat was still tied to the dock.

"We need to get out of here." Mike said, putting his arm around Kaysee's waist moving her a little faster down the dock.

"Where are going now?" she asked.

"Didn't Bert say he had an apartment around here?" Mike asked, swinging the gate open.

"Yeah, it's up on the seventeenth floor in that building." Kaysee replied, pointing up toward the balcony.

"Let's go see if he is at home." Mike said, starting to trot.

ↄ৲

CHAPTER FIFTEEN

Earlene went to the back door, leading to the pool area, saying "Dinner is ready. Come and get it."

Everyone entered the dining room, followed by Bert and Dale. Everyone took seats around the table.

"Earlene is a good cook, especially when it is unexpected." Dale said, taking a seat at the head of the table.

"We really didn't want to stay for dinner, but your wife, wouldn't take no for an answer." Dave said, giving Earlene a smile.

After giving thanks, Dave asked, "What do you call this dish?"

"It is Bert's second favorite meal. Our mother called it Goulash." Earlene replied, patting Bert on his back.

"It is made with fried hamburger, tomatoes and macaroni, but I add V8 juice now." She explained, dishing it out.

"It tastes good." Joan stated, lifting her fork as a salute.

"It's filling if nothing else." Earlene replied, getting up to answer the phone.

"Yes, she here." Earlene said, then motioned for Linda to come to the phone.

"Who is it?" Linda asked, taking the phone for Earlene's hand.

"It's Tim, from your office." she said, going back to her chair.

"This is Linda." she said, putting the phone to her ear.

"Hi Tim, what's up?" she asked.

Bert could tell there was something wrong, as he watched Linda's expression.

"He did?" "Were you able to find it?" "Yeah, that's good. You did?" Thanks Tim." "They are?" "You did." "Well, just hang up, and I will call you right back. Then you can Bill, we are all going out to dinner. Tell him we are meeting at that Cuban place, down on Front Street. You know, "The Flamingo." "Yeah, that's the one." "Thanks again Tim. Now hang up." Linda said, pushing the end button. Then dialed her office.

"We have a problem." she said, while she waited for the number to be answered.

"What kind of problem?" Bert asked, watching Linda's face, as she held up one finger.

"Bill this is Linda." "Yeah, we're fine. I'm just calling to let you know we are all meeting in about an hour, at that Cuban place on Front Street. Yes, that's the place. Ok, see you there." Linda said, as she hung up the phone, and returned to the table.

"So, what's going on?" everyone asked, as Linda sat down.

"I can't believe what Tim told me." she said, putting her hand over her mouth.

"You've got our attention. Tell us what is going on." Earlene said, clearing the dishes from the table.

"The good news is. Tim was able to catch Mike and Kaysee as they came out of the elevator, in Bert's apartment building. He said he told them where you live, also the phone number here. The bad News is, Tim over heard Bill telling, two guys from the DEA, who came to the office, everything about all of us. Tim went on to say, these guys said something about impounding our boats, and bring us in for questioning. Bill told them we are all here. Even gave them the address." Linda told the group, handing her plate to Earlene.

"Bill did all that?" Dale asked, then added, "Jim has been wanting to get rid of him. I wonder if Bill is DEA. If he is, that would explain how those kids, who came to rent an apartment, was arrested so quick."

"Yeah, even Doc. O'Malley, was stopped by the Coast Guard." Earlene added.

"One thing for sure. We must get away from here." Dave said, slipping his hand into Joan's. Then said, but were are we going?"

"Good question." Bert replied, getting up from his chair, going to the front door, and looking out.

"We must get our boats out of the marina, right away." Rose said, looking around the table.

"We could take them to Bimini, but I'm not sure the Feds., wouldn't just follow us." Dave interjected, moving next to Earlene.

"I'm sorry, we have involved you, and Dale with the government." he said.

"Not all. We glad we can help." she said, giving him a big smile, saying, "John O'Malley has a place, somewhere in Bahamas Islands. I don't know where, but I bet he would help you." Earlene stated, finishing placing the dished in the dishwasher.

"Perhaps. He knows we are looking for our island. He also knows we don't have much time. Can I call him?" Dave asked, pointing to the phone.

"Sure. Help yourself." Earlene replied. Pulling the phone closer to him.

ↄ৲

CHAPTER SIXTEEN

"Is there a Bill Davis here? Paul asked, the guy behind the counter.

"My name is Tim." the man said. "Can I ask, who wants to see him?" he asked.

"Just tell him, we're the guys from DC., he'll know." Paul instructed.

A couple of minutes passed, and Bill Davis walked out of his office with Tim.

"I'm Bill Davis. Why don't you gentlemen come into my office?" he said, opening the gate, to let them through.

After they entered the office, Paul told Bill Davis, he wanted to know if Mike Ryan, was on his boat. To which Bill told him about the two of his men, who had checked Ryan's boat and found nothing. I have a feeling we may have tipped our hand. I know Ryan spends most of his time on the boat, or with a group who are planning to look for some island.

"Yeah, I know all about the island. I have been told, to stop these people, from leaving the marina. Your headquarters, are getting the paper work to impound all of their boats." Paul told him, as he closed the door to the office.

"If your going to do that. We are going to need a bunch of guys down here, to guard the docks. I'm not sure just what that will take." Bill confessed.

"You make the phone call, and get them moving fast. This Ryan is no foul. If you have tipped him off, that we're looking for him. He'll be wanting to move his boat, and all the rest." Paul explained.

"Just than Davis's phone rang, and answered it at once.

"This is Bill Davis." he said, looking at Heilman.

"Hi Linda. What can I do for you? I know their not. Yes I'm sure.

"The parking garage? Ok, a Red Mustang, a rental. Ok, is that Earlene's number? Ok use a pay phone. Got it. Yeah, see you in the morning." Bill finished the conversation, and went to the office door telling Tim to run an earn.

After Bill explained what Tim needed to do, he turned back to Heilman and said, "I think we just lucked out. The whole group is at Linda's boyfriend's sister's house. It's not far from here. Maybe you can get over there and catch everyone at one stop. Besides that, Mike Ryan, maybe still in the area. I'm having Tim check it out now."

"Do you think we might get a break?" Big Bill asked, looking out the window, and said, "Here comes your man now."

As Tim entered the office the phone rang. But before he could get to it, Davis had already picked it up.

Tim knew it was Linda calling back. He heard Davis say just what Linda had told him to tell Davis. Tim smiled as he went on with his filling.

Then Davis came out of his office asking, if he had found Mike Ryan's car.

Tim told him, He had left the note on the windshield, but had not seen Ryan.

"You sure it was the right red car." Heilman asked, walking into the office.

"Yeah, I'm sure. I know a Red Mustang, when I see one." Tim said, in an indifferent voice.

"Come on, Big Bill maybe can get Ryan right here." Paul said, heading for the door.

"Wait, Davis said, "I need to give you the address where everyone will be.

Heilman and Big Bill stopped, letting Davis give them a slip of paper with the address for the "Flamingo" on it.

"Thanks." Heilman said opening the door.

☙

CHAPTER SEVENTEEN

Captain Mike picked the story with him and Kaysee at Bert's apartment, as they came out of the elevator.

As we exited. There was Tim, from the dock office. We knew him from being in and out of the office.

We asked him why he was there, and what he told us we couldn't think of any reason for Bill Davis to turn us in.

Tim told us he had over heard Bill telling the to guys from DEA, where the group was and they could catch everyone if they went to Bert's sister house. He gave us the number to contact. Stated we should use a pay phone, because Linda thought the office phone was tapped.

I couldn't see how or why, but Tim told us Bill had talked to Linda. She had told him they were meeting at a Cuban place, but they were really going someplace else. Then he told us the government wanted to impound our boats, and arrest us.

"How can they do all that?" Kaysee asked, in an agitated voice.

I told her they weren't going to take our boats, but at the time I had no idea, how we were going to get away, this time. Nor where we would go, until time for me to go looking for the door.

Instead of making the phone call, Kaysee and I got in the rental car, and following the instructions, Tim gave me. We were on our way to Bert's sister's.

Turning down Earlene's street, I saw the group leaving, and heading in my direction.

As they got closer, I stopped, brought down the driver's window, signaling the lead car to stop. It was Dave, Joan and Rose.

"Where are you headed?" I asked, Dave, as he came to a stop even with me.

"We were going to look for you." he stated, with a big grin.

"Ok, now what?" I said, watching the other cars come to a stop.

Rose got out of Chadwick's car, and came over to Kaysee's window. "They want to take our boat." she said, frantically.

"It will be alright, Rose." Kaysee replied, in a vary composed voice.

"Let's go across the causeway, into the city. There must be someplace we can sit down, and figure out where to go from here." Dave said, motioning for Rose to get back in the car.

"We'll talk later." Kaysee told Rose, as she got back into Dave's car.

"I know a place we can go on the other side." I told Dave. "We can go to the marina where I had the bottom done, on the "Windjammer", Linda knows the place. They did the work on the "Witchcraft" also.

"Sounds like a plan. Let's go see the city." Dave said, pulling his car forward to let Bert pull up even the us.

I told them where we were going to meet, telling them to take the lead.

With in a hour the group had reassembled in the boat yard. We knew the government didn't want us to go looking for the island, but couldn't understand why.

At the time, we thought maybe they really were concerned about our safety. But quickly put that out of our thoughts. If that was the case, then no one would be able to sail in or out of Biscayne Bay.

We decided our main problem, was to get our boats out of the Del Ray marina, before the government impounded them. Thus cutting off our only means of looking for the island.

I explained to everyone, what we needed was a way across the bay to the marina. We could rent a boat, but we would need to wait until morning. We needed to do at night, if we were going to have a chance to out wit Heilman, and the men he had working with him.

Linda suggested we talk to the owner of the boat yard. Maybe he would take us. Dave, and all, thought this was a good idea, so Linda and I went to see the owner.

After pleating our case, and Dave's fat wallet, the guy agreed to take us to the marina by water, after dark.

☙

It was 1 AM when the group left from the boat yard. It had been agreed that Joan, would go with Bert and Linda, while Kaysee and Rose would take their boat. This left me, and Dave to take the "Windjammer".

We planned to sail from the Del Ray Marina out into the bay and anchor until daybreak. Then we would sail to the Bahamas islands. Where Doctor O' Malley had a cabin, on one of the small islands, of the Berry Islands Chain. The only ones who knew where and what we were doing, was those in the group.

Linda had talked to Esther. She ask her if she had any information from the chart and book.

Esther had informed her, the program was running, and she should have something the next day. Esther told Linda, to call her back the next afternoon.

Everything was set, and the plan was put in motion. We reached the boats about 1:45 AM. The boat Captain, killed the motor on the boat, just as we entered the Del Ray Marina's main canal. He let the boat drift to the dock. I was on the bow. I checked to make sure no one was around. Seeing the dock was clear. We tided the boat to the dock and everyone disembarked, heading for the boat they would be taking out.

I had instructed Kaysee, and Linda; we would all start our Aux engines at the same time. Hoping if someone was watching our boats they would be confused as to which boat to try and stop. I checked my watch and saw it was time. Dave had all the lines loosened, and was ready to cast off.

"Here we go." I told Dave, and with a turn of the switch the motor on the "Windjammer" came to life. At the same time the other two boats started to glide out of their slips.

The boat, which had brought us over was the last to leave the marina. He kept his boat behind us to block any boat that would come out the main canal.

When we cleared the intercostals waterway, all three boats turned on their running lights, and followed the

"Witchcraft" to one of the anchorages around Biscayne Bay.

By this time it was almost day break. We took turns keeping an eye out for a Coast Guard cutter, or one of the Dade County Water Patrols, while the others got much needed sleep.

Dave gave me the coordinates for O' Malley's island. It only took a few minutes to set-up the GPS, and the course for the Lorene.

∾

CHAPTER EIGHTEEN

I interrupted the story by asking "Do you know what happened with Bill Davis, after you took all of the boat out of the marina?"

Bert said, his sister had talked to Bill the next morning, and he was very up-set with Mike and Dave for not telling him they were leaving.

According to Earlene "He was spiting nails." She went on to tell me; He had called Heilman trying to explain how we were able to get away without anyone knowing.

"All three boats are no longer in the marina. They must have taken them out last night." Bill Davis said, shifting around his chair.

"What? I thought you had people watching those boats." Heilman screamed.

"We had agents watching the people, not the boats." Davis shouted back.

"If you had the people being watched, where did they go?" Heilman asked, his voice getting back to a normal pitch.

"According to the report I'm getting...they drove across the causeway, into the city. They went to the boat repair yard, and spent the night. No one left the yard, the agent is telling me." Davis replied, looking out his office window.

"If that is the case; why aren't these people still at the boat yard?" Heilman asked, reaching for a chart of Biscayan Bay.

"I don't know." Davis replied, still looking at the empty slips. Then went on telling Heilman, at the time the group went into the city, their boats were still in the marina, and that they had gone in cars across causeway.

"Ok! Ok! This is getting us no where. Tell me where these people would have sailed off to." Heilman said, in a commanding voice.

"The last I knew of what they had planned was to wait until they had the information from that computer wiz at South Florida U." Davis explained.

"Did they get the information they wanted?" Heilman asked, making a note to call Esther Easterday.

"As of yesterday, they hadn't." Davis stated, turning away from the window, and sitting down in his chair.

"Ok, let me make some phone calls. Maybe someone has a lead on where the door will show up." Heilman said, hanging up the phone.

He looked at the chart. He found the boat repair yard. He guessed it was some 35 miles across the bay. He took a pencil and drew a line from the boat yard to the marina. Then from the marina out to the ocean. He knew they wouldn't go back to the repair yard after they had their boats underway. So where would they go... someplace where they would be safe and they could get the information Ryan needed to find this dammed door, or cloud, what ever it was.

He made a call to Esther, hoping he would be able to tell if she had gotten the information for Ryan. Hoping she hadn't passed it on to him yet.

"Ms. Easterday this is Bert Williams. I'm a friend of Linda Carrie's. She wanted me to see if you had the information she had asked you to run for her." Heilman said, in the sweetest, respectful voice.

"Not yet." Esther replied, "I told her I would have it some time in the late afternoon. Please have her call back then." she added, and then hung up on him.

"Great...Heilman thought; Ryan doesn't have it yet. Maybe he is still around and I can catch him yet."

Picking up the phone again. Heilman placed a call to the Coast Guard, telling them he thought he might need their help to stop three boats from leaving Miami Beach. He was told they had received a request from his office to have a boat ready, and he could board it at the station anytime. Heilman thank them and said he would be there in an hour.

He then dialed the number for the motel to reach Big Bill. He told Big Bill to come pick him up at the DEA headquarters. Then he called Bill Davis back telling him he thought the group was still someplace in the area. He asked Davis if Linda had showed up for work. To which Davis told him, she had taken vacation time to check out her boat, and would not be back for a week.

"Boy nothing is going my way." Heilman said, putting down to phone, just as Big Bill came into the office.

"What's up?" Big Bill asked, as he sat down in a chair in front of Paul's desk.

"Those people got away with their boats, and now we have to find them again." Heilman stated, giving Big Bill a funny grin.

"What's so funny?" Big Bill asked looking around the office.

"I was just thinking how we thought we had them nailed and now we aren't any closer than when we came down here. Even with all of the help…I also think we would've been better off doing it by ourselves." He replied, picking up the chart from his desk. Telling Big Bill they were going to the Coast Guard station.

As they started for the door the phone rang. Heilman went back picking it up on the third rang, he said, "Hello," this Paul Heilman. The voice on the other end was Emily…the Director wanted to talk to Paul about Ryan and the search for the door. Then the Director came on the line and asked for an up date on this Ryan. When Paul told him about the group taking their boats out of the marina, and that he didn't know where they had gone. The director told Heilman he had information about the door everyone was looking for. He said he would have Emily fax the information and they should concentrate on Ryan, that he was the one most likely to go looking.

Paul and Big Bill waited for the fax. When it arrived they were off to the Coast Guard station.

കൈ

CHAPTER NINETEEN

As daylight creep across the blue water of Biscayne Bay, the boats came alive. We were close enough, so we could talk loudly to each other.

Linda, Joan and Bert were sent North, when we sailed into the Atlantic. They were told to meet up with Dave's boat the "Topic Bay II" as it was come South. They were told the Captain's name and was to use it as a password just in case Heilman took over the Schooner. I asked Bert, if he knew the difference between a Ketch, and a Schooner. He told me, he did saying, the rudder control on a Ketch was in front of the Mizzen Mast, and on the Schooner was behind. "Very good." I told him

As we were getting ready to split our ways, Dave decided he wanted to go with the "Witchcraft" and his wife. Stating he would know the Captain on sight. Feeling the "Witchcraft" would have a better chance of evading Heilman, should he have captured the "Topic Bay II".

Bert brought the "Witchcraft along side the "Windjammer" and Dave jump ship.

After saying our farewells, it was a Sloop against a Ketch. Linda had made it very clear, it was a race to Doc. O'Malley's cabin.

The wind was blowing 20 knots to my stern, so I engaged the auto pilot, went forward and put up the Spinnaker sail, which gave the "Windjammer" a fighting chance.

Linda was not to be out done, as she raised both Jibs, and an oversize Main Sail, plus her Mizzen sail.

I thought to myself…that's why she had broke her mast during the storm.

We were both making a good run, when the "Kaysee Rose" cut across my bow. I came off the wind, as quick as I could, and just missed clipping her stern.

As I recovered, and found the wind again. I could see there was a problem with the "Kaysee Rose". It looked like Kaysee had lost control. The boat was sailing very erratic. We had been running without using our radios. But I went to the radio, and yelled for Kaysee to drop her sails. The way the seas were running, and with the wind changing, she had to much sail out.

I could see, Rose, fighting her way forward to bring down the Main, and I saw the Jibs poop, and the boat righted itself.

I quickly lowered my Main Mast, with the pump, dumped the Spinnaker, and put the fenders over the side. I eased the "Windjammer" along side the "Kaysee Rose". Tossing a line to Rose, who pulled the two boats together.

My first concern was for the girls. I wanted to know they were alright. Then I asked Kaysee what had happened. She said the wind had caught her by surprise her boat started side slipping. She tried to come off the wind, but couldn't. That was when she cut across my bow.

I explained to her...she was carrying to much sail. So we agreed not to continue the race.

Rose tossed the line back on the "Windjammer" and I pushed off, after giving Kaysee a big kiss.

We set sail again, but not as fast as we had been running. I moved the "Windjammer about a half mile off of the Kaysee Rose. This was fine until night closed in on us. I decided to move in closer as the sun set in the west.

With our early morning start, and the cool evening breeze, I became very sleepy. I set auto steering, and checked the rigging. Went below, retrieving a blanket, and cat napped on deck.

Somewhere around midnight, I snapped awake, with a start. I could barely make out the outline of a larger vessel off my stern. It had a big search light on its' deck. They were swinging it back, and forth as if it was looking for something. The beam of light wasn't close to me yet, but shortly it would be.

I had been sailing without running lights, and didn't want to turn them on, just in case it was the Coast Guard. I set the tact so my course would bring me closer to the "Kaysee Rose", they were without lights also. I had to be careful not to get to close.

On my new course, I could vaguely make out the "Kaysee Rose". I saw Rose at the helm. She didn't see the "Windjammer", and I didn't want to scare her, but she also hadn't seen the search light.

When I was about 100 yards of, I whistled as loud as I could. It still made Rose jump, but she saw the boat astern, hollered "It's coming on fast. Do you think it has seen us."

I told her to change course to the West and I would lay back, just in case it was Heilman. I had no idea what I would do if it was, but I wasn't going to let him get Kaysee or Rose.

With the "Kaysee Rose" tacking to the West it gave room to move in the same direction. I watched the spotlight still searching, but they didn't change course. In a short while, the light despaired in the darkness. I kept an eye on the "Kaysee Rose" through my binoculars and could see Kaysee had taken over the helm. I brought the "Windjammer" upon the wind as clean as I could. I was gaining on her.

❧

CHAPTER TWENTY

Heilman arrived at the Coast Guard Station. Checked in at the main office and was told where to find the Coast Guard Cutter, "Nantucket" was docked. He was also told the commanding officer was Chief Warrant Officer John Tibbett.

Paul and Big Bill hurried down the dock to the gangway of the boat, where they were met by a First Class, who asked for their ID. Then quickly showed them to the Duty Officer. Heilman explained what he needed. He was told CWO Tibbett was expecting them and would meet them on deck shortly.

Big Bill and Heilman walked to the rail and gazed out over the Port of Miami. They could see, many boats coming and going. Heilman wondered if one of the sailboats was Ryan's. His thoughts were broken as he heard footfalls behind them.

"Mr. Heilman welcome aboard the "Nan" Tibbett said as he extended his hand toward Paul.

"Thank you, Sir." Paul replied, giving his hand.

"What is it we can help you with this bright and sunny day?" Tibbett queried, making a gesture to the sky.

"There are three boats we must stop from leaving port." Heilman replied, retrieving the chart from Big Bill.

"I think we can best accomplish it by going to Fisher Island, just pass the Mac Arthur Causeway and Virginia Key." Heilman explained, showing the commander the chart.

"I know the area well." Tibbett said taking the chart, glancing at it and then returning it to Heilman. Then stated the currents around the causeway sometimes caused problems for sailboats, as there were eddies and ebb tides. Most sailors would ease their way through this area by using their aux. motors, so they would have better control.

"I will know one of the boats on sight, if we can find it." Heilman said, looking around as the crew was making ready to get underway.

"Good, we can be in the area you want in about an hour." Tibbett told Paul. "In the mean time you can come up to the bridge where you will have a better look ahead."

Paul and Big Bill followed Tibbett to the bridge wing on the port side. He looked around, and watched as the boat moved away from the dock, as Tibbett gave orders to stow all line and half speed ahead.

The boat glided out into the intercostals waterway. Paul heard Tibbett tell the radio operator their area of operation.

Tibbett turned to Heilman asking, "Why are we stopping these boats?"

Heilman looked at Big Bill, giving him a smirk, saying, "Drugs. We believe a guy by the name of Ryan is smuggling cocaine out of Miami, to an island some place in the Bahamas. We got word from an agent who saw this Ryan put the packages on the sailboat called the "Windjammer" out of Charleston, South Carolina. DEA agents were watching the shipment come into the airport, where Ryan picked it up. This was sometime early morning today. We want to board the boat, and catch him red handed." Heilman explained.

"Roger that." Tibbett replied, turning to the helmsman, saying kick up, we're on a run. At once the boat picked up speed, and Big Bill turned his back to the increase of the wind.

Seeing this, Tibbett told the two they could steep into the bridge where the wind would be less.

The "Nantucket" was running flat out, making about 25 knots, as they can upon two sailboats, sailing together. Tibbett had the boat to slow, so they could get a good look at them.

As the Cutter came along side the first sailboat, Heilman could see two people in the cockpit. There were a man and a woman. The boats stern stated that the boat was out of Miami.

"Their not the one we are looking for. They are about the right size, but the name isn't right." Heilman said turning his attention to some boats farther ahead.

The Cutter picked up speed again, as the helmsman brought the boat back on course.

"It's a good thing this is a weekday, otherwise, we would have a hundred sailboats out here" Tibbett said, coming back in the pilot house.

"We may not catch up to them before we reach Fisher Island. They may have left early, but I would think they would have waited until they had the information." Heilman replied, picking up the glasses, and scanning, the water for a mile around the Cutter.

"There!" Heilman shouted, "About a half mile off the Portside. That sailboat just behind the Cabin Cruiser and the Ketch, or Schooner." Heilman said, pointing in the direction of the sloop, now about a quarter of a mile from Fisher Island.

"Looks like it is tacking to the South, around the point." Tibbett replied, taking the glasses from Paul.

"Can we catch it, before he makes the open sea?" Heilman asked, straining to see the boat, he wanted them to pursue.

"It will be close, but as long as we can see the boat, we can get him." Tibbett replied, heading for the deck, to alert the crew to the overtaking of the sailboat.

Heilman could see the crew getting ready for a boarding party. Big Bill and Heilman went down to the deck, so they would be ready to board the "Windjammer" once the cutter stopped it.

"How much do you think he is carrying?" Tibbett asked, already to log a drug bust, into his log book.

Paul looked at Big Bill, who held up three fingers. "Three pounds, maybe more." Heilman replied, giving Big Bill a smile.

Tibbett gave orders to the crew to hail the boat as they came a long side.

The sailboat lowered it's sails and heaved too, as the "Nantucket" eased closer. Tibbett ordered the crew to secure lines to the sailboat. Then announced that he was

Chief Warrant Officer John Tibbett, of the United States Coast Guard, and wished to come aboard.

"Come ahead on. You're wasting your time, but come aboard." the man said, stepping back from the rail.

Mike watched as the "Kaysee Rose" and the "Witchcraft" made their way around the other side of the island. He also saw Heilman standing at the rail. Mike knew it wasn't the time or the place to confront Heilman, but at this point the didn't care.

A crew member climbed down the ladder, onto the deck of the "Windjammer". He held the ladder as Tibbett came on board, with Heilman right behind him.

"Welcome aboard." Mike said, as he side stepped Tibbett, and came face to face with Heilman, who barely had his feet on the deck. Mike hit him in mouth, with all the power he had. Followed with a power kick to Heilman's chest.

"Hold on there Captain!" Tibbett exclaimed, moving between Mike and Heilman.

Heilman fell back, bouncing off the ladder, he had just came down.

"I told you what would happen the next time we crossed paths, and I meant it. Now get off my boat, before I throw you in the drink." Mike said at the top of his voice.

Heilman recovered from the punch, and kick slowly. Then said to Tibbett, "It's alright, we've had some misunderstandings in the past, but have your men search the boat. I know there are drugs on board. I want this boat impounded, and the Captain here handcuffed. We will tow the boat back to the Port of Miami." Heilman said, calmly, then turned to Mike Ryan saying, "I never would have thought you would be so stupid, to think you could out smart me. You dumb doughboy.

Tibbett told his men, who had came on board, to search the boat for drugs.

"Start at the bow, they should be easy to spot." Heilman said, smiling at Ryan.

"Try not to miss up my boat to much, guys." Mike said, stepping back from Tibbett. "There are no drugs on this boat, Chief Warrant Officer." Mike said, turning toward the ladder where Big Bill was coming down.

"You want me to go check? Paul", he asked, stepping up Mike.

"Help yourself, Big boy." Mike said, with a grin, then said to Heilman, "Another flunky, Paul, for you to blame things on?"

"Be careful Ryan. I'll turn him lose on you. You might have caught me off guard, but Big Bill can handle himself." Heilman threatened, taking a steep forward, but Tibbett, put up his hand, telling Heilman to hold off until they found the drugs.

"Mr. Tibbett, I say again there are no Drugs on this boat. The only way Heilman, here would know there was drugs, is if he or one of his buddies tried to set me up. Another one of your CIA tricks? Heilman." Mike snarled.

"It sounds like you have had more than a misunderstanding." Tibbett stated, looking at Heilman in disbelief.

"You don't know the half of it, Mr. Tibbett. This SOB, pulled the rug out from under 15 of my men. Good men, who didn't deserve, dieing; because of him, and his cronies back in Washington." Mike said, with vengeance in his voice.

"That was a long time ago, Ryan. I had nothing to do with it. You know there just wasn't time to call off the operation." Heilman responded.

"Sure! I know you were just following orders. While I got to write letters to the Mothers, Sisters, and Wives of the men you had killed." Mike said, trying to get around Tibbett.

"Now over there, to the wheel Mister, or I'll have my men cuff you to it." Tibbett said, stepping in front of Mike again.

Just then Big Bill came back up on deck, with a sorrowful look on his face.

"What is it?" Heilman snapped?

"We have checked every where, but there aren't three bags of drugs, not even one." Big Bill told Heilman. Then turned to Mike Ryan, and asked, "What did you do with them? I know there was three pounds on board."

"Maybe you put them on the wrong boat. They all look alike in the dark." Mike replied, with a big smile.

"I know it was this boat. I'm not dumb, you know." Big Bill said, walking over to where Heilman was standing.

"Shut-up Bill." Heilman sneered.

Tibbett's men came back on deck, and gave the same report, saying, "Mr. Tibbett, we looked ever where. There just isn't any drugs on this boat.

"Ok men, Thanks. Now get Heilman, and Bill here, back on the "Nan". We'll be out of here." Tibbett said, moving to where Mike was standing.

"Looks like we were mistaken, Mr. Ryan. I'm sorry to have delayed you. Where were you heading anyway?" he asked, as he headed for the ladder.

185

"Thought I might sail down to the Keys. If I don't get detained all the time, by the CIA." Mike replied, giving the Chief Warrant Officer a little hand salute.

"We will be out of your way shortly." Tibbett said, as he ascended the ladder.

."Thank you." Mike said, getting ready to raise his sails, and get underway.

ভ

CHAPTER TWENTY ONE

"After your run in with Heilman at Fisher Island, how did you catch up with Kaysee and Rose? They must have had a big lead on you." I asked, looking at Captain Mike.

"Yeah, well, I had seen them clear the island on the other side. When the Coast Guard was done playing around on the "Windjammer" I headed out to sea. I was sure I could sail straight to where I knew the girls were going, because the Coast Guard was sure Heilman had tried to set me up for a drug bust" Mike stated.

"So were there drugs on board the "Windjammer?" I asked, not sure what had taken place.

"Oh, sure. Heilman had Big Bill stash them in the bow compartment, right where anyone coming down here would see them right off; but I came down to get a blanket and found them. Right away I knew it had been Heilman, so as we sailed off in the morning I threw them over board, in the middle of Biscayne Bay. I spread the coke across the water. And just kept sailing, hoping no one saw me." Mike explained.

"Then you met up with the girls and then what?" I asked, picking up my pen.

We had to make our way to a port in the Bahamas, where we could get a visa. We don't want any trouble with the Bahamians. We had the US government looking for us, we didn't need another.

Over my better judgment, we decided Bimini, was a closer port of call than Nassau. We had eluded the boat with the searchlight, but wasn't sure they hadn't spotted us, and would be waiting for us to surface someplace looking to get the entry visa. We had to take a chance.

As we came to anchor in the harbor at South Bimini, we used our rubber rafts to go ashore. The girls and I entered the Custom House together. After answering questions about what we were doing in the Bahamas, and how long we were planning to stay. We paid our fees and was on our way. We hadn't told the officials where we planned to anchor. But told them we were sailing for the week and would be returning to Key West the following week. My thought was maybe they would lead Heilman to Key West, and we would be in the Berry Islands. At least that's what I hoped. They wanted to inspect our boats. They would have an inspector go aboard and would issue our visas within the hour.

True to their word, the inspector showed up, and boarded the "Kaysee Rose", finding everything in order, he came to the "Windjammer" making the same inspection. While he was going through my boat, I asked him about pirates in the Bahamas. He told me they are here, but if you are careful they shouldn't be a bother. He also said that firearms aren't allowed in the islands. I should hide the 9mm Glock better. Adding another inspector might not over look such things. I slipped him a hundred dollar bill, as he was leaving. He gave me a big smile, and wished me a safe voyage.

With all of the paper work completed, we sailed to the Southeast until we were out of sight of land then swing the boats, to the North-North West. We tacked back to the Northeast. With about 75 Miles to go and our speed at 12 knots, we kept our tacks to 30 minutes in each direction. According to the chart it would take us about 20.5 such tacks. With the last tack, taking us into the cove where the cabin would be.

When Mike entered the cove, the "Kaysee Rose" was setting at anchor. He eased the "Windjammer" close in. There was no one on deck, which made Mike uneasy. The first thing that came to mind was the girls had taken the raft to the dock and were in the cabin. He couldn't see a rubber raft at the dock. Had Heilman found out where they were and beat him to the cove? The answer came quickly.

Two Zodiac type rubber reinforced assault boats came charging from outside the cove. Mike quickly got his Glock from below and took up cover in the cockpit of the "Windjammer". He could make out three men in each of the rubber boats. He took aim at the lead boat. His first shoot took out the driver at the outboard motor. His second went through the rubber float, at the front of the boat. The lead boat turned, heading back the way they had come. The second boat kept charging, and opened fire on the "Windjammer". Mike look around as the "Witchcraft" came heading into the cove. A shot came from it's deck. Mike knew it had to be Bert. As the rubber boat seen they were out gunned turned and ran for the open water.

Mike look at the "Kaysee Rose" and saw the girls just peeking over the rail.

"What's going on?" Kaysee yelled, at Mike as he brought the "Windjammer" in closer.

"You were going to have visitors. We just sent them packing." Mike replied, giving a little laugh, and pointing to the "Witchcraft".

"We saw those boats, as we came into this cove." Kaysee said, jumping on board the "Windjammer". She throw her arms around Mike's neck, giving him a big hug.

"We were ready for them." Rose said, waving a baseball bat, so everyone could see.

"I didn't know what else to do, but drop anchor and hope we could beat them off." Kaysee said, putting her head on Mike's chest.

"It'll be alright, for now. I'm sure they will be back with more troops." Mike replied, giving Kaysee a reassuring kiss.

The "Witchcraft" eased along side the "Windjammer". Bert was standing with a 30/30, in his hand.

"Not bad shooting." Mike said, giving Bert a big smile. "They'll be back." Mike told him, "How much ammo do you have on board?" He asked, steeping away from Kaysee.

"Maybe 100 or so rounds for this rifle. We also have two 357's with another 150 rounds." Bert replied, picking up the handguns.

"How about you? Got anything more than that pea shooter." Bert asked giving Mike a smirk.

"Let me go below and brake out the guns and ammo I have stored in the oil tank. But Yeah, I have two AK47's with about 500 rounds, another 9mm, with a couple hundred rounds, and 4 Rocket Propelled Grenades." Mike replied, giving Bert, the Boy Scout Salute.

"Always be prepared." Bert said, in a laughing voice.

Giving Bert a little bow, Mike told the group they should get the boats to the dock.

With the boats all secured, and everyone on the dock. Mike did a head count. He knew he was missing two bodies. "What did you do with the Chadwicks?" Mike asked, turning to Bert, who had just finished climbing from the "Witchcraft."

"Dave went on board the "Topic Bay II". Bert replied, resting his rifle in his arm. "They should be along anytime. It sure is a beautiful boat. I'm not sure there is enough room at this dock for it. But we will know for sure when they get here."

"We can always tie it off along side the "Windjammer." Mike told him. "Let's see what this place looks like. It sets high enough above the water and dock." Mike stated, starting to climb the stairs.

"This place doesn't look like a cabin to me. I have seen houses smaller then this place. It must be at lest 3,000 sq ft." Bert said, as they reached the deck at the top of the stairs.

The girls had went into the cabin, before the guys had finished on the dock. When Bert and Mike walked into the cabin, Rose came out saying "You must see the quarry tiled floors, and the vaulted ceilings in the 5 bedrooms. It has an open kitchen that opens on to another deck with a pool. What a place!" she exclaimed, as she lead them into the cabin.

"Mike looked around at the deck in the front of cabin. He could see a good mile out to the entrance to the cove. He knew it was going to be a long night. What with the Chadwicks still sailing, and the chance that the pirates might come back. He could see they weren't going to get much sleep.

Mike caught up with Bert and Rose as they were coming in from the pool. "What's out back? He asked, sitting down at the kitchen table.

"There is a lot of trees out there. What a get away." Rose replied, still excited about the place.

"I think I know what your thinking." Bert said, setting down across from Mike.

"You more than likely do. We are going to set up guard duty shifts. Those guys who met us as we came in, could come back anytime." Mike told them.

"Does that mean we don't get to sleep in those water beds?" Kaysee asked, walking up beside Mike.

"It means we take turns, keeping eyes on the boats, and everyone here." Mike explained. "We will take 4 hours each. The others will sleep at least through the hour of dark."

"This is starting to sound more and more like an army operation." Kaysee said, wrinkling up her nose.

"What would you suggest we do? We have Heilman still trying to stop us. We now have pirates wanting what they think we have…namely money, and I'm not real happy with the way our boats are setting ducks for those guys in the rubber boats." Mike replied, rubbing his forehead, looking up at the ceiling.

Linda came in with an arm load of boxes. "Isn't anyone going to help me move all of the food off the boat?" she asked, setting the boxes on the kitchen floor.

After everyone moved everything off their boats; Bert took Mike off to the side and asked, "Have you gotten your weapons off the "Windjammer"?" Mike told him it would take about an hour to open the Hyd. Tank, and remove the weapons.

"Maybe we want to do it before dark. We may need them to defend ourselves.

"Your right! I just want both of us to be involved in moving everything up the stairs. You stay with the girls, and I will get started. We must clean the rifles once I bring them out. It will be messy, but a least we have them, and no one knows it" Mike explained, and headed for the dock.

Mike could hear his name being called, by Linda. He had the cover off the tank, and had his hands fishing around for the weapons. He pulled out one of the AK47s, with one hand, and brought out a box of ammo, with the other. They were dripping of oil as she came down the ladder, saying, "The Chadwicks are coming into the cove. They look like they ran into some bad weather. They aren't using their sails. You had better come take a look."

Mike laid the weapons on some towels on the deck, and followed her topside.

He could see the "Topic Bay II" was come in using their motors. Then he saw a rubber boat trying to get close to the boat. The skipper was cranking the wheel one way and then the other, trying to make it harder for the men in the rubber boat to come along side.

Bert already had the engines running on the "Witchcraft" and was undoing the lines, as Mike came running up the dock, with the AK 47 and the box of ammo. He climbed over the gunwale, and was wiping the oil from the weapon as Bert came onboard.

"Looks like those guys aren't going to wait until dark, before they want action." Bert said, trying to catch his breath, as he got the boats underway. In short order he had the Chris-Craft running flat out toward the Chadwicks.

With the "Witchcraft" speeding to the mouth of the cove, the pirates decided the "Topic Bay II" wasn't worth the trouble, and began heading for cover out side the cove.

"Stay with them." Mike shouted, moving to the forward deck, taking up a prone position where he could get a good shot at the rubber boat.

The rubber boat was traveling as fast as they could, but the "Witchcraft" was much faster, with it's twin screws turning at 2200 RPMs, Bert had caught them within a few minutes.

From his position, Mike took aim and let lose a blazes of rounds which found their mark in the side of the rubber boat. He could see the boat starting to collapse as the "Witchcraft" made a turn back to the Chadwicks' boat.

"Good shooting." Bert shouted, slowing the speed of the boat, as he came up alongside the "Topic Bay II", where the Chadwicks were on deck waving.

"Thank You, gentlemen!" Dave exclaimed, as the "Witchcraft" slowed their speed.

"Nice Welcome. We got much the same, when we came in." Mike stated, adding "There is room for your boat at the dock."

Mike turned to Bert and said, "I think we had better keep your boat closer to the stairs, so we can get it underway quickly if we need to."

"Roger that!" Bert exclaimed, giving Mike a thumbs up.

"Nice driving, Captain." Mike said, extended his hand to the Skipper of the "Topic Bay II" as he stepped onto the dock.

"Thanks, it was the only thing I could think of to do. I knew I didn't want to let those people get close enough to board." the Skipper replied, as Dave Chadwick walked up.

"Mike Ryan this is my friend and Skipper of my boat, Dirk Carson, he was one of the first people, Joan and I met when we returned home. He is also a Lawyer. But he loves taking care of the boat." Dave explained then added, "This is Johnny Weston, he helps Dirk with the boat when they go sailing or bring the boat when ever or where even I need it."

"Great to meet you guys. Your just who we need; if those guys in the rubber boat come back for another round." Mike replied, giving Johnny his hand.

"I don't think they'll be back, after the rounds you put in their boat." Johnny said, following the Chadwicks, who were heading for the stairs

With everyone safe at the cabin. Dave wanted an update on what was happening with the information from Esther Easterday.

"I'm trying to call her now. I put in a call from the phone over by the hammock, and the operator told me she would call me back as soon as the call went through. I'm hoping we hear from her tonight. I had called her before we left, but she didn't have the spot yet." Linda replied, as she finished open the can of soup.

"We can stay here for as long as we need. Doc. O' Malley told me he doesn't get out here very often." Dave told the group around the kitchen table.

"I want to thank you men for coming to our aid this afternoon." Joan said, getting up and going to Mike and Bert giving them a kiss on the cheek.

"I'll second that." Linda said, walking to Bert's side. "You run my boat really well." she added, giving a big kiss, and a hug.

"Ok folks, we need to get our watches setup. Who wants too take the first watch?" Mike asked, and went on to explain they need two people on guard, for 4 hours each. There needs to be one out front, and the other someplace out back, in the shadows. He added, "The idea is to stay close to the cabin, so if someone comes from the woods, you'll be able to sound the alarm.

"The Skipper and I can take the first watch" Dave said, looking for approval from Dirk. "Sure, it works for me." he replied, giving Dave a nod.

"I want to check out back." Mike stated, turning to Bert saying "Let's recon the area to see just what we can expect. If those guys decided to come up from the rear. With their boats flat they might try to get to us on land."

"We have something on the boat which might help watch the woods out back." Dirk said, giving Mike a smile.

"Sure, the Night Scope." Johnny said, getting up from the table, "I'll go bring it up."

"It's like the ones we used on "Fire Fly" mission in Vietnam. We hung them in the door of the Hues. It would let us see the VC moving at night. It work well. Later they used them around firebases to see the buggers coming through the bushes." Skipper explained.

"You were in Vietnam?" Mike asked, walking around to where the Skipper sat.

"Yeah, a couple of time." he replied, giving Mike a big grin. Then added, "I flow Hues, with the 199th, out of Saigon. I was attached to "The Capital Military Assents

196

Command." until I rotated back to the States, in the early 70's."

"Great!" Mike exclaimed, patting the Skipper on the back, then said, "I spent a couple of days in country, myself."

After Mike, Bert and Dave walked the back of the cabin, Mike could tell their biggest problem would come from the cove side of the area. The backyard had lighting around the pool, which covered the back of the cabin for about 100 yards out from the pool.

"If we keep the lights on, who ever is watch our backs, should be able to see anyone trying to come through the woods, and over the little fence." Mike told the group. "We need to make sure no one comes near our boats at the dock. I think we should put the "Night Scope' on that side. We can hang it from the decks ceiling. It should give us warning enough."

Then the phone rang, getting everyone attention. Linda ran to answer it, in the next room. When she returned, she informed everyone that it was Esther. She had the information, they had been wanting, but Esther was worried that her phone had been tapped. Someone had called her earlier asking for the information. She told who ever it was the information wasn't available yet. Esther said she thought it may have been Heilman, as he told her he was Bert.

"Anyway," Linda said, "Esther said she will get us the information by morning."

"How is she going to get to us? Does she have a boat?" Dave asked, pacing the floor.

"No," Linda replied, giving Bert a smile. "She'll wing it, is the way she put it."

"What does that mean?" Dave asked, getting impatient.

"She said, just trust me" In a round about way I told her about the berries we picked a month ago…I hope she understood, I was talking about the "Berry Islands". I asked her to check on the test I had taken from Doctor O' Malley, and to tell him I needed help." Linda explained, setting back down at the table.

Turning to Mike, "How soon can you be ready to make your search?" Dave asked

"There are a few things I need to do to the "Windjammer", but it wouldn't take very long." Mike replied.

"Johnny and I can help." Dirk stated get up.

"Thanks." Mike said, walking to the front deck. There isn't that much to do. I just have to reassemble the Hyd. Tank, and make sure my fuel is toped off."

&

CHAPTER TWENTY TWO

I stopped the story with a question, "How are you going to find the island?" "I'm get to that part of the story. But first I needed some place to start looking." Mike replied, getting another cup of coffee.

"We had no ides what Heilman was going to do next. I knew he couldn't use the Coast Guard anymore."

"Why not?" I asked, ready to make more notes.

"For one thing we were outside their area of operation. Secondly they can not enter Bahamas waters, unless they are asked to help. Normally it must be an emergency." Mike explained, setting down again.

"We knew the DEA was helping Paul, but didn't think he could find out where we were." Kaysee interjected.

"True, but when the government has it's mind set on something, it's only a matter of time, before they have their way." Mike replied, then went on saying, "According the Heilman, Big Bill was the one who set me up in Miami. I thought with cutting Bill Davis out of the loop, we stopped the leak. Not so, Washington had others working on their problem...

"Paul I know absolutely, I put those bags on Ryan's boat. I don't understand what happened to them. But I know what I did with them." Big Bill told Heilman, as they climbed into their car. They had returned with the Coast Guard.

"How is your chin?" Big Bill asked, as he started the engine. "Where too?" he asked, looking around.

"We need a boat." Heilman said, taking the fax from his pocket. Then asked, "What did you do with the chart I gave you on the Cutter?"

"It's in the backseat." Big Bill replied, turning around trying to reach it."

"That's alright we'll get it later. Right now we need to go to DEA Headquarters. I know they have all kinds of boats they have confiscated in drug raids." Paul said, as Big Bill headed the big black car, toward the building on South Beach.

"What is in the fax you got from the director?" Big Bill asked, once he pulled into the parking lot.

"It tells us where Ryan will be, or should be in two days. But only if he get the information from that Easterday woman, in time." Paul replied, giving him smile.

After making three phone calls to Washington, and visiting the same number offices. Paul had the boat he needed to make a sea trip to the Bahamas. The boat was a 40 foot "Welcraft Cruiser" called "Betty Lou II", who's previous owner was doing ten to twenty for drug running. He went to the holding docks to pick it.

With in the hour, Big Bill and Heilman were headed for Bimini with every thing they needed for Deep Sea Fishing.

"This sure is a nice boat. I would like to have it, when we are done with this case." Big Bill said, as he adjusted the course on the GPS.

"Remember we are on vacation." Paul told him, as Paul brought the boat around the North end of Fisher Island.

"Why are we going to Bimini?" Big Bill asked, leaning forward to look at the chart on the chart in front of him.

"We are going to check in at the Customs House, on South Bimini. You need to go below and put all of the weapons in the secret compartment in the bow. The Biminites don't like Americans having guns in their islands." Paul instructed.

Big Bill made his way down from the flying bridge, and through the solon to the forward compartment. There was a panel next to the bunk, it was where the drug runner hid the drugs. Now it was used to hide two AR 15, assault rifles and four 357 handguns. He carefully replaced the panel, and checked to make sure it look natural. He was already on Paul's list, for the drugs, he didn't need anything else.

"As he rejoined Heilman on the bridge, Paul was muttering something under his breath.

"What's wrong?" Big Bill, asked, not knowing if he truly wanted to know the answer.

"It's this GPS. It keeps telling to change course. I have laid in the waypoint from Miami to a point at the channel at South Bimini. The GPS tells me the line should be 96o relative to North. It holds for a few minutes, and then the stupid thing tells me to change course to the South by 3 or 4 degrees. It's back and forth every few minutes." Paul complained.

"Are you taking in account for the Gulf Stream?" Big Bill asked, looking at the GPS.

"What does the Gulf Stream have to do with GPS telling me to change course?" Paul asked, looking at Big Bill as if he had lost his mind.

"Paul, the Gulf Stream is pushing us North, and the GPS reads that drift. With the drift it tells you to go South to stay on course. Change your course by 9o to the South, and see if that doesn't help." Big Bill explained, giving Heilman a big smile.

"Where did you learn so much about GPS." Paul asked, making the change to the GPS.

"I don't like to fly…boats, and the water is another story." Big Bill replied, steeping back.

Paul watched as the GPS showed they were back on course. But then it flashed another change. "What is wrong with this thing." Paul shouted, looking over his shoulder at Big Bill.

"Have you put in the difference between True North and Magnetic North?" Big Bill asked, looking at the compass.

"No!" Paul exclaimed. "I thought they were the same of Florida." Paul stated.

"On land they are almost the same, but out here there is a 6 degree variation. Just add another 6 degrees to your course, and that should do it." Big Bill explained, looking at the chart.

After an hour and a half, the "Betty Lou II", made the harbor at South Bimini. Paul and Big Bill went into the Customs House to clear the islands. Much to his surprise the Royal Bahamas Police Force in Bimini had a capture and hold on the "Betty Lou II".

It took Heilman another three hours, before the true story was told, and Big Bill and Heilman were given clearance to enter Bimini waters.

While going through all of hassle with the boat, Paul did find out that the "Windjammer" and the "Kaysee Rose" had both passed through the Customs House. They were sailing the Bahamas and then back to Key West.

Paul knew where Mike Ryan was going to be in two days, but at present he had no idea.

"What are we going to do for two days?" Big Bill asked, taking the chart in hand.

"See the X I have marked on the chart?" Paul asked, pointing to the mark. "That spot is where we must be in two days to stop Ryan. Until then…we are going fishing somewhere close." Paul explained, starting the engines on the "Betty Lou II".

⁓

CHAPTER TWENTY THREE

With the coming of the early morning light the blue green water of the cove was a beautiful sight to Mike. It had been a long and uneventful night. He hadn't slept much. Every change of the guard he had heard. He and Kaysee had taken the late watch. He was sure if the pirates were going to attack, it would come about day break.

Bert came out on the front deck. Mike turned to see him stepping up to the railing saying "Morning, anything going on?"

"Nope." Mike replied, handing Bert a cup coffee. And added, "Keep an eye out on the cove. I'm going out back to see how Kaysee is doing."

"I looked out there before I came on this side, but I didn't see Kaysee." Bert replied, taking a sip from his cup.

"She under the deck. I took a chair to her earlier." Mike informed him.

Mike walked around the side of the cabin, and peeked around the corner. He could see Kaysee standing under the stair to the deck. She was watching something in the direction of the woods.

"What do you see?" Mike asked, in a low voice, as he crept closer.

"I don't know. I thought there was movement in the trees, but I'm not sure.

The two waited, and watched. Mike drew his 9mm from his belt, just as a man stepped through the gate in the fence. He walked toward the pool, as if he owned the place.

Mike stepped out from under the stairs, pointing the gun at the man. "Who are you?" Mike asked, as he moved forward, still pointing the gun in the direction of the new comer.

"Oh man...I take care of the cottage for the Doctor. I come here three time a week. I clean the pool and trim the grass, clean the inside. My name is Jose. Who are you...are you pirates?" Jose explained, putting his hands in the air.

"Put your hands down." Mike said, then answered with "We are friends of Doctor O' Malley. We will be here a few days."

"I didn't know anyone was here. Doctor never told me." Jose said, walking up to Mike, as Kaysee came out from behind the stairs.

Jose tipped is hat, as Kaysee came closer. "We thought you were pirates." Kaysee said, giving him a little bow.

"No, I'm not a pirate. I work for the doctor. He only comes one or two times a year. Can I clean the pool now or should I come another time?" Jose asked, putting his hat back on his head.

"Do you know any pirates who live around here?" Mike asked, looking deeper into the woods.

"Some bad men stay in a cave by the sea. Out there by the point of land." Jose replied, pointing to the front of the cabin.

"They attacked us yesterday, when we came into the cove." Mike told, Jose as they walked to the cabin.

"I use the phone. I call the Bahamas Police. They will take action, so they don't bother you anymore." Jose told, Mike as he walked to the phone in the front of the cabin.

By the time Jose had finished with his phone call, the rest of the group were up and ready for breakfast.

"Mr. Ryan, the Police say they have been watching those men in the cave, and will have a patrol boat in the area, just in case there is trouble." Jose explained, walking back in the kitchen.

"Thanks Jose." Mike said, and proceeded to introduce the rest of the people.

"You have a big group. If there is anything I can do for you, just let me know. I'm a good fishing guide. I know all of the good fishing areas." Jose informed the group, heading back for the pool.

"Great!" Bert said, "maybe we will go fishing later."

The girls had been cooking breakfast and had it on the table. Mike invited Jose to eat, but he declined saying, "He had the pool to clean, before the bugs took over."

Following breakfast, Dave took Mike down to his boat. "I have some things I would like you to take with you when you find my island." Dave told him, as they went aboard the "Topic Bay II". I know we survived for over fifty years, without any of these, but this time we can have a little of the comforts of the outside world."

"I'll have Bert and Johnny help me move them to the "Windjammer." Mike replied, taking note of the things Dave had set aside.

"There is something else I want you to know. Once you find the island, and have taken Joan and I back to it. I have informed Dirk, who handles all of our holdings, that Joan and I want you and the rest to share what ever is left after this undertaking is over." Dave said, putting his hand on Mike's shoulder.

"Dave there is no reason you and Joan need to do that. If I find the island, there is no reason to think, I will get back. Let alone be able to take you and Joan back in." Mike explained.

"I have every reason to believe you will." Dave assured Mike, then added, "You people have put your lives on the line to help Joan to return to "Topic Bay". I have learned; you never know how good you have it, until you loss it. If I had realized, what we had, I would have stayed on the island. You will see once you find it."

"Well, Let's talk about this after we accomplish, as you put it, undertaking." Mike replied, offering his hand, which Dave took and gave it a shake.

Walking back to the cabin, Mike's thoughts went to what he had gotten himself into. Kaysee was part of the problem he faced. He knew he wanted to be with her, but he also knew he could not take her with him. He decided to cross that bridge when the time came.

Mike was brought back, from his thoughts, with the sound of a plane circling the island. He stood watching it come in low over the cove, right over the cabin. He could see it was an amphibian, and looked like it was a "Cessna Caravan". The plane made one more pass, before it went out beyond the cove. It banked around and within minutes it was gliding up to the dock as the pilot, killed the engine.

Linda hearing the plane coming. She ran down the stairs and was standing on the dock next to Mike as the plane came to a stop.

"Now I see what Esther meant, when she said she was going to wing it." Linda said, as she walked forward to help Esther steep up to the dock.

"Welcome to the Berry Islands." Linda said, grabbing the pilot's hand.

"Thanks." Esther said, shaking her hair loose, as Linda put her arms around her, giving her a hug.

"Esther, this is Mike Ryan." Linda told her, sliding her arm around Mike's waist.

Mike stepped forward extending his hand, which Esther took saying, "You're the one who needs this." showing a stack of papers in her other hand. "and this is Doctor O' Malley. I think you know him." Esther said, to Linda, turning back to the plane.

"What are you doing here Doc.?" Linda asked, going up to him, giving him a kiss on the cheek.

"Esther told me you needed me. So here I am." Doc. O' Malley said, with a big grin. "Actually, I came to see how Joan Chadwick is doing." he said, in a more serious voice.

"Oh yeah, She's up in the cabin. I mean your cabin." Linda replied, point to the upper deck.

"Let's tell Dave the information is here. We'll need to go over it." Mike said, taking Esther by the elbow, moving her in the direction of the stairs.

"There isn't much time, before the cloud will form about 50 natural miles from here." Esther said, as she walked up the stairs.

Once everyone was in the kitchen, Esther spread out the computer printouts along with the chart of the area.

"Wow! All that information just to find a spot where the door will open?" Dave asked, looking over the printout.

"Yes, I took all of the disappearances and wrote a program to locate the spot where they all may have crossed the same spot." Esther explained, and then went on to say, "Tomorrow at 3:37 PM a cloud will form at the spot I marked. I'm pretty sure of my findings, but I don't have enough information to tell you for sure if or when this door will open again. Taking the information from some others who have reported being in a magnetic storm, I went a head and ran the possibility of the cloud forming in the same area. The computer says seven days three hours and forty two minutes after you enter the cloud it will be back at the same spot." Esther reported, looking around at the group.

"Guess I had better get things ready." Mike said, getting up from the table.

"We can help you." Kaysee said, moving to his side.

"It means you need to leave early tomorrow morning." Bert said, as he walked out on the front deck.

రు

CHAPTER TWENTY FOUR

"I must leave for the door now, or I will lose it." Mike told the group.

Kaysee protested but to no avail. Mike sailed out of the cove. She knew he would be alright, but she wasn't sure she could handle the suspense of not knowing what the out come would be. A chill slithered up her spine. She hoped it wasn't a sign, like the one when someone had walked on your grave.

She was confident Mike would be alright, but she couldn't understand why he wouldn't let her go with him. He knew she loved him and wanted to be with him forever. If he found Chadwick's island maybe forever would be there.

Dave Chadwick slowly approached Kaysee. He could tell she was in deep thought, but felt he had to console her. Affirming, Mike decision to go into the cloud alone.

"Kaysee you know Mike is right, about going in on his own." Dave said, putting his arm around her. She turned to face him with tears in her eyes. "I know your right, but I could have brought him coffee when he needed a cup.

What if he can't find his way back through the door, or if the door opens in a different place. This is a big ocean how do we know it will open here again?"

"Mike knows what he is doing, that's why I got him involved.

I had him checked out. If anyone can work his way through the cloud and find Our Island, it is Mike Ryan." Dave told her.

"I know I should keep a stiff upper lip and all that, but I'm concerned that Heilman may still cause us problems. From what Mike told me this guy will stop at nothing." She bleated out.

ᴄᴈ

Mike Ryan sailed off to the Northwest. Then tacked back to the Northeast. Passing the North end of the island. Then set his course to the East. He would sail between the Great Abaco island and Eleuthera island off his port beam. The spot marked on his chart was about 30 miles due East. He had left the group early enough to make sure he was not late to meet with the cloud. He planned to return to the same place in 7 days, 3 hours, and 42 minutes. Mike would contact the other boats and have them all meet at Doc. O'Malley's cabin.

Mike now turned his attention to the job at hand. Namely, what was a head of him as he sailed into the cloud? He looked at his watch. He still had an hour before the cloud would form, but he still had a few miles to go to the mark.

Off in the distance he could barely make out a boat coming at high speed. It looked like it was coming straight at the "Windjammer. He checked the distance before the X. He was still a mile from to point. He guessed the speeding boat would be on him just before the cloud could form.

Boat a fast Well-craft was less than two hundred yards from him when a streak of lightening flashed between them. It caused the speeding boat to veer off, as Mike saw the cloud directly in front of him. Entering the fog, Mike looked behind the "Windjammer, and could see the "speed boat would be on him shortly. He heard gunfire coming from the speedboat.

Mike had his hands full as the wind gust became very strong, and the waves started rolling to 12 to 15 feet. Mike checked his GPS, it read the right spot, and his compass was going wild, just like on his trip to St Simon's Island.

He went below and set the Seven Day timer, which he and Dave had made out of two, one-gallon milk jugs. The tops had been, glued together and a 3/16th hole drilled through the two caps. They had timed the flow of sand from one jug too the other, and set the weight for exactly 7 days, 3 hours, and 42 minutes.

With Mike back in the cockpit, the fog began to in gulf the boat. As he sailed on the fog got so thick, he could hardly see the bow of the boat. The sound of the wind in the sails lessened and Mike could feel the pressure on the Tiller was lost.

The running lights on the boat flickered and than went out completely. Mike anticipated he would lose electronics, so he had designed a compass much like the original compass, made of a cork and a needle, floating in a large deep pan of water.

On the pan, he had marked the degrees of a compass, so he could hold a heading.

He knew whatever force caused his main compass to malfunction he could use this handy dandy compass, no matter what force came on the boat.

Mike looked at the compass and it was spinning, all of the electronic equipment was out. The wind stayed steady; as Mike held the "Windjammer" on the same heading, But the "Windjammer" pitch and rolled, first to Starboard, then back to Port. It seamed like only a few minutes had passed, when he sailed out of the cloud, into a vast area of deep blue, ocean. At least it looked like the Atlantic Ocean.

Mike leaned over the rail, sticking his hand into the water. Wetting his hand, he brought it to his mouth tasting it. It was salty.

The wind was still blowing strong, and the "Windjammer" sailed on. The compass was now steady and the lights came back on. Mike checked the GPS. It gave a reading of No Contact with Seattleites. He was not surprised, so he went back to the compass heading 85 degrees, NNE.

Mike made a note of this heading, so he could come back on the reverse, when he would be trying to get out. He scanned the horizon, for some kind of land. Looking straight a head he could see what looked like a dot of land. Looking back over the stern Mike didn't see the speeding boat. Maybe it missed the door. He sailed on, and noted the time.

Timing would be the only possible way the group could know where he would be when he returned. Thoughts of Kaysee ran through his mind. From the first time he saw her standing on the deck of the "Kaysee Rose" he knew someday she would become the most important person in his life.

Until he met her, his life had been very practical. Now with an ocean between them, he had to keep his mind set on the task-at-hand. He kept sailing in this strange new world. He thought of Columbus on his first voyage to the new world. How he must have had doubts about where he was going, and what he would find when he arrived in the New World.

If this was the area of Atlantis, Mike thought, what kind of land would it be? Would the people who had been lost welcome him, or had they been conditioned to distrust outsiders. Onward he sailed hoping for the best.

He reminded himself he was looking for the Chadwick's Island, and finding the De Longs. He had promised Mrs. De Long he would bring them back if possible. Mike always kept his word or would die, trying.

He felt everyone was counting on him. He couldn't, or wouldn't let them down. The "Windjammer" still headed for the small dot, just off the horizon. It looked as if it was getting larger, but Mike knew vast areas of water play tricks on your eyes. He took out his binoculars thinking he could get a better look.

The sails of the "Windjammer" were still full and Mike saw it was making 10-knots. Not bad, he thought going below for a cup of coffee. Coming back on deck, he heard something he hadn't heard for a long time.

He heard the sound of the boat cutting through the water; the wind snapping the sails, but he also heard a bell. It was clanging with the wave motion. Mike felt the boat raise and fall, the bell clanging in the same rhythm. Was he still outside the door, or was the channel marker on the other side. He wondered could he find the bell and leave this same way. Could the marker be marking the opening? Would it be there when he tried to find his way back? All these thoughts made Mike more aware of what he had gotten himself into.

He decided to change course find the marker and sail on from the bell. He knew there had to be a reason, for the channel marker, but what?

A few minutes on the new course, he saw Maker #17, swinging on the waves. Mike turn the "Windjammer" back on line to what he thought was an island off the bow and the marker off the stern. Now he felt better about his chances of getting out.

Onward he sailed. He watched the sun, hazy but also didn't look like it moved. It was like sailing off the coast of Norway at midnight, when the sun still shown and it should have been dark. He could tell how many days would pass, but not the hours.

He mentally took inventory of what the group had loaded on board. He knew he had enough water for a month. Food he could eat from the can. Dried food where he just added water. Pots, pans, and two camp stoves, with 18 small bottles, of propane. Extra batteries all specially wrapped. Three rifles, a crossbow, two compound bows, all with arrows. He was sure he wouldn't need the weapons, but he kept two handguns on deck.

Dave Chadwick had also insisted Mike take three life rafts stored in drums and tents. It was Dave's thoughts, when Mike found the right island; he could leave all of these supplies on the island, as it would be less they would take when they returned.

The way Dave had put it, "We have grown accustom to many of the new products this world has to offer. It will take awhile to be satisfied with living on the island again.

From the way Dave had described the Island, Mike was sure he would know it when he found it. One of the things Dave had told him was the Bi-plane was still setting on the beach when they left.

Dave was sure it would still be there, because he had used the pontoons for the raft.

Sleep did not come easy for Mike. He knew he had to try. After what seemed like hours of tossing and turning, he dozed off into an restless sleep, only to be startled awake by the slapping of the sails.

He had no idea of how long he had been asleep, quickly he went up on deck to find the wind had dropped off, but the "Windjammer" was still on the course he had set at the Marker. He glanced at the bow and could see the dot had grown to a very high mountain. He couldn't see any movement on the land leading up the mountain slope. It looked to be some miles ahead. He brought the "Windjammer" parallel to the mountain's peek, so he could watch as it passed on the port side. He was looking for some kind of activity.

He couldn't tell if it was an island. On the other hand, it could be a strip of land.

He held the boat well off shore in hopes he could see something, and yet not be, seen from the land. Mike knew from his travels in the Caribbean. Pirates could appear at any time, from nowhere.

Mike checked the compass and brought the "Windjammer" on a heading, which would bring him closer to the mountain, which loomed off his port side.

The mountain looked like a big green finger sticking out of the water, with a sandy beach surrounding the shoreline. He was sure this couldn't be Chadwick's island. The mountain was too high and the beach to short.

Mike stayed on course until he could see, it was truly an island. He kept watching the land for some kind of movement, human or animal, but saw nothing.

He could see the rich green foliage that covered the whole island. Mike remembered reading somewhere that there had been three main islands, which made up the area of Atlantis. According to legend, the god of the sea, had five sets of twins, and gave each set, an island. Perhaps this island was one of them and no one had done anything with it. Much like kids now days, do with things their parents give them.

Mike held his distance from the island, but turned the "Windjammer" so it would circle around to the other side of the island. He kept watching the tree line just off the beach, but saw nothing.

He took a long look up the beach, still not seeing any movement, he went below, made more coffee, and grabbed some lunch meat, bread along with a cup of coffee and was back in the cockpit.

Taking a quick scan of the beach again to make sure he hadn't missed anything. He settled into having some lunch, but always watching the beach. He checked the makeshift compass he could see the "Windjammer" had only made a quarter of the way around the landmass.

He told himself, he was wasting valuable time going around this island looking for an airplane that couldn't be on the beach. He made another sail change and continued circling. He thought he would sail on this heading until he knew the boat had made it three quarters the way around, than he would put the "Windjammer" back on it's original course.

With a cup of coffee in one hand and the glasses in the other, he watched the beach. His arms were getting

217

tired and his cup was almost empty. He wanted to take the glasses from his eyes, but something made him hold on a little longer, and there it was. Setting on the beach just as Dave had described it.

Mike felt like the little guy on "Fantasy Island." He shouted "The Plane"..."The Plane"

After jumping for joy, Mike quickly made ready to bring the "Windjammer" in closer to the beach. He could see the wings of the plane, so he knew it must be the right island after all. He looked over the side of the boat, making sure he had enough water to keep the "Windjammer" from running aground.

When the boat was about 500 yards off the beach, Mike furled the main sail and furled the jib. Going forward he dropped the anchor and let the "Windjammer" take up the, slack. Then went below and brought out one of the rubber rafts, Chadwick had insisted he bring.

Over the side with raft, he reached for one of the hand guns and stuffed it in his shorts. He looped the tie rope around one of the cleats. While holding on to the running end, he climbed the ladder and gently stepped into the raft. He pulled the oars from their retaining straps, and pushed off from the "Windjammer".

With his back to the island he began to row toward the beach. It had been a long time since Mike had rowed a rubber raft, so it took a few strokes before he got his rhythm going and the raft moving in the right direction.

In Mike's mind 500-yards was not all that far, but as he rowed, he realized how much out of shape he was. He rowed harder, and steady, before his arms gave out. He felt the sand of the beach moving under the raft. With movement of the waves, the raft easily floated on shore.

Putting the ores in the raft, he looked over his shoulder and saw what looked like a cabin just off the beach, about two hundred yards from the plane.

He didn't remember Dave saying anything about a cabin, but than there was more likely a lot that Dave didn't think important to finding his island. Dave had told Mike "You will know the island when you find it. The plane is the biggest thing you will see from the water. Find it and you will have found the right island.

Mike looked around to see if there was any sign of tracks in the sand, but found nothing. He walked to the plane and checked it out. There was nothing in the plane.

"What did you think you would find after sixty years?" He asked himself, shaking his head as he walked in the direction of the cabin.

Approaching the cabin he could see at one time there were people who had taken time to build, so it would last a good long time. Looking around Mike could see a clearing and knew the logs had been cut to clear an area for a garden. Mike wondered what Dave and his wife had grown.

He made his way inside the cabin. It looked like someone had gone for a walk and would be right back. The table in the center of the main room was set for dinner. The plates were made of wood, as were the fork, spoons, and a knife, and a Bible at one end. There was a fireplace at the back of the room. Mike could tell this was where they must have did all of the cooking as there were two big pots fashioned from some parts of the plane.

Mike found tools in a chest by the front window. As he took each tool out of the chest, Mike could see how

Dave had built the cabin and knew it had to have taken him a long time to finish it.

He closed up the chest, and walked to another room just off the side of the main. He found a large bed. Mike felt like Goldie Locks from the three bear's fame, but the room also looked like everyone would be right back. He couldn't understand why everything was so neat. Dust hadn't set in even though it had been over ten years since Dave and his wife had left the island.

Suddenly an odd sound came from the main room. He spun around to fine an old man, standing in the doorway, staring at Mike.

"Who are you Sir?" was the question on the man's face, but he asked, "Is Dave and Joan back?" were the words that Mike understood.

"No. Not yet." Mike replied. "I'm Mike Ryan, a friend of the Chadwick's.

"My name is Zen Ben Noah. I am also friend to Dave and Joan. I have been looking for them to return for sometime now." He stated. "They did not come with you?" he asked, walking to the table and sat down on one of the chairs.

"I didn't know anyone else lived on this island." Mike said, taking up another of the chairs.

"I have been here before the Chadwick's came. I helped Dave build this house, and build the raft to leave. I was sure they would be back, but I thought they would return long before now."

"Your name is known to me. if I remember right it means son of Noah…are you the son of the real Noah, the one from the flood time? The one, who built the ark, and had the mammals, and birds on board?" Mike asked, watching the man's eyes.

"You think I must be either very old, or not telling the truth." The man said, with a big smile on his face and a twinkle in his eyes. "But the truth being I am five removed from that father Noah.

It took Mike a few minutes to think the statement through. Then the light went on. "Oh you mean you are the Great-Great-Great-Great Grandson of the Noah of the flood." Mike asked, rubbing his beard.

"I don't understand those words but if you think you are right then it must be me." Zen replied, walking to the front door.

"What kind of boat did you arrive in?" he asked, turning back to face Mike.

Mike got up, walking to the doorway, next to Zen, saying "the one you see out there in the water."

"We call it the "Windjammer" Mike explained, looking at his boat which seemed to be calling him back on board.

"How do you tell the passing of time on this island?" Mike asked.

Zen looked puzzled, then asked Mike to explain what he mentioned.

Mike repeated "passing of time." Then thought for a few minutes, but couldn't explain what he was saying. Without the sun, raising, nor setting, there seemed to be no pasting of time, but Mike knew he must get back to the "Windjammer" to check his timer, because he didn't know how long he had been in the cabin. He knew he was tried, but not as he would have been on the outside.

"I need to go out to the boat." Mike told Zen. "I have many supplies on board, which I need to bring in to the cabin. When Dave and Joan return they will want them. Mike explained.

"Do you want assistance?" Zen asked, turning to look Mike in the eye.

"I could use some help, if you would like to help." Mike replied, turning back to look at the "Windjammer".

"I will have some men come to assist you." Zen stated.

Hearing this, Mike thought to himself … it will take a bit to get men down here to help."

"That will be great, but I will start now, while you go get the men." Mike said heading for the raft.

As Mike reached the beach, and the raft, there were fifteen men standing by his side.

"Wow!" Mike said, it was the only thing he could think of to say as Zen joined them.

"Tell me what you need and I will explain it to the men." Zen told Mike, as he helped Mike put the raft back in the water.

Following the instruction, Mike and two of the men rowed out to the "Windjammer" and boarded her.

Mike quickly went below and began hauling the equipment to the upper deck. The men put it in the raft as fast as Mike could bring it up.

He took a look at the time jugs and could see he had more than half the time left.

When the raft was loaded, Zen's men would row the supplies to shore. The other group would carry them to the cabin. Within a short time, all of the equipment and supplies were in the cabin. Mike returned to shore joining Zen.

"Thank you very much for the help." Mike said, "it would have taken me many trips to the boat and back, to get all this equipment ashore."

"I do not understand why Dave had you bring all these things. The island has everything they would ever need. God provides all the food and water we need. We need only what we have here. If there something we need, God gives it to us.

"I have no answer." Mike said, scratching his head. Then asked, "How did you get the men here so quickly?" Looking at the men as they walked back to the cabin.

"They have been here since I first entered the cabin to talk with you." Zen answered with a smile.

"I didn't see, nor hear them." Mike replied, looking around. "Where did they go? I don't see them now."

"They have gone back to their homes. I have no need of them." the old man said, putting his hands in his sleeves.

"Where is home?" Mike asked, looking at the water where the "Windjammer" was anchored.

Zen turned and pointed to the inter part of the island. "Would you like to see?"

"Sure." Mike said, with a look of bewilderment. "How far is it. I must leave here before very long. I must reach the cloud before the sand in my jug runs out." he added.

"Not to worry. Zen replied, "it is only a touch of my robe. Take hold, and I will show you."

Mike touched Zen's robe, with his right hand, and was at once in a village on the top of the mountain. The men who had helped Mike move the equipment from his boat to the cabin, came running to meet their leader.

"Wow!" was all Mike could say.

I do not understand the word, "Wow", Zen said, with a big smile.

"How did you do that?" Mike asked, getting his thoughts together again.

"We can move about without much walking. Zen replied, then added "If we would have walked up the mountain, it would have taken three rest periods, this way we could be here in a twinkling of your eye.

Zen bow, and walked to the group of men who had been standing a few feet away. They seem to be giving Zen some information, but Mike could not understand the tongue.

Mike looked around the village. He could see houses or rather cabins, much the same as the one on the beach. Mike now understood how Chadwick had built his cabin. Mike didn't understand why he hadn't been told of the people who lived on the island.

"Did Dave know of this place?" Mike asked, as he followed Zen to a larger build that rose to a height of twenty feet. It was in the shape of a triangle on each side. The stones and logs made it look like some of the temples in the far east or Asia.

"No, I never brought him here. Him and Joan where happy on the beach. We wanted to stay out of their way. It wasn't until they were ready to leave on the raft, they found out there was more than myself on the island. We worked and talked many time. They taught me about the outside world, of the Bible…being the word of God. They even showed me where the book talked about father Noah and the flood. We knew of this passing, but didn't know about other people knowing of it." Zen answered, opening a door to the very large building.

"Please enter my house. I would like you to meet my kin. I have many kin, most of the village are of the same clan." Zen explained.

Zen introduced Mike to a woman, who Zen said, was his wife Sari. She look to be about the same age as Kaysee.

She had long black hair, that hung down her back almost to the ground. Her dress was more like a robe. Brightly colored, with reds, greens and yellows. She bowed deeply, as Mike was introduced. Then raised her head giving Mike a bright smile.

Sari is God's gift to me. She is what Joan said a good wife is to be. She makes my food good. She tends the house good and neat.

Zen bowed to her, and she left the room only to return with glasses of water and lemons, placing them on a short table. Zen gestured for me to have a seat on a high stack of pillows and to drink some water.

I was told of how the clan came to be on the island. Zen told of there being other islands not very far away, but he could not go there as the king of that island had taken many of Zen's clan, and they had never returned. His men wanted to go after the ones they called Firbolgs. Their king named Eochaid was said to have a crystal which when held to the sun would give powers over everyone.

Zen told of God coming to his aid and the Firbolgs were no more. They no longer raided Zen's clan...but the island disappeared during one night and no one knew what had happened to it.

Zen's wife brought in some food. Mike didn't know what it was, but after he tried it, he was glad he had. It was very good.

Zen explained that his clan now had a different problem. His word just couldn't get the idea across to Mike. Finally he took Mike by the hand, and lead him to the outside. He then had Mike touch of his robe. In a flash the two stood on a cliff over looking; what looked like a buildings being erected on the island, close to the water.

Mike asked who were down on the beach. With a wave of his hand, Mike was standing on the edge of the project. The men looked be Americans, but why were they build on this island, which the government said could not be found. "Can they see us?" Mike asked, looking at a man, some twenty feet away.

"No." replied Zen, going on to explain, "There is a shield. Their eyes can not see through it. As long as you stand near me, they are unaware of us." Zen replied, taking Mike's arm.

How long have these people been here?" Mike asked, looking at all of the men working.

"They came shortly after Dave and Joan left on their raft. At first we were going to help them. Then a big boat came with much equipment. Much more than you brought. The clan wanted to chase them off the island, but God told us to let them be." Zen answered.

"Now I understand why the government didn't want me to find this place. They wanted to keep it for themselves.

"They are not taking up much of the island, but I'm worried my clan may want all the things they have down here." Zen stated, turning toward the cliff. Then said, "You must go back to your boat."

രൗ

CHAPTER TWENTY FIVE

"There he is!" Big Bill exclaimed, seeing the "Windjammer" entering the cloud. "It looks like we missed him."

"We will follow his wake and get him on the other side." Heilman said, as he increased the speed on the "Betty Lou II". "See if you can get a shot at him." Heilman said, handing Big Bill an AR 15.

Big Bill grabbed the rifle and headed for the bow. The fog was closing in on the stern of the "Windjammer" as Big Bill opened fire. The rounds fall way short of the target, as the "Betty Lou II" sped into the cloud.

Heilman could hardly see Big Bill at the bow, so he cut his speed. The boat responded and heaved to the right, as if it had hit a rubber bumper. He spun the boat harder to the right and headed back into the cloud.

Again the boat ricocheted to the right. It was all Heilman could do to turn the boat back to the left, trying to enter the cloud. Just when he thought he had the "Betty Lou II" headed back into the cloud, a huge black object appeared in front of him. His reaction was to turn away, just in time to see a Navy Destroyer bearing down on the "Betty Lou II".

"Oh shit! Big Bill scream, as he rolled back into the cockpit.

"It's alright." shouted Heilman, as he brought the boat out of the way of the destroyer. The waves of the wake splashed over the stern.

It took Heilman a few minutes to recover from the near miss.

"I guess we should get back to land, before we get run over in this fog." Heilman confessed, bring the "Betty Lou II" round in time to see how large the destroyer was compared to their boat.

"Where did that ship come from." Big Bill asked, as he picked himself up from the bottom of the boat.

"I have no idea." Heilman replied, pushing the throttle forward, bring the boat up to full speed.

"The Director isn't going to like us missing Ryan." Big Bill stated, taking the clip out of the AR 15. "I tried, but he was to far out of range."

"I know." Heilman said, then added, "The information we were given, was wrong by twenty minutes."

"Do you think that destroyer was trying to stop Ryan or us?" Big Bill asked, watching the ship disappear.

"I think we need to find out, and we had better do it fast." Heilman, told Big Bill. "It looks like bad weather is moving in."

The "Betty Lou II" raced to the port of Nassau, where Heilman knew he could get to a phone. He wasn't sure how the director was going to take, missing Ryan entering the cloud. He knew the longer he put it off, the worse it would be.

ट्र

228

CHAPTER TWENTY SIX

After saying his goodbyes to the clan on the island; Mike ready the "Windjammer" to sail back to the door, which he had entered five days earlier. He hoped it had only been five days. The time jugs showed time was running out. He didn't know how long it had taken him to find the island, but he now knew where he was going.

Mike couldn't believe he had out ran Heilman in a speedboat. Heilman must had taken a wrong turn as they came into the cloud. Mike now wondered if Heilman or someone else would be waiting for him as he exited the door. He knew the group would be either at the door or they would be waiting in the Berry Islands, which ever place, wouldn't matter.

Mike was amazed at the people on the island. He still didn't understand how they could move from one spot to another so fast. He couldn't understand why the government wanted to keep the location of the island a secret, nor why were they building a compound. For who was it built to accommodate? His thoughts ran to a conspiracy by CIA, FBI, or an international group.

Mike had heard of groups who wanted to start a one world government…maybe they were behind the buildings on the island. Even the Bible told of a conspiracy. Where the Antichrist would appear, take over the world. Could this island be the place where the antichrist comes from. Zen had said, God told them it was alright for these people to be on the island. According to Zen; God protects them.

He told Mike of people who lived far to the North of his island. Zen explained, these people were the raiders who came looking for wives and slaves to work their fields on this island. Mike wanted to check out this other island but time was not on his side…it would wait until another time.

All these thoughts went through Mike's mind as he sailed to the door. He needed to get back to the real world, and bring the Chadwicks to their island. What ever the reason the government wanted to keep him and the Chadwicks off the island, must be dealt.

He kept an eye, on his make shaft compass, as the "Windjammer" made it's way to the door. He looked around trying to find the cloud, which he knew he must go through. He listened for the channel marker. He didn't hear the bell, he had heard on his way to the island. Handling of the boat was much easier now, with the supplies off loaded. The "Windjammer" was much faster. giving Mike the sense, he could make the portal, in time to pass through, and on home.

With a loud crack of thunder Mike saw the dark cloud form directly in front of his boat. The lighting struck with such force it caused the water to flash white. The fingers of the lighting starched across the horizon. He ducked out of a conditioned reflect.

Recovering he could see the black cloud just off the water. It was rolling straight for him and closing in around the "Windjammer". Mike was sure he was at the right spot.

The seas became moderately heavy, with the winds picking up speed. Mike kept the "Windjammer" head-on into the waves. He knew he had to slow the speed of the "Windjammer" in order to ride up and over the waves rather than driving the bow into them. If the waves got much worse, he would heave to. On one of his trips with Doreen, the swells became so heavy and the "Windjammer" was running before the sea. The waves were coming from directly behind him. It was all he could do to keep the boat from racing down into the trough of the wave, and the bow going submarine. It had almost cost him, the "Windjammer", his and Doreen their lives.

Mike quickly lock the wheel and went below, grabbed another sea anchor.

Back on deck he ridged it to a line at the bow and threw it overboard. With the one at the bow and the one his harness was attached too, slowed the "Windjammer" to a speed where it was just making headway. Mike brought down the main sail, reefing it midway and furled the jib. With all this accomplished, he guided the boat through the cloud. Heavy rain began falling and with the wind blowing in Mike's face, it was hard to see what laid ahead.

By this time, Mike was not sure where he was…he could still be in the door, or had he sailed out into a storm. He knew storms came up quick in around the Bahamas.

The fog was so thick Mike couldn't see anyway but up. He saw the clouds swirling over head. He sailed on, keeping a close eye on the waves and the wind.

Mike watched as the last of the sand ran out of his plastic jugs. He sailed out into a bright sunny afternoon. The waves had returned to just a roll and the wind had dropped to about 25 knots.

Raising the "Windjammer's" mast and sails, Mike checked to see if his GPS was working. It showed he was 3 miles, from the spot he had entered the cloud. The compasses were now showing him the same heading. Mike corrected his course to take him back to the Berry Islands. He felt good about the adventure, and was sure he could bring the Chadwicks to their island.

As Mike cheeked his surrounding, he could see white fluffy white clouds over head. He was watching the horizon, when he also saw what looked like a large boat, about half mile or so off. His first thought was his friends were coming to meet him. He put his binoculars to his eyes and could make out an overturned boat. He changed his course to bring him closer to the boat. It looked like there were two people setting on the overturned hull.

Mike wanted to get back to Doc O'Malley's cabin and Kaysee, but he couldn't sail pass these poor people stranded on their boat. He knew the Bahamians had a Police Boat which would answer emergency radio calls, but maybe they hadn't had a chance to send out an SOS.

With the approach of the "Windjammer" the people on the overturned boat began shooting and waving, for Mike to come closer. As he brought his boat closer Mike could see the people were two men. One was shorter than the big one, who out weighed the first by a hundred pounds.

At 1000 yards, Mike lowered the mainsail, popped the jib, and started his aux. engine He ease up to the Speed Cruiser, which Mike could now see was a Wellcraft. At first Mike didn't recognize the men, but as the distance closed, he could see they were Heilman and Big Bill.

Mike pulled up short of the overturned boat He began to laugh, as he put the "Windjammer" in reverse to stop it from getting to close.

"Boy, are we glad to see you Ryan." Heilman said, as Mike stood at the rail, laughing.

"Fancy meeting you two out here, in the middle of nowhere." Mike said, steering the "Windjammer" around the other side of the Cruiser.

"Come on Captain. Get us off this hull." Big Bill cried, motioning for Mike to move in closer.

"Why so you can stash more drugs on my boat? Or because you guys are such good human beings?" Mike asked, turning the "Windjammer" away from the two men on the overturned boat.

"Mike, it wasn't our idea to try to stop you or have you arrested." Heilman replied, at the top of his lungs.

Mike fought the urge to just sail away, but knew they couldn't last very much longer the way things were.

The more he thought about all of the men Heilman had let die in Vietnam, and how they had tried to kill the others in his group, the more Mike was ready to leave them.

He could just sail away and no one any the wiser. Just another boat lost in the Bermuda Triangle.

As Mike readied to raise the main sail, the pendent which Zen had given him, started to heat up against his chest. He looked down, it seemed to be glowing. Right away he knew what was happening. He had to do the right thing, even if he didn't want to.

"I guess God wants me to help you guys. For the life of me, I don't know why." Mike told them, as he brought the boat close to the hull. Big Bill slid down the over turned hull, landing on the front deck of the "Windjammer" while Heilman came closer to amidships.

"Thanks, Captain for saving of lives." Heilman said, setting down in the cockpit.

"You are lucky I happened to see your overturned boat." Mike stated, readying the "Windjammer" to get underway.

"How did you end up losing your boat?" Mike asked, turning away from the hull.

"I guess you haven't been listening to your VHF radio. We are in the eye of a hurricane." Heilman replied, pointing off to the Southeast.

"Why didn't you tell me that in the first place?" Mike asked, looking in the direction Heilman was pointing.

"How long have you guys been setting on the hull of your boat?" Mike asked, trying to get an idea of how large the eye was.

"Some time during the night, the wind started blow very strong. I miss judged how far we were from the Great Abaco. By daybreak, the waves were rolling so high I couldn't keep the boat from falling to the bottom of the waves. I tried to turn into the wind but I loss power and that was when a big wave caught us on the side, and over it went. We were lucky to get back on top. After about two hours or more everything changed. The wind eased and the waves became what they are now." Heilman said, making room for Big Bill.

"Yeah, the waves had to be running at least 30 feet." Big Bill said, setting down next to Heilman.

Mike check his course, then went to the radio. He selected the International Emergency Channel #16, and listened for any traffic. He knew the NOOA of Miami broadcasted weather information every half hour, when there was heavy weather.

"Attention, all ships in the area Northeast of the Bahamas Islands and all out islands. The radio stated, "there is a category 4 hurricane...it has winds over 120 nautical miles per hour and has forward movement at 18 knots. The seas in the effected area are running at 25 to 30 feet. All small craft are advised to seek shelter in the closes safe harbor. The track of the hurricane is to the Northwest and is projected to make land fall between Helton Head, South Carolina and Charleston, South Carolina over the next 12 to 15 hours local time."

"That doesn't sound very good." Mike told them, as he checked the chart. The way the hurricane was headed didn't surprise Mike. He had been through storms in and around the Bahamas, but a hurricane was something else. He knew with winds at 155 miles per hour, the seas would be moderate as far as wave action, because the water was so deep. If he could get the "Windjammer" moving at it best speed, he might be able to make 12 to 14 knots. With the forward movement of the storm at 18 knots, it would over take them in maybe 10 hours.

"I think our best bet will be to try to stay in the eye as long as we can. I'll keep our heading to the Northwest. I'll try to get us to Charleston, before the back edge of the storm catches us." Mike explained, changing course to the Northwest. He watched as the "Windjammer" started to sail. He put out as much sail as he could…knowing when the storm overtook them he would have to reef the sails.

The knot meter showed the boat was making 12 knots, with the wind coming on a short reach. Mike wanted to put up the Spinnaker, but it would mean, he would need to change his heading. He really didn't want to sail more to the North, and he knew even with the larger sail out, the "Windjammer" wouldn't give him that much more speed.

"Ok, gentlemen, this is what we are going to do. Mike stated, spreading the chart out on the upper deck of the "Windjammer". "We are going to Charleston, as fast as this boat will get us there. It means we may have heavy seas at our back before we get there." he explained, then went on to say, "Paul you and Big Bill need to go below, put on foul weather gear. There are harness down there, with safety lines. I want you guys to be attached to the boat at all times."

"We aren't in bad weather yet." Big Bill said, gesturing with his hands, feeling for rain.

"Not this minute." Mike said, then pointed to the stern. "See those clouds they are full of water, and they will be here by the time you get the gear on. So just do it." Mike said, in a commanding voice.

CHAPTER TWENTY SEVEN

Dave Chadwick paced back and forth. First he would check his watch, then he would look out the back, off the deck. He paused only long enough to watch the weather channel as it tracked, Hurricane Hugo.

"Mike should be coming out of the door by now." Dave said, turning to the group, who were also watching the weather.

"Do you think he is in this storm?" Kaysee asked, holding Rose's hand.

"What do you think Doctor?" Dave asked, as he passed.

"I think you need to set down. You are going to wear a grove in the floor." Doc. O'Malley replied, looking up from the TV.

"I mean, what about the storm. Do you think we should get the boats moving back to Florida?" Dave asked, stopping in front of Joan.

"I think we should be alright here." He replied, turning the Esther, saying, "You might want to fly back, before the storm get much closer."

"I was thinking I should leave, or at least move the plane away from the dock." she told the Doctor.

"From the looks of the track it should miss us by 30 or 40 miles, but we may still get a lot of wind. Maybe upwards of 60 miles per hour," he stated, looking back at the TV.

"Maybe I should get my aircraft back to the mainland." Esther said, get up and walked to the front deck, just as a huge bolt of lighting struck somewhere close.

Bert came in off the back deck saying, "I think we had better batten down the boats. It's going to start pouring down rain."

Everyone headed for the dock. Esther was the first to reach the dock and her plane.

"I'm out of here." she said, as the others joined her.

"Thanks for everything." Linda told her, as she put her arms around Esther, giving her a hug.

"Are you coming with me Doctor O'Malley?" Esther asked, opening the door to the plane.

"No, I think I will stay here." he replied, holding the door as she got in the pilot's seat.

Within minutes Esther was speeding out of the cove and heading back to Miami.

"Doc. You know these waters. Do you think we should move our boats away from the dock?" Bert asked, as they watched Esther takeoff.

"We're on the leeside of the island, so the storm surge shouldn't be all that bad. The wind will be blowing out of the cove. They will be alright." Doc O'Malley explained, as he helped Bert and Linda put the canvasses on the "Witchcraft".

Rose and Kaysee took down their "Bimini Top" and stowed in to bow compartment. As everyone finished closing up their boats, loud claps of thunder could be heard a long with flashes of lighting off to the East.

"Come on Rose." Kaysee said, taking her by the hand, "Let's run it is going to start raining hard any minute."

Everyone made a dash for the cabin, with Kaysee in the lead. More thunder, and the wind picked up as they all entered the cabin.

"Any change on the hurricane?" Kaysee asked Dave, as everyone took up their spots around the TV,

"Not much. It is brushing pass us about now. They say it will make land fall someplace on the South Carolina coast. Most likely around Charleston." Dave replied, setting down next to Joan, who was drinking a cup of coffee.

"We need to close up the back of the cabin." Doctor O'Malley told the group, as the tropical rain and the wind became stronger. They all started closing windows and bringing in the deck furniture. Bert ran to the pool, and moved all of the tables and chairs to the storage building.

Reentering the cabin, Bert was soaking wet. Linda handed him a towel, saying "It's a good thing we started when we did. Look at the wind and rain coming down now." pointing to the tree-line. Tree branches were braking and were flying toward the cabin.

"We are in for a big blow." Doc. O'Malley said, getting himself some water.

"This is a good day, to just set back and relax." Bert said, then adding, "We are on a tropical island."

"I wish Mike was here." Kaysee replied. "This setting around, even if it is a tropical island, is getting old."

"Maybe he will call." Rose said setting down in a chair by the front deck.

"I'm sure he has his hands full, about now." Dave told the girls. adding, "This will all be over before long."

Bert was at the sink, rinsing out his cup, when there was a banging on the French Doors leading to the back deck. It was Jose and he had a young girl in his arms.

Bert quickly opened the doors, and Jose came in saying, "Sir can you help me? This is my daughter, Maria. I think she has a broken arm. The wind blew a tree on her. She cannot move her arm, and it banged her in the head."

"What is it Jose?" Doctor O'Malley asked, as he came into the kitchen.

"Oh! Doctor, you're here. It's Maria, her arm. I don't know she's not moving. She screamed when I picked her up, but now she isn't crying anymore." Jose said, rocking his child.

"Take her into the bedroom, and lay her on the bed." Doctor O'Malley instructed. The doctor told Bert to go to the hall closet, and retrieve his black bag.

Bert quickly returned carrying the bag, and handed it to the doctor. The girls all came into the room, to see if there was anything they could do to help the doctor.

Doctor O'Malley checked the little girl's, eyes and her arm. As he moved her arm Maria's eyes popped open and she began crying and tried to thrash around. Kaysee placed her hand on the girls' chest, and began to talk to her in a soft voice.

Turning to Rose the doctor asked her to get some warm water, so they could clean her broken arm.

Doctor O'Malley carefully pulled on her arm to get the bones back in line. He then cleaned the arm and then mixed Plaster-of-Paris making a cast for the arm. The little girl was still afraid and couldn't understand where she was, or what had happened to her. Jose came into the bedroom telling her how the wind had blown a tree on her, and the doctor had fixed her arm, but she wouldn't be able to use it for some time.

Doctor O'Malley smiled and told Maria her arm would be all right in about six weeks.

"Thank you so much." Jose said, as he leaned over and kissed his daughter. "I must go check on my wife and son."

"You can leave her here and we will look after her." Doctor O'Malley told Jose.

The heavy rains had slacked off, and the wind dropped to were it was just a strong breeze.

ᏀᏯ

CHAPTER TWENTY EIGHT

The "Windjammer" was cutting through the 25 foot waves at about a 45 degree angle. Mike had lowered the mast and reefed the main sail and the jib. With 45 mile an hour winds coming over the starboard side he kept the main on a short reach, and was still making 14 knots.

The torrential rain had been beating him in the face as he tried to hold the course he knew well. The GPS gave him the fix 31.7 North and 78.8 West. Mike knew he was real close to the harbor at Charleston. He told Big Bill to keep a close eye out for the channel markers for the harbor.

Mike tried to see the lighthouse at entrance, but with the rain and the wind blowing at gale force, the only thing he could see was big Bill holding on to the bow rail for all he was worth.

Mike had Heilman below keeping check on the radio and the plots on the chart. Negating in heavy weather was very tricky. The wind was trying to blow him one way and the waves are fighting to drive him in the other.

For 8 hours the three men, changed off, taking the helm. As the "Windjammer" got closer to Charleston, Mike was fighting the 20 to 30 foot swells. During the daylight hours, it hadn't been to bad. The three men had time to work out the hostility Mike and Heilman felt between them.

While Mike still felt Heilman had done his men wrong in Vietnam, he knew Heilman would do things different if he could do them over. But time and tide...Mike also knew he would need help from Heilman to convince the government to let Chadwick go back to the island.

"Land straight ahead!" Big Bill shouted, waving his hand and pointing off the starboard side.

Mike look close, but couldn't make out any landmarks. From the position Heilman had given him, Mike knew he was near the Fort in the harbor. The lights in the city were out. He thought that was about right, as the lights would go out from a little storm, and this hurricane wasn't little.

"Bill," Mike shouted, "watch for the seawall to your right. Don't let me get to close. I need to be about 100 yards off the wall. The water get real shallow around here, quick."

The waves were still striking the stern and wind was kicking the waves to 30 feet. It was all Mike could do to keep the "Windjammer" in the channel as he made his way toward the end of the harbor, some 10 miles inland.

Mike could see that Hugo had hit Charleston hard. He could hear the wind screaming all around the boat. He knew tornadoes would spin off of the main part of the hurricane. They had seen water spouts while it was still light.

The lighting was off to the North of the harbor, which didn't bother Mike.

Heilman came up into the cockpit, as Mike made the turn into the channel which lead to Buzzard's Roost. The waves were still running 10 to 15 feet and it was all Mike could do to keep the "Windjammer" in the middle of the channel. Just around the bend, he knew there was a drawbridge. Normally there were lights lining the channel, but with the power out in all of Charleston, there were no lights.

"Bill watch for the bridge...it should be just ahead. Sound off as some as you see it." Mike shouted, over the wind.

"Do you think we can make it to the marina?" Paul asked, standing, looking forward for the bridge.

"Yeah, we are only a few miles from it." Mike replied, watching the edge of the channel, as they passed.

"If there is no power in the area, how are we going to get under the bridge?"

"I'm going to put the mast all the way down, and run the motor until we clear the bridge." Mike replied, giving Heilman a smile.

"I'll have to see this." Heilman said, looking up at the mast.

"Bridge dead a head." Big Bill, hollered, standing up to stretch his legs.

Mike could see the outline of the bridge, because of the lighting. He centered the "Windjammer" on the bridge. He lowered the mast as low as it would go. Started the engine and eased the boat under the bridge. Clearing it by 10 feet, even with the raising tide.

Once on the other side of the bridge, Mike raised the mast and reset the sails. He kept the engine running as it aided in control of the boat.

"What would happen if we got hit by lighting." Heilman asked, watching the lighting sticking around the area close to the channel.

"Probably nothing, the hull of the "Windjammer" is Fiberglass." Mike replied, checking the channel ahead.

The words had hardly gotten out Mike's mouth, when a very loud crack struck the mast on the "Windjammer". With the flash, everyone on the boat ducked.

"I wish I hadn't asked." Heilman said, dusting the parts from the anchor light, from his hair.

The engine coughed and sputtered to a stop. Mike had to quickly change the sails, as the wind swing the "Windjammer" to the side of the channel.

Mike could hear the keel slam acutance to the bottom of the channel.

"I think we had better get the boat back in the middle, and drop anchor." Mike told Paul and Bill.

He quickly turned the boat, into the wind. He had Paul and Bill secure the anchors, both forward and aft. He hopped there wouldn't be other boats trying to use the channel. He had Big Bill tie a flashlight to the bow. Paul got the flashlight with the red lens and tied it to the stern.

"We'll get some sleep, while we wait for daylight." Mike informed them.

"Why are we stopping here?" Heilman asked, turning to look at the water ahead.

"We almost ran aground. We can't get out and walk." Mike explained, going below to get a cup of coffee.

❧

At daybreak, Mike was awaken by the Coast Guard. They wanted to know if everyone was alright, and if their boat had weathered the storm.

Mike assured them that everything was shipshape, and they would be moving the boat shortly. To watch the Coast Guard informed him that the channel about 1000 yards ahead was partially blocked by three boats, which had broke loss from their docks.

With the coming of daylight, Mike went to the engine compartment to see why they had loss power following the lighting strike. He could see the battery and charger had been destroyed. Further checking showed the lighting had burned three of the shrouds where they were attached to the deck. The anchor light at the top of the mast had been blown off. He knew these would need to be replaced before they tried to sail back to the Berry Islands.

First he needed to get to the marina, to make repairs. He raised the main sail, had Paul and Big Bill pull up the anchors and he eased the "Windjammer" up the channel toward the marina.

"It's a good thing you stopped when you did." Paul said, as the boat slid pass the wrecked boats that hadn't made it through the hurricane.

"I had a feeling there was something in our way last night." Mike replied, as they cleared the area. Within a few minutes they were approaching the marina. It hadn't faired very well either. Boats were blown upon shore. While others were setting on the bottom. Docks were torn up. Many people had came to the marina to see if their boats had survived the storm.

As the "Windjammer" came into the main channel of the marina, Mike saw the office building was still standing, but the roof of repair shop had been torn off.

All in all the place looked like it had been hit by an A bomb.

He slipped the "Windjammer" into one of the only slips that didn't have a sunken boat in it. He went to the repair shop, where he was able to buy all the parts he needed to repair his boat.

The guy in the repair shop told the three, how the strong winds and tornados had wrecked everything. He told them how hard Charleston and North Charleston had been devastated and the whole area was without power. Most of the business were closed, and it would be days, if not weeks, before they would back operational. Mike went to the parking lot to check on his jeep. It was still where he had parked it, but the windshield was cracked and the canvas was torn. The interior was wet, but the seats were leather. He pulled the plugs in the floor boards to drain out the water.

"We have what we need to fix the "Windjammer" and it will only take a little bit to get us back on the water." Mike informed, Paul and Big Bill.

"Where are we going once we fix the boat" Paul asked, as they walked back to the boat.

"Well that's up you. I know I need to get back to the Chadwicks." Mike replied, as he climbed back on board the "Windjammer."

"I need to get to DC, and let my director know that Big Bill and I are alive. Also that we didn't stop you from going into the cloud." Heilman stated, following Mike.

"You could fly to DC. The Air Force, and airport are about 20 miles from here. I can drive you the airport." Mike said, looking around for a pair of gloves, so he could get the battery out of the compartment.

"Yeah, that would work for me, but Big Bill doesn't fly." Paul said patting Big Bill on the back.

"Well, Bill could go with me. You could fly to DC., and pave the way for the Chadwicks to get approval to return to their island. I need to get you and the government off my case. Then I will be able to get the Chadwicks on their island." Mike informed, the two.

"You know! I'm on your side, now." Heilman said, looking at Big Bill.

"I'm with you Mike...even if it cost me my job." Big Bill said, then added, "I was looking for a job when I got this one."

For the next four hours, the men worked on the repairs to the "Windjammer". With the mast in it's lowered position, it was easy to replace the light, and the shrouds.

The weather was still cloudy, rainy, and the wind was still blowing at around 40 miles per hour.

Mike took Paul to the Air Force's Base Operation building where Paul was able to get a hop to Andrews AFB., just out side Washington. Big Bill and Mike went back to the marina and finished cleaning the "Windjammer".

Mike didn't want to leave the marina, with the weather so bad, but according to the area weather reports it would be another three days before it would clear enough for the "Windjammer" to get underway.

Mike went to the marina's office to make a phone call to the Berry Islands. He was sure Heilman, and Big Bill had changed sides, but he still didn't want Big Bill to know where he was calling the Chadwicks, and Kaysee.

CHAPTER TWENTY NINE

The interview was interrupted by a man sticking his head into the gangway asking, is anyone down there?"

"Yeah, we're all down here, Paul. Come on down and join the party." Mike shouted.

A man in his late fifties, with salt and pepper hair. He was under six feet, dressed in a pair of dark slacks and a white shirt. He was carrying a package in his left hand. Mike got up from the table, and struggled to get up to shake the man's hand.

"We are being interviewed by this man." Mike said pointing to me. "His name is Mickey Mc Guire. We have been telling him about how we found Topic Bay for the Chadwicks. Mike then said, Mickey, this is the infamous Paul Heilman."

I turned and stood, offering the man my hand, saying "I've heard a lot about you. I'm glad to finally meet you."

"Not all good, I suspect." Paul said, handing the package to Captain Mike and taking my hand.

"I was just getting to the part where you left Big Bill and I in Charleston." Mike explained.

"Hey speaking of Big Bill, where is he?" Paul asked, looking around.

"He's over on Doctor O'Malley's boat. He's getting it ready to take to the Doctor." Rose replied, before anyone else, could speak.

"This place is getting crowded." Mike said, putting his hand on Heilman's shoulder. Let's go up to the restaurant. I'm getting hungry and I know Mickey must be also. He has been down here since breakfast, with only me and coffee."

As everyone crawled up and out of the "Windjammer's" cabin, the sun had began to set over Biscayne Bay. I asked Paul if he had time to tell me; what had taken place when he went back to DC., and told his director he had failed to stop Captain Mike.

"I guess…Did he tell you about dropping me of at the Air Force Base?" Paul asked, as we walked to the restaurant.

"Yeah, but not much." I replied, trying to keep pace.

The following is what Paul Heilman remembered after being dropped off at the Air Force base in Charleston South Carolina.

"At the Base Operations, I show my ID, and asked them if there was a plane headed East. I was told they had a C-130 aircraft, leaving in a half hour. They were carrying cargo, but they would make room for me.

The takeoff was a ruff one. The wind was still strong and it was still raining hard, off and on. The plane was empty, so it was just that much harder to takeoff." he explained.

The pilot told Paul there were 27 C-130's making the trip from Andrews AFB to Charleston, bring in water, ice, and food to help out the residents.

It was a three hour flight to the base in Maryland. Paul had time to catch up on sleep and rest. In talking with the men on board the aircraft, Paul found out how lucky he was to have survived the hurricane.

Paul arrived in DC, and went straight to the directors office. Emily was at her desk when Paul walked in.

"There you are!" she exclaimed, getting up and rushing to his side. She put her arms around his neck and kissed him on his cheek. "I was worried you had gotten lost in the "Bermuda Triangle". The Director has been in contact with the DEA wanting to know what they knew about you and Big Bill...where is Big Bill?"

"I left him in Charleston...with a friend. You know he doesn't like to fly...no he won't fly." Paul stated, as the door to the director's office opened, and a bald headed man stepped into the outer office.

"Where in the world have you been the director asked. "Come into the office you can have a reunion later." he said, going back into his office.

Paul gave Emily a hug, then quickly followed the director into his office.

"Ok, fill me in on what took place in Florida." the director stated, as Paul came in and sat down in a chair in front of the director's desk.

Paul started with how the DEA had tried to take Ryan, Chadwick and some others into custody, but only had alerted them to the fact that the government wanted to stop them. He went on to explain that Big Bill had dropped drugs on Ryan's boat. The Coast Guard had stopped Ryan as he was sailing out of Miami, but the

Coast Guard didn't find any drugs on board Ryan's boat.

Big Bill and I got a fast boat from DEA and tried to caught up with Ryan using the information his office had supplied. but the information was twenty minutes off, so he had missed stopping Ryan only by a few minutes.

Paul knew what Mike had found when he was on the island. He went right to the point by asking, "Why was it so imperative, for me to stop Ryan from finding the island…that isn't there in the first place?"

"It isn't anything you need to know. Has he returned?" he asked, giving Heilman a strange look.

"Your damn right he returned. It's a good thing he came back when he did…I wouldn't be here now." Paul said, and on went to explain, how his boat had been overturned by the hurricane. How Ryan had came to his rescue and sailed all the way to Charleston.

"Did he tell you anything about his trip? Anything about what he may have found? Did he find an island?" the director questioned.

"Yes!" Heilman exclaimed, "And now I want to know just what this is all about. You either tell me the whole story, or I will raise so much hell…I will go to the media. I'll blow this whole outrageous thing, sky high; spending tax payers money building a resort on an unknown island, and about stopping American's from sailing where they want, and when they want.

"Now hold on there a minute mister. Just who do you thing you're talking too. I'm still the director, and you work for me. You do what you are told or I will find someone who will." the Director screamed, getting up from his desk.

It was at this point Paul jumped to his feet so fast that the director thought Paul was going to hit him. But Paul stepped close to the desk, keeping the director from pushing a panic bottom, on the side of his desk, which would tell Emily to call the guards.

"Ok, Ok,!" the director said, raising his hands in the air, and sat back down in his chair.

"This is bigger then you think...I only know what I've been told. It's not much, but the orders came from way up the chain of command. For all I know, it could have came from the President.

"The President?" Paul asked, shaking his head. "Why?" Paul couldn't believed what the director was telling him.

"The way I understand it. There is a group of about six very wealthy people, who think this island has something that will let people live forever. According to Chadwick himself; told everyone they had been on the island for over fifty years. Somebody must have passed this information to the these people, and they want the island for themselves." the director explained.

"Who are these people?" Paul asked, trying to get as much information as he could for Mike Ryan and Dave Chadwick.

"You can't say anything about this island...they will know where you got it, and we both will disappear forever." the director said, with a very nervous and serious look.

"When I was trying to get into the cloud, following Ryan, I was almost run down by a destroyer. It didn't have Naval markings, but if I hadn't reacted quickly, Big Bill and I would have been on the bottom of the ocean. It came out of the cloud, or at lest looked like it had came out at almost the same spot Ryan had gone in." Paul told the director, watching his reaction, but there was no change, Paul could detect.

"Listen Paul...these people have enough money they can buy their own Navy, or anything else they need. Equipment, or people." the director replied. "You need to get Big Bill and keep up with Ryan. If he or anyone else make a move to go back into the cloud, I want to know. You had better carry out this order, if you want to keep working for me." director stated.

Paul took the director's statement as a good time to leave. He wasn't sure what he was going to do, but he was sure the first place he would go.

"I guess I had better get out on the road." Paul said. Getting to his feet.

"Stay in close contact with this office. I want to know where Ryan and his group are at all times." the director said, as Paul reached the door. He turned and told the director he would be hearing from him.

Paul walked out of the office, to find Emily standing by her desk.

"I heard you shouting in there, is everything alright?" she asked, giving Paul a big smile.

"Oh yeah, everything is just peachy. I'm going to need a car and more expense money. How about 4 or 5 grand." Paul replied, setting down in a chair, putting his hands on his head.

"Sure, but I need you to fill out some paper work on your expense account, before the end of the month." She told him, as she signed a voucher.

"Emily have you heard anything about the operation I have been working on?" Paul asked, watching her make out the paper work.

"There was some guy from the White House in here the other day. It was after you called from Charleston. I didn't hear what he talked to the director about, but after he left, the director told me to take the rest of the day off. In twenty years, he has never said that before." she replied, handing him the voucher.

Paul thanked her for the money, then left.

"So you were still working for the same people? You didn't quit?" I asked as everyone filed into the restaurant.

"No I thought I could do more to help, if Big Bill and I were still working." Paul replied, as Jim Chapman, walked pass saying, "I see you caught up with Mike Ryan." then turned to Bert and said, "I just talked to Earlene; she said she was expecting you and Linda for dinner. Said you father and stepmother are here."

"Yeah, we'll get there." Bert replied, looking at Linda as she sat down at a table. After everyone was seated, and drinks ordered Paul returned to his story.

A quick call to Andrews and Paul had a flight back to Charleston AFB. He wasn't sure if Mike and Big Bill were still at the marina. He had checked the weather reports which told him that the hurricane had swung to the North, but there was still a lot of rain and wind in the area. He took a chance and flew to Charleston.

Once in Charleston, he took a cab to the marina. As he got out Paul could see the jeep was parked in the same spot it had been when Mike had taken him to the Air Force Base.

He walked to the marina office to check on the "Windjammer". They told him it was still in the slip. He walked down the docks until he saw Big Bill rolling up the hosepipe. He was still wearing fool weather gear.

"Hey! You got room for one more on the boat?" Paul asked, as he got closer to Big Bill.

"Sure." a voice said from behind him. "We are just getting ready to take her to sea again." Mike said, walking up beside Paul.

"Thought I might have missed you." He replied, climbing on board.

"You might want to change out of that suit." Big Bill said, shaking Paul's hand.

While Paul was changing, Big Bill and Mike got the "Windjammer" underway. Mike had checked with the Coast Guard, and found that the channel to the Edisto River was open, so Mike took it because it was a quicker way out into the ocean.

By the time Paul came back on deck, the "Windjammer" was well down the river.

"Did you find anything out, while you were in DC?" Mike asked, as Paul took up a seat in the cockpit.

"Not much." he replied, "But from what the director told me, there's allot of big money people, who don't want you or the Chadwicks on the island. According to Emily, someone from the White House came to see the director...even gave her the day off...unheard of." Paul explained.

"Maybe these people don't know there are other humans on the island. When I talked with Zen, he said they had a shield. If I can get the Chadwicks through the door, and on the island, no one would know they were there." Mike said, checking the sails as the "Windjammer" struck out for the open sea.

"That might work." said Paul, as Big Bill came back to the helm.

"Where are we headed?" Big Bill asked, looking at the compass.

"I think our best bet is to sail Southeast, and see where we end up" Mike replied giving the two men a smile.

"I hope this trip will be quieter than the other day was." Big Bill said, ducking as the main boom passed over his head.

"We sailed Southeast for hours and hours. At one point I was temped to ask Mike; are we were there yet? But I thought better, because he was in deep thought about something." Paul said, as he continued his remembrance.

"Mike had laid in a course on the Lorain and the GPS. The coordinates showed we were going, someplace in the Bahamans. By late afternoon the next day, we were on another small island." he told me, as Big Bill walked through the door and sat down at the table next to Rose, who leaned over and gave him a kiss.

ॐ

"Now all we need is the Chadwicks and the party would be complete." I said, getting up and shaking hands with Big Bill.

"They won't be here. They're on their island." Big Bill said setting down.

"So, you did get them to their island." I said, setting down and starting to take notes again.

Mike took over the rest of the story saying, "Once we got back to Doctor O'Malley's cabin, and I told Dave

Chadwick, what I had found his island. It was all I could do to keep him at the cabin long enough to contact Esther to find out the next time the door would open." Mike explained, "Linda made the call, back to Miami and talked to her friend. Who told her, she had already started working on the problem, but the government had raided her office, taking the book and her copy of the chart. She also said, it hadn't been Heilman, but was someone with more clout, because the guy had the FBI with him.

Esther said they had also taken her computers that had been in her office. She said, who ever it was didn't know she had copies on her computer in her apartment. It would take a day to get the information as she had to check it with the first time the door had opened." Mike replied, giving the waiter his and Kaysee's order for food.

"We were worried that the government would find her other computer. I was sure they had her phone tapped." Linda said, sipping her drink.

"Yeah, it was decided Linda and Bert would take the "Witchcraft" back to Florida, and get the information from Esther." Kaysee said, as Bert and Linda got up.

"We must go to my sister's house for dinner. My folks are going to be there." Bert said, turning to Mike he added, "We'll see you in the morning at 6 AM."

"Yes, that will be good…we must be at the spot around noon, give or take thirty minutes." Mike told Bert, with a wave they were off and Mike got back to the story.

"Esther brought us the information. She didn't want any thing to happen to it. Bert and Linda had already started back to the cabin. They were followed out of Biscayne Bay, by a larger cruiser. When they were out of sight of land, this big boat tried to sink the "Witchcraft", but Bert was ready for them. I had given him one of the

RPGs. When this boat tried to get close, Bert let go with the rocket and sent the larger boat to the bottom. He told me it didn't have any markings and it had three men in black outfits, with hoods. He felt bad about it, but didn't want to put Linda in harms way." Mike explained, looking at Big Bill, who went on with the story.

"When Bert got back to the cabin, Rose and I took the "Kaysee Rose" headed back the way Bert had come from Miami, but we didn't find anyone, not even an oil slick. It must have been someone working for the group, who were on Chadwick's island." Big Bill, told me.

⁊

CHAPTER THIRTY

"What about when you took the Chadwicks to the island?" I asked, trying to get back to the story.

Mike started by explaining; at the time he felt the Chadwicks wouldn't get to their island, if they didn't leave quickly for the cloud. Esther had bought the information on when the cloud would open, and where. The location had changed, a little closer to the Berry Islands, but the government would also know about the change.

Mike had Heilman and Big Bill go back to Miami with Bert and Linda. They were to keep everyone in the government thinking he and the Chadwicks were having trouble getting the information on the cloud. Esther was to put the word out to Heilman, that she needed the book and the chart, to be able to pinpoint where and when the cloud would open. They used land-lines to commutate, hopefully the government had them tapped.

It must have worked, because when Dave, Joan, Kaysee, and Mike left, they had no trouble entering the cloud. "We didn't even see a bird in the area. The seas were

260

ruff, with the clouds swirling, but the "Windjammer" drove through it all." Mike stated.

The journey to the island went with out a hitch. With in a day they were anchored off the island. Joan's health had gone from bad to worse, and getting her off the "Windjammer" took a little bit of a strain, but with Dave's help, Mike was able to get her into the raft and onto the beach.

When they landed, Zen was there to greet them. It was like an old homecoming. Zen knew right away what Joan needed. He had some of the women, bring fresh fruit, and water for her. He prayed over the food and water, and prayed for Father God to heal her sickness. It was like magic…with in minutes Joan was better.

"When we carried her into the cabin, she couldn't walk. She was shaking so bad she couldn't hold a cup; without spilling what was inside.

We were amazed at how fast she had recovered." Mike said. When Mike had a chance, he talked with Zen about Joan's recovery, he was told that her problem was; "She had been missing the goodness of Father God's food."

He went on to tell Mike, how Father God provides for all on the island. "They have everything they need. Father God will take care of them forever. Father God wants us to live for Him and only Him." Zen explained.

"How did you come to be on this island?" Mike asked, as they walked on the beach.

"Long ago we were part of another world. A world were humans fought other humans. They were looking for something, but didn't know what it was, nor how to find it. We had many gods for everything. My brothers each had their own lands, but one of my brothers, wanted all of us to do his wishes. He went against the commandments of our Father God. There was a time when much information was known. This brother used this knowledge to lead our people away from our Father God.

This went on for a long time, but the people wouldn't turn back to Father God. In one day and night, my brother's land was taken away. We don't know how this happened, as it was long before my Grandfather's age.

Our Father God came to his father, in a dream telling him that the world as he knew it, would be done away with, but because my Grandfather had tried to do our Father God's wishes, he would be placed in this land forever and ever." Zen stated, turning to look out to sea.

Remember, me telling of a land out there." Zen said, pointing to the North. "a place where the people came and took members of this clan? Well this went on, until Father God sent the Guardians of the sky, to stop it. They placed a shield around us, to keep us safe.

This shield cannot be seen by the normal eye, but hides us unless we need to be seen. That is why you could see me when I first came into the Chadwick cabin. This is also why the people on the other side of the island don't know we are here. They are on the outside of the shield. We are watching over them, but until Father God, or the Guardians return, we cannot interfere with what they have planed." Zen explained, then asked, "Why are you so concerned about what those few people have planned?"

Mike didn't have a good answer, but tried. "I guess it's because of the trouble these people can cause the world... My world."

"But you don't understand; Father God is in control of ever thing, in your world...as you call it...as well as here and every place in the stars." Zen told him, then said, "Take hold of my sleeve there is a place I have been told to bring you."

Mike took hold of Zen sleeve, and in a blink, the two were standing in front of a huge structure. It was larger than any building Mike had ever seen. The outside was pure white, which shown like a bright light.

Mike look to the right and to the left, but couldn't see either end of it. He looked up, but couldn't see the top, and when he looked at the base, he saw that it seemed to be floating.

"What is this?" Mike asked, finishing his survey of the structure.

"This is the place where our Father God stays when he comes to be with us." Zen replied, taking Mike by his arm, moving him forward.

Mike was so struck by the size, and it's brightness that his legs didn't want to step forward, he stood like a stone statue.

"It's alright." Zen said, pulling Mike forward, in the direction of a large gate, which had a smaller gate in it.

To Mike's surprise the small gate was very narrow. As he got near, it opened and Zen pushed him through it.

Once on the other side, Mike could see rolling hills with green grass, which seemed to go on forever. The path leading away, was very bright and gleaming, but he couldn't see to where. He looked around for Zen, but he wasn't there. In his place was a man slightly taller than Mike. At that moment Mike knew exactly who had joined him. It was as if Mike had seen this man many times, and yet not.

Then Mike asked the dumbest question of his whole life…"Are you who I think you are?"

"I Am." He replied, in a gentle voice, resting his hand on Mike's shoulder.

"You are really, the Jesus of the Bible?" Mike asked, starting to shake.

"You know me, and I know you Michael Ryan. Take your hand, and place it here." He said, pulling his white robe aside. "You are not the first who doubted."

Mike fell to his knees. He was shaking so bad he could not speak. Jesus lifted him to his feet, and placed his hands on Mike's head.

"Oh! Lord…forgive me; I knew it was you from the start, but then I wasn't sure." Mike stammered.

"You are forgiven. Come walk with me. The Father wants to talk with you." the Lord said, taking Mike's arm to steady him as he walked down the path.

Mike's mind was racing, and he could feel his heart pounding in his chest…"Am I dead?" Mike asked, not knowing if he was dreaming or if this was what happened when you die.

He had always heard "absent from the body present with the Lord." Was he still breathing? He couldn't tell.

"No, you will be returning. The Father has work for you to do. HE will explain everything. There is no need to be frighten or fear. HE is our Father. You were not frighten of your earthly father, why should you be frightened of Our heavenly father?" Jesus explained.

Before Mike knew what was happening he was standing before GOD. He wanted to fall to his knees, but Jesus was holding him so tightly he couldn't. Tears began rolling down his face, so much he couldn't see beyond his nose.

"Michael, I want you to spread MY word about MY SON. Tell everyone HE is coming on MY behalf soon. Tell them not to fear what lies ahead. I AM in control and I hear their cries."

"But, Lord God, who am I to tell anyone anything. There are so many who could do it much better than me." Mike bleated out, lowering his head.

"Where have I heard that before?" God said to Jesus. "Use the words of my faithful servant Matthew. He did a good job writing what I told him to write. Now be on your way and don't worry, We are always with you."

With that, Jesus took Mike from the presents of God, to another room. The room was as white as the outside of the structure he had been standing front of with Zen. In the middle was a stand, which held a large book.

Jesus walked to it and opened it. Mike looked over the shoulder of Jesus, and could see his name on two pages with four columns on them. In each column were marks. The first column had words Mike could not read. The second had many red marks. The third column had many black marks. And the forth column had what looked like zeros.

"What is this book?" Mike asked, as he looked down each column."

"This is the Book of Life. It contains everything you have done in your life." Jesus explained, as he place a red make, at the top of the second page.

"What are the marks?" Mike asked, knowing full well, what they were.

"They show everything you have done in your life, so far. The red ones are for things you have done good, and the black ones are for things you haven't done so good." Jesus replied, putting a zero in the last column.

"What is the last column for?" Mike asked, truly not knowing what information it contained.

"Oh, the last column is the balance on your account." Jesus replied, putting another zero in the column, and then went on to explain…"Every time you do anything, good or not so good, you get a mark, but because I paid the price for your Sins, your balance is always zero."

"Is everyone's name in that book?" Mike asked looking around the room.

"No, this is the Book of Life." Jesus replied, pointing to the walls covered by rows and rows of other books. "Those contain the names of everyone who don't believe in our Father or who will not accept his gift, that I paid for on the tree. Our Father has made it so easy. All anyone must do is have a change of mind…turn back to God, by faith, believe, I paid the price for their Sins. Their name was put in this book, the Book of Life. Before we made time, or the world as you know it." Jesus explained, then added, "They can never be taken out."

"So, How do I stack up with other people?" Mike asked, not sure he wanted to know the answer.

"About average." Jesus said, in nonchalant voice, putting his arms around Mike, "It's time to go."

"But, there are so, many questions I want to ask." Mike said quickly, not wanting to leave the side of Jesus.

"There will be time to answer all you want to know, soon enough." Jesus replied, guiding Mike from the white room and down a long hall.

Before Mike could say another word, he found himself standing back beside Zen, who said, "That didn't take long. Are you alright?"

"I don't know. Was I really with the Lord? Did I really see God?" Mike questioned himself, as well as Zen.

"Yes!" was the only word which Zen expressed.

ა

CHAPTER THIRTY ONE

"What an experience. Did you leave the island as soon as you came back to the village?" I asked, Mike as I started making more notes.

"Not right away. Dave and I walked and talked with Zen. We showed him how the book of Matthew traced the Family line of Jesus, from the first man, to his Great, Great, Great, Great, Grandfather, and then to King David, and finally to his earthly mother. Zen understood and told us he believed all which we explained. Before I left the island all of the clan was learning about Jesus, and how the Bible told about others of their family tree. Those who helped had shaped the other world."

"We had the best sailing weather on our return trip. The waves were rolling as we went through the cloud, but once we cleared the fog the breeze was great, the ocean was beautiful." Mike said, as the waiter brought our food.

After Mike gave Thanks for the food, he continued to pray for everyone at the table for a long life, and fair weather and following seas. Then said, we ask this in the name of Jesus, Amen.

As the group began eating, Mike went on with his story by saying, "When we were about 10 miles away of the cloud, the Navy showed up with two Cruisers. At first I thought they were American ships, but when we were closer, I saw they had no markings.

My instinct was to try and make a run for it. I had Kaysee take the helm, while I put up more sails. The "Windjammer" was making 14 knots, but she was no match for the bigger boats.

I tried to head for shallow water, but that didn't work either. I was watching over the stern as one cruiser came up to within five hundred yards, it fired a round over the "Windjammer". Kaysee screamed and I ducked, as a second round landed fifty feet astern. I knew the next one would be right in the middle of our boat.

As we came off the wind, and prepared to lower the sails, the lead boat slowed, and came along side ordering us to follow them back into the cloud.

Kaysee wanted me to lose them in the cloud. The thought came to mind, but I wasn't sure what kind of orders these people on the boats had been given. They could send us to the bottom, or take us to their leader.

"Following in the wake of the cruiser, was difficult, to keep the "Windjammer" on course. The Captain on the lead cruiser must have seen my struggle, because he stopped and had a line thrown to me on the "Windjammer", and order me to tie it to the bow. They towed us through the cloud.

When we cleared the cloud, they let me detach the "Windjammer" from them. I could sail the boat free again. I knew we were on a course which would take us back the exact same side of the island, we had left shortly before. I hoped I remembered where the shore met the deeper water. I wasn't sure just how close I could get the boat to the shore. If I could get close enough, to the shore, we could jump, and swim to the island.

When we got close to where I could see the plane still on the beach, I turned the "Windjammer" to port, bring it off the wind. Then started the engine, and popped the jib, it furled. Then dropped the main sail and it furled. Then I swung the bow straight for the beach. We were ready to jump ship, as the "Windjammer" came to rest on the bottom, we went over board. I jumped with the anchor, and set it to keep the boat from drifting away.

Kaysee had reached the beach before me. She was standing waiting for me to come ashore. I shouted for her to head for the tree line, just off the beach. I looked back, and could see the cruisers were trying to come around. They had trouble, because the water became shallow a long way from the beach.

I swam as fast as I could for the beach, and stumbled to the tree line. At first I couldn't see Kaysee, but there was Dave and Joan standing in the doorway of their cabin.

They were watching the men from the cruiser coming ashore. I turned in time to see them heading up the beach toward the plane.

"Where is Kaysee?" I asked, when I reached the cabin.

"Welcome back," Joan said, stepping a side as Kaysee spring from the door, throwing her arms around my neck.

We stood watching the men race back and forth, looking first at my tracks and then back at the "Windjammer".

"I hope they don't do anything to the boat." I told Dave, setting Kaysee back on her feet.

"I see they didn't let you out." Dave said, walking to the edge of thee trees.

"Nope, we were going to make a run for it, but I knew we couldn't." Mike replied, stepping up next to Dave.

"Why didn't you asked God to protect you from the evils?" Zen asked, joining the two at the edge of the trees.

"I didn't think about it." Mike said, rubbing the top of his head. "Do you think God would?"

"You two are the ones, who showed me the Bible. The Word said "You have not because you ask not." Zen said, giving me a big smile.

They prayed; asking God to blind the eyes of the ones who meant harm to Mike, Kaysee and the "Windjammer".

As the three stood watching the men come running into the trees. They went right pass Mike, Dave and Zen, as if they weren't even there. The men kept going right up hill as far as Mike could see.

Within a few minutes they came running back to the beach. Got in the rafts and headed back to the cruisers that got underway to the other side of the island.

"Great!" Mike exclaimed, walking back to the cabin. He motioned for Kaysee to come with him back to the "Windjammer".

"Thanks Zen. I won't forget it again." Mike said as they passed.

"Remember, the Lord is with you always." Zen replied, giving a wave.

Mike and Kaysee swam back out to the "Windjammer" and crawled on board. He looked back at the beach and could see Dave and Zen still standing there. He started the engine, put in reverse, pulling the "Windjammer" off the bottom where Mike had beached it.

Kaysee waved to the men on the beach as Mike headed for the door and home.

"Excuse me, Captain Ryan, we are about to close." the waiter said, steeping to the table. "Can I get you or your friends anything?"

"Hey, look at the time" Mike said, finishing his coffee. We have an early call."

"I thought you were going to tell Mickey, how you made the wrong turn, coming back the last time, we went to the island." Kaysee said, as everyone was getting up from the table.

"Yeah Well, that's another story." Mike said, giving the waiter his credit card.

"We are leaving in a few hours, but we will be back in about three weeks." Mike said signing the bill and getting his receipt.

"Yeah Right, if you don't make another wrong turn coming back." Heilman said, giving Mike a pat on the back.

ca

I spent the night going over all of my notes, and listening to the tapes of the interview. I wanted to make sure I hadn't missed any of the story about the Return To Topic Bay.

As the sun was starting to rise above the horizon and true to his word Captain Mike Ryan, and the group were all on the dock ready to leave. In the short time I came to know them, I knew I would be waiting for their return.

Bert and Linda introduced me to Bert's father and step-mother. They were not in good health. Mike had arranged with the Chadwicks and Zen for them to live at Topic Bay.

According to Paul Heilman, Big Bill had cancer, and if he didn't go to the island he wouldn't live much longer. That was why Doctor O'Malley suggested, Rose and Big Bill, also stay on the island after they delivered the Doctor's boat.

As I watched the white sail of the "Windjammer" fill with the wind, I waved to the people as they went out into Biscayne Bay. It's always a sight to see a sail filled with wind and the boat to heal to one side. It makes you want to be on board.

Like Captain Mike said as he was boarding the "Windjammer", some go out and do it, while others stay behind and write about it.

I think there might be a lot of truth in those words.

ᑍ

About the Author

H. Mickey Mc Guire lives with his
wife, just West of St. Louis MO.
He served in Vietnam with the
101st Airborne Division,
as a Photographer &
Information NCOIC
also with
82nd Airborne Division
173rd Airborne Brigade &
503rd Airborne Battle Group
He is an active member of
InJOY Christian Fellowship
&
A servant of Jesus Christ